THE FOURTH LEVEL

JEOPARDY

BOOK FIFTEEN

I0553253

NICHOLAS HUNTLEY

First Edition, November 2020

nichhuntley.ca

WHITEWOLF PUBLISHING

Paperback ISBN 978-1-988765-40-2

Digital ISBN 978-1-988765-41-9

The text of this book is set in Times New Roman.

"Live so as not to fear death, for those who live well in the world, death is not frightening, but sweet and precious."

— St. Rose of Viterbo

Act 1, Scene 1

Vehicles sped left and right, left and right along Penultimate Bridge, which stretched across the two closest points from where the mainland of Harlech reached King Island. Penultimate Bridge was a narrow multi-lane suspension bridge with cables that spread from two central towers constructed out of metal beams. From afar, the bridge could be faintly seen through a thick fog that came with the cold, dismal evening weather, which included the scatter of intangible snow by sharp winds. Along the cable suspensions, bright red lights could be seen like Christmas lights. The bright LED lights on lampposts provided a thickness of light for the drivers who all drove with a mutual focus in mind.

The coniferous pine trees of King George VI Park were frosted with snow. The promenade along the seawall was quiet with not a single pedestrian in sight. The condos and apartments from Camross all the way across Whitney Harbor were bright with plenty of lights on in the homes inside. Within Central Harlech, there was an insufferable and immovable traffic that clogged the major streets of Campbell Street, Hardwicke Street, and Durham Street. Main Street and the highway were in an equally poor state. However, in the hours that passed, that soon changed to present the opposite as the streets cleared and the people of Harlech returned home from a day's work on Christmas Eve.

Below, within the district of Keswick, tied up in a wool black coat with hands tucked firmly in the side pockets, a woman walked through the quiet streets with her head down to avoid the onslaught of razor-sharp snowflakes that cut at her cheeks. Her hair was somewhat covered in the same flakes of snow like sparkles that didn't shine, but simply contrasted the darkness of her almost black hair. This young girl, or young adult it should be said, walked through the crippled slums of Keswick with a straight back and a confident pose as she wore leather boots that stomped into the snow that attempted to form before her. She was very reserved and avoided glancing around to the various festive lights and garland decorations that had decorated a part of the city that was so poor, but rich in the Christmas spirit. This woman raised her head up, exposing her light fair skin and rosy cheeks as she smiled and turned towards the old familiar building on her right.

Diana held a quaint smile over her face that caused her to glow. She entered through the foyer of the apartment building and proceeded to climb up the stairs as she smelt the strong odor of cloves and ham. She removed her hands from her pocket and ran her hand over the rail guard of the old stairs she knew so well. Once she reached the top, she turned to face a wooden door that was scratched out, but still in fair condition. At the front of the door, underneath the peephole, there were the numbers one and two of the twelfth unit of the apartment building. Diana did not take keys out from her pocket, but instead simply touched the brass handle of the front door and opened it to enter the bright and lit corridor of the home she grew up in. She then walked forward and began to take off her jacket, placing it on a hook to the right where there were other coats hung. Diana then removed her leather boots before she continued forward to come into the living room where it was warm.

Diana took a deep breath and smiled as she looked forward to see the makers of her existence, her mother and father, on the couch ahead turned to face the television. Diana's mother held her husband by the arm and tipped her head over onto his shoulder as they watched TV. Willis Cambridge wore a collared shirt, navy blue sweater, and jeans. His dark hair was slightly balding, and he looked older than when Diana had last seen him. He was clean-shaven too. The same was true for Scarlett Cambridge whose dark golden blonde hair was fading back to its natural light brown shade. She wore a blouse and white pants as well as her glasses as she watched TV lovingly with her spouse. She also wore a gold ring at her hand and a golden necklace. Diana walked over to them and placed her keys in a bowl behind an armchair to the right of the sofa.

"It's pretty dead out there," Diana remarked to them.

Diana looked into the kitchen and smiled as she saw Tristan. Tristan looked as youthful as he was the last time that Diana had seen him. His hair was cut short, however, and like her father, he wore a collared shirt, but with a red sweater that matched his strawberry-blonde hair. Both of them had plain gold bands around the fingers next to their pinky on their left hands. Tristan held a sincere and bright smile – a smile that had become lost to both of them over the last year and a half. The smile brought inner joy to Diana as she saw it. Diana walked over to him and kissed him on the cheek as he dried his hands on a kitchen towel.

"Don't worry about it," Tristan replied, looking to her lovingly. "I told you not to worry about it."

"I had to try, didn't I?" Diana questioned, going over to the kitchen to pick out some fruit from a bowl in the corner.

"Oh, Diana," her mother chanted, standing up from the couch and going over to her. "You work too hard, you know. It's Christmas! Come, sit down with us – the two of you."

Diana smiled back at her mom. She took Tristan by the hand and followed her to the couch. They sat down in a second loveseat on the left of the sofa where Willis was. Tristan stretched his arm around Diana, and she snuggled up to soulmate with more than content in her eyes. She looked around the refurbished living room and kitchen. In the left corner of the room, next to the table with the bowl, there was a beautifully decorated Christmas tree with glistening ornaments and a royal red ribbon. The walls were painted, covering the graffiti that the vandals had left since the house had been abandoned, and there were various souvenirs that Diana had collected over the years, which had since become objects of decoration in her home. For example, Diana's katana was on display over the table behind the armchair and the nutcracker that Tristan gifted to her was on display on a bookshelf on her left, next to the flat screen TV. The sofas were brand new, slightly modern, but comfy. The TV stand was made of a firm dark wood. Before them was a clean, simple rug and a glass coffee table. The kitchen had been redone just as it was, the cabinets restored, but the fridge, microwave, dishwasher, and stove were all new. Diana took a deep breath and then pressed her head into Tristan's side as she stretched an arm over his stomach.

"What are you thinking about?" Tristan politely asked Diana.

"Nothing," Diana said in a soft voice, closing her eyes. "Life is… life is just really good right now."

Diana opened her eyes at the sound of the doorbell. She stood up and went towards the front door, leaving everybody behind. Diana put her hand around the door. She then opened the door and looked to the elderly gentleman who was on the other side. The man had short hair and a thick moustache in the same shade of whitish-grey. He wore a black winter coat, a scarf around his neck, and a hat over his head. In his right hand, he held a paper bag filled with gifts.

"Charles," Diana greeted with a smile. "Come in."

"Hope I'm not too late!" Charlemagne remarked, walking in.

"Never…" Diana replied.

"Here is my tribute," Charlemagne said, pulling out a wine bottle from the brown bag and presenting it to the couple.

Diana took the bottle into her hand.

"You shouldn't have," Tristan said.

Charlemagne followed the couple into the main room. Diana and Tristan went into the kitchen where she sat the bottle down on the counter. She looked at the bottle with suspicion, lowering her smile. She then felt a hand in hers and was turned around. Tristan looked to her and placed his hands at her waist. He gave a flirtatious look to her.

"What's with the look, Captain Hook?" Tristan teased, looking down at her.

Diana did not respond and instead looked back at the love of her life with wide eyes. Her deep blue eyes stared into his jade greens, and then their lips drew together. Diana felt the pounce of Tristan's heartbeat as his chest touched hers. She closed her eyes, and they kissed.

Suddenly, Diana opened her eyes again, torn from her love as the loud and irritating beeping from the alarm from her smartphone went off. She sat up, pressing her body into her spring-loaded mattress, and brought a hand to her face as she took her hair and moved it aside from the front of her face. She breathed deeply and then took a long deep breath, closing her eyes and then falling back onto her bed. Diana groaned and buried her face into her pillow as she sought to avoid the reality around her.

Diana stretched a hand out and grabbed her smartphone. She then tilted her head up to look and then silence the alarm. She sat her phone down and turned herself back around. The bedroom of the same, but different desolate and old apartment that she was in had a grey overtone to it as light poured in through the translucent blinds. Diana stared up to the ceiling.

Diana's bedroom was different to how it had been little more than a month ago. For a start, the old mattress that had been in the corner had been tossed and in lieu of it, a slightly wider-sized single bed had been placed in the middle of the room, towards the left wall from the window. The walls had been painted to a color that suited her, grey. Next to the bed there was a desk with Diana's laptop, two computer monitors behind, a lamp near the bed, and some other personal belongings scattered around. Across from the desk, next to the door into the bathroom door there was a wardrobe to the left against the parallel wall, and to the right on the other wall next to the door, a messy bookshelf with a few books already placed inside, most of which were textbooks from school. On the other side of the bed there was a night table with a Bible overtop and a picture of Diana's mother and father behind.

Diana took a deep breath and then pulled her feet out from her bed to go and pull the blinds up at the window, bringing in a bit of the cold sunlight that hit the town through the fire escape. She looked across the rooftops nearby and towards downtown to see that it was grey out with a thick layer of snow that covered the city. She continued to look outside for another moment before deciding to enter the washroom. Diana turned on the light and looked at herself in the mirror as she didn't wear nightgowns anymore, but instead simply pajama pants with any t-shirt she could find.

The bathroom in the apartment was very small with barely enough room for one to close the door as they stood inside. In the corner there was a shower, to the left from the door there was a sink attached to the wall, above the sink there was a mirror that Diana had bought and placed to replace the old cracked one, and behind that there was a toilet.

Diana looked at herself and pulled her t-shirt down, bringing it over her stomach. Over the last month, she had developed a minor curve at her stomach that was firm as the extra space came from inside and not outside. She breathed in and held her stomach, which somewhat made up for the weight she had gained in the last month and hid the ever-growing abdomen. Diana looked at herself with displeasure and sighed. She then attended to her personal business, showered, and then got changed.

As Diana attended to her business, she held a flat emotionless face. She walked out from her bedroom and into the living room, which had seen little progress in the last month. The walls were painted into a caramel color. The kitchen was just like it was in her dream as she had the kitchen put back together just as it was, using the money she had earned in the last several weeks in her new position with the Harlech Syndicate, and she had also bought new appliances. The dining table had been outright replaced with a newer, more modern one. There was a TV stand, but no TV, and there was only one sofa to replace the broken old one, but no carpet. Where there could have been an armchair, there was a table against the wall, but not even the bowl for keys to rest in. The apartment was thus very austere.

Diana entered the kitchen and turned on the kettle. She then went to the countertop on the other side and began to look through a folder set atop where there was some intelligence passed on to her by her supervisor, Scot Sutherland. Diana rubbed her neck as she read through the reports and then she went to pour herself some hot water and make some instantaneous coffee. Afterwards, she gave the coffee some sugar and cream, and then she went with the mug and folder to the table to sit down. Diana sifted through the papers and then gave a deep sigh.

Diana's phone vibrated in her pocket. She took it out and turned it on, looking at the wallpaper which she had yet to change and displayed both her and Tristan together at a beach on Isla Paraiso. Diana looked at the wallpaper for longer than she should have, ignoring the text message that she had received from her boss. Diana sat the phone down and closed the report, pushing it aside. She then grabbed the mug of coffee and stirred, looking around the vastness of space around her that she shared all to herself.

Act 1, Scene 2

"It with a great honor that I am here today in lieu of my dear brother, Charlemagne, to open the Judith Lambert Memorial Research Center," Allodia announced from a podium within the lobby of Cabernet Tower. "Dr. Judith Lambert was a close family friend, hard worker, and passionate scientist in her field who will be remembered for the breakthroughs and all her contributions to the sciences. Through the generosity of our investors, we have been able to put money into the development of this state-of-the-art research and development laboratory deep within the confines of this tower that is a part of the Cabernet legacy found within the Harlech skyline. To our investors and the public, I place my assurance to you that the works led by Dr. Barry Lambert and his team of experts have sought to continue the vision and mandate of the Cabernet family to develop better and healthier lives for all. On behalf of my brother, I must extend his apologies that he could not be here on this momentous occasion, but he assured me his work at the moment could be pivotal for all of humanity in the near future."

"Yeah, right," Tristan muttered. "He's downstairs in his private lab doing whatever the hell it is he's doing... he won't even say."

"It's pivotal work," Finn assured him jokingly.

Tristan smiled and shook his head. Both Tristan and Finn were among the attendance of less than a hundred people and journalists. They were both in suits and both at the front of the two groups of foldable chairs before the stage where Allodia was. There were also four chairs on the stage that Allodia was on, one was empty, the other occupied by Barry, the third occupied by Richard Huxley, and the last occupied by Joseph

Gilbert. Tristan shook his head in disbelief and continued to focus on Allodia's speech.

"Jeez, I'd love to get to land an internship in a place like this," Finn remarked. "Imagine the technologies that are being developed here."

"I'm not even sure if Cabernet Industries still has an airline division, or if was liquidated because of the setbacks now that we're technically in a recession, or depression, or whatever the hell people are saying we're in," Tristan stated with slight concern in his face. "Unemployment is through the roof, and inflation isn't looking too good either. Not to mention there's still this virus that people – sorry, the media, is freaking out about and all the other crap that's going off around the world."

"Yeah, the world isn't looking to good, is it," Finn replied. "Everybody is mad. It is perfect."

Tristan looked back at Finn and didn't respond.

"And now," Allodia expressed to the crowd. "I would like to invite our current Chief Scientist, Dr. Bartholomew Lambert, who to say a few words."

Allodia moved away from the podium to sit down. Barry stood up. He was dressed in a fine-pressed black suit. He wore the same slim glasses as always, but his beard was neatly trimmed and his long hair combed. Allodia, Huxley, and Gilbert clapped with the crowd as Dr. Lambert approached the podium with a paper in hand.

At the end of the speech, Finn and Tristan met with Allodia as some champagne and food were being served.

"How was that?" Allodia questioned Tristan, smiling to him.

"Not bad," Tristan replied. "Sorry Charles made you do his job for him."

Allodia sighed.

"It was worse five or six years ago before he adopted you and disappeared from public life, but it's been a while since I stood before a crowd like that. I hate speeches."

Allodia looked to Finn.

"Hi there," Allodia remarked to Finn.

"Hi," Finn responded in his deep Suffolk accent. "I'm Tristan's roommate"

"Nice to meet you… Tristan's roommate."

Tristan sighed and expanded to say, "His name is Louis."

"Oh, well, nice to meet you, Louis."

Finn looked at Tristan with sort of distaste. He looked at him back with annoyance. Allodia took in a deep breath and then looked to Tristan.

"Where's Diana?" Allodia questioned. "Is she busy with school? I was hoping that I'd get to see her."

"Science has never been Diana's interest," Tristan deflected. "Neither has Cabernet Industries, really."

"What?" Allodia questioned in disbelief. "Isn't she doing a science degree?"

"What Tristan meant to say is that he hasn't seen Diana in over a month," Finn clarified. "Nobody has."

"What the heck does that mean?" Allodia then questioned. "Tristan?"

Tristan didn't immediately answer.

"He's got no idea," Finn answered in his place. "Nobody has any idea."

Tristan sighed.

"Charles said that the Protection Squad have been keeping some tabs on her and that she's not living at Declan Walham anymore," Tristan finally said. "She's living over at her folk's old home in Keswick."

"Okay…?" Allodia responded. "Why though? What's with the loss of communication, and the P.S. watching her? What happened while I was away?"

Tristan groaned and replied, "Last time I talked to Charles, he said he wasn't going to have the Protection Squad spy on her anymore because he felt immoral about it."

"Tristan, you aren't being very clear about what's going on with Diana. Did the two of you breakup, or?"

"They broke up," Finn clarified.

"Oh my God," Allodia exclaimed. "How? Why? I thought the pair of you were perfect together, so what happened?"

"We… drifted apart," Tristan simply said. "And that's why we're not together anymore."

Allodia looked puzzled.

"Just like that?" Allodia questioned.

Tristan shrugged. Finn rolled his eyes.

"Ever since the pair of them arrived here and went to their separate universities, they barely spoke to each other. And then in October, they stopped talking outright until Diana walked in on Tristan with another woman."

"Finn!" Tristan shouted, annoyed at him.

"What? Is this true?"

Tristan looked aside.

"Tristan," Allodia remarked in an annoyed manner.

"Yes," Tristan quietly admitted.

Allodia frowned. She brought a hand to her temple.

"I don't like this," Allodia said, shaking her head as she removed her hand.

Tristan shrugged and replied, "What do you want? She's technically a resident of Alberta, and in Alberta the age when you become an adult is eighteen, so she's free to do whatever she wants. She's not Charlemagne's problem anymore."

"Diana never was a problem," Allodia stated with a deeper frown. "I don't really understand what is going on. I should try and talk to her."

"Hmph," Tristan responded. "Good luck. She doesn't want to hear from anybody. Charles said that she's 'emancipated' herself from the family because she can't be with you or Charlemagne because of me. It wouldn't be 'healthy' for her and prevent her from moving on. I'd just hurt her again."

Allodia sighed and replied, "Whether Diana likes it or not, she is still a part of this family. She can't just abandon us as if the last three years were for nothing," she said, shaking her head. "She's being overly dramatic. What about Christmas? Where is she going to go home to on that day? She's going to be all alone. I won't stand for it."

Tristan was silent. Allodia sighed again.

"I can't stay here," Allodia remarked. "I need to… find my phone and send her a message. Ask her to meet for some coffee or something… I need to find my idiotic brother and get him to explain to me what the heck is going on…!"

Allodia left Tristan and Finn. Tristan looked to Finn scornfully.

"She seemed nice," Finn remarked, sipping his champagne. "For an aunt, you know?"

"What the hell was that?" Tristan questioned.

"What?" Finn responded. "Are you mad that I told the truth? You're still pretty clueless, aren't you? How the hell did Diana survive three years with you? I've barely been able to last four months…!"

Tristan's annoyed frown turned to one of slight sadness. He finished his glass of champagne with a straight shot and then let out a sigh.

The elevator doors opened, and Allodia walked out with both hands at her smartphone. She lowered the phone and then looked around from the top of a platform that looked around an open space below where there were various machines, cabinets, tool cases, and computer stations against the wall. She was in a sort of workshop with a platform directly below her where there was a rectangular object hidden behind a tarp. The elevator door closed behind Allodia.

"Charles!" Allodia shouted, going left and coming down a set of stairs to confront her brother.

Charlemagne looked over to her from where he was at a workbench, sat on a stool with a magnifying headset as he focused on carefully soldering an object. He lifted up the visor and looked over to her. Charlemagne looked much as he did the last time the two saw each other, except his skin was looking sickly pale and his eyes baggier than usual. His hair was also whiter.

"Charlie, what the hell is going on between Diana and Tristan? I've heard they've split up!"

Charlemagne looked aside and then nodded to her.

"Seems to me that you know what's going on," Charlemagne simply said.

"He's also told me that Diana's 'emancipated' herself from the family? How could you let her do that?"

"She's old enough to care for herself, and from what I've heard, she has been doing just that, and a remarkable job at it may I add. She's both studying and working full-time, and she's excelling in both fields without any sign of harm to herself. I was so impressed, I've began to think that all of this has been for the better."

"What?"

"I played my role in her life," Charlemagne said. "I took her in from the streets. She was educated. She fell in love. She had her experiences, and she learned from them and took with her both wisdom and knowledge, which she is now putting to good use. What parent could ask for more? All that's left is for her to settle down and have children…"

"How are you okay with this?" Allodia questioned. "Do you even imagine the sort of mental harm that she may have had to experience on her own?"

Charlemagne shook his head and replied, "When it comes to Diana, I'm not even slightly worried about subjects of the psyche. She's experienced a difficult childhood and with it, she's developed a thick skin and an unmoveable faith in God. It's Tristan that's been my worry more than anything… that's part of the reason why I've spent the last month or so in Harlech… to keep an eye on him."

"Oh my God…" Allodia simply said, looking to her phone. "Poor Diana… I've sent her a text to meet me for coffee. If she won't talk to you or Tristan, then maybe she'll talk to me. You men… what have you done while I was away? This needs a woman's touch. I'll make her feel comfortable…"

"Hmph," Charlemagne grunted, looking back to the piece he was working on. "Good luck."

"I don't need it," Allodia replied with a smirk. "She's already replied."

Charlemagne looked back over to her. He stood up and approached her with haste.

"Please, do something for me then," Charlemagne begged. "Please, watch over her and let me know that she is okay. Ever since she left, I've worried for her, but as her former guardian there is nothing that I can do. I had Heavner spying on her, but I couldn't bear to invade her privacy in that manner when I learned how well she was… at least from afar. However, you'll be at her side… You've always been like a second mother to her, so please, let me know that all is well with her when you learn more from her."

"Relax," Allodia remarked. "Of course. Look, I've invited her out to have some dinner later."

Allodia put her phone away and looked to Charlemagne, crossing her arms.

"I promise you that I'll have everything sorted again," Allodia said with a smile. "Just leave it to me."

Act 1, Scene 3

Oswald Montgomery gave a long, hefty, and thick hack of a cough from his bedside where he laid half-slouched and propped up by the pillows behind him. An oximeter was attached to his index finger and the wires from nodes attached to his chest protruded out from underneath his silk red pajamas. On a dresser at the side of the room there were various cards from friends and family that expressed hopeful sentiments for the mob boss to get better soon.

The Leader of the Harlech Syndicate appeared exhausted and resigned with large bags underneath his yellow eyes. He looked to be sickly pale and had developed a stubble around his cheeks and away from his moustache. Blankets were up to his chest and a private nurse at his side kept check of his vitals.

The room that the old man was kept in was his private office at the top of the Calypso Tower in Lincoln. His desk had been moved aside so that he could operate his business from his office, although he could only wheeze and mutter in a hoarse voice. The office was a dim room with brown wooden floors set up in square tiles and brown wooden panel walls. Most of the furniture in the room was made of a similar dark brown while lamps and picture frames were made of brass. Above a fireplace to the left from the bed the leader was in, was a portrait of him in his youth with his dark hair and thick moustache and dressed in a suit and with a confident look on his face. He held a hand at his waist and another against the side of a column in the picture, looking stoic and proud with a stiff upper lip.

The double door at the other end of the room from the bed opened quickly as Damian Jerrick Lachlan 'Scot' Sutherland entered, arguing with a man in a lab coat. He was an old man with slightly tanned, olive skin and grey hair. He had a firm jaw and medium-length grey-white hair. He looked like he was of Middle Eastern descent, while at the same time looking to be possibly European. Scot was dressed in in a black tactical uniform. At the back of his ballistic vest were the words 'Security' and on the front was his name, 'D. Sutherland.' His face was unshaven and had grown a bit of a beard, but he appeared healthy and youthful with medium-length dark hair and grey eyes.

"He is not in a state to speak with anyone," the man in the lab coat argued, speaking in a coastal New York accent. "He has to heal – I won't let you put his recovery at risk."

"That's out of the question, doctor," Scot bickered, pointing a finger at him. "I'm his second-in-command and the field commander of all operations, and unlike the military, this isn't a place where medical staff can overrule an officer."

"What is all the fuss there," Montgomery croaked in a raspy voice.

"Forgive me," the doctor apologized, "but your son refused to give you the time of rest that I have prescribed to you."

"Nonsense, doctor," Montgomery replied, attempting to raise a hand, but struggling. "Please, Dr. Bishop, you've done quite enough for me at the moment. Thank you for your consideration, but I need to speak with my dear boy. Leave us."

"As you wish," Dr. Bishop replied, bowing to him.

Dr. Bishop left the room as Diana appeared. She was dressed in her own tactical uniform with her hair tied in a bun. She looked at the doctor as he left, and he gave her a scorned look. He then promptly disappeared down the hall while Diana went to join Scot.

"What in God's grace do you want, my dear boy," Montgomery requested, looking over to Diana. "Diana, please, the door."

Diana nodded and then went to close the door. She then went to finally join Scot. Diana stood next to her old friend and looked around the office to get a closer look at the decoration and view. On the opposite-side from the fireplace there was a cabinet with various items inside. On the left from this cabinet was a bookcase, and to the right was a small bar with various crystal drink containers. On the wall that the bed was pushed against, there were tall windows with the blinds lowered and slightly shut. Diana could make out a view of the surrounding neighborhood going as far as Port Burnes and over the Pacific Ocean.

"Commissioner Game is getting suspicious of your health," Scot said to Montgomery. "He was asking a lot of questions about you and why you haven't been able to meet with him. We were barely able to speak about much, and he wants another meeting as soon as possible, but not with me, but you. Our intel suggests that he might defect and leave the Syndicate."

"For forty years we've done business with the police department, and this man, Game, has never sat easy with me. He's always wanted more and more... He's a reformer, and we are going into an election year. If our enemies elect someone like him, we may lose our protection."

"Not to mention the council," Scot replied. "If we lose another seat, we could be finished. Local media has been adamant to defund the police despite the spike in crime, and given the changes that have occurred worldwide, the revolution might spread here as well."

"The media has always been our enemy. They are the enemy of the people. The masses are so easily manipulated that they would easily eliminate the Harlech Police Department when crime has never been worse. Of course, our enemies understand this... what they want is to control the citizens. If we're careful, we may be able to hijack control or be a form of resistance."

Montgomery looked over to Diana with a smile.

"What brightens my prospects for the future is the will and determination of such young people as yourself, Diana. You have done so well to become a part of my organization – I'm both sorry, but glad that you are with us at such a critical moment."

Montgomery laid his head back to look up to the ceiling.

"I must confess... I don't have much life within me left," Montgomery confided. "I've been avoiding the prospects of succession, but I must now consider the definitive future of this organization without me."

"You are going to get better," Scot insisted.

"I do not believe so. I am getting worse not by the day, but by the hour. It is only a moment until my conditions worsens to the point where I am no longer conscious. I had that lawyer in here earlier today... the one that is friends with your sister, Hyacinth. However, within it, I left the matter of my succession as the Chief Executive Officer of this company. I have not told her, but tomorrow it will be official because I will have to step down as the head of Paladin. I will continue my role within the Syndicate but act mostly in an advisor capacity. The next Chief Executive Officer of Paladin Group will be you, Damian. You have the integrity and strength to lead this company over your sister. Only you can overcome the challenges that are to come... with your title you will also take my place as the Leader, and I will entrust in you to keep together the Syndicate that I have crafted over the last forty years. Can you do this?"

Scot looked at his adoptive father with compassion. He nodded.

"Thank you," Montgomery muttered, looking over to Diana. "There will be a time, I hope, where you too, Diana, will come to succeed this corporation. The pair of you have been my favorite children. Come tomorrow, these walls and my men will be yours," he remarked, looking back to Scot.

Scot nodded.

"However, while this is the business that I have set out, I will continue to be the Leader of the Syndicate until the day that I pass in which you will then definitively takeover. You are to continue to act in my capacity under my advice until then. What other news do you have for me?"

"Well, as I was saying," Scot replied, "the police are showing some resistance, and there are some newer senior officers within their ranks that haven't been able to understand the rules and which Game is too weak to exert his force against."

"Treacherous fool," Montgomery responded, shaking his head.

"And because of that, our spy within the Harlech Nuclear Power Plant was arrested after an investigation led by a Senior Detective Langstrom arrested on charges of espionage."

"Hm," Montgomery croaked. "This is unfortunate news. If our contact in Russia does not have his demand satisfied, we could lose our reputation among the international market. Mr. Patrovich can be a sour man that does not show remorse."

"Shall we continue with the operation?" Scot questioned. "My men are ready to deploy as we speak. I just need your permission."

"No," Montgomery denied, shaking his head. "We cannot risk it at this time. What we should do instead is petition and extension from Mr. Patrovich until we are able to re-establish our network in that area. I'm afraid of what our contact within the nuclear plant could have said to police by now…"

"My intel says that he hasn't said anything…"

"Still," Montgomery said, "it is too risky. Has our shipment from Hong Kong arrived?"

"Not yet," Scot replied.

"Hm," Montgomery groaned. "We will have to have a word with Mr. Lingzui then. In the meantime, continue all regular operational activity. That is all."

"Yes, sir," Scot responded, looking over to Diana for them to leave.

The two of them left. Scot closed the doors behind him. He then turned back to Diana as they continued to walk down the hall. The hallways of the tower were bright in contrast to Montgomery's office. They consisted of beige panel walls and yellowish-white marble tiles. The lamps that hang from the ceiling were brass.

"He really isn't looking good," Diana remarked as they approached the elevators.

"Yeah," Scot sighed, "I know. I knew he would make me his successor. He never trusted Hyacinth ever since she married that American."

"Then why is she technically Acting-Chief Executive Officer?" Diana questioned as the elevator arrived.

"To give her something to do, I suppose."

The pair entered. Scot hit a button for the sub-basement. He then tapped his ID on a card reader. The doors closed.

"I've got a lot on my shoulders, and this isn't the best time to be given the keys to both Paladin and the Syndicate. Still, I have a job to do – an opportunity to turn this Syndicate around for the better. I've waited years for this opportunity."

"What do you think Hyacinth is going to say when she finds out that Montgomery's chosen his adoptive-son over her biological daughter?" Diana asked.

Scot shrugged and replied, "If she were sensible, she should have seen that coming. To be honest, she had the efficiency of an administrator, but never the tactical decision making that's needed to run both, especially in these trying times. I'll be honest, but I'll miss the field once I'm in charge."

"I can see that. You live so that you can be out there."

"At any rate, Hyacinth is a lot like her mother. If Matilda were alive, she would take the Syndicate into a different direction. I want to steer it away from that direction while Hyacinth wants to continue its radical path. Believe it or not, but I didn't used to be an advocate for the Syndicate… When I was your age, shortly after my father died, I ran back to Scotland and joined the British Army. I later joined the Special Air Service (British special forces) and fought in the Gulf War. When I was injured and put on leave, I came back to Harlech because I found myself not where I wanted to be. I joined the Harlech Police Department when I healed, and then the Emergency Response Team, but even then, I was still not where I wanted to be. Eventually, I came back home to Montgomery, joined Paladin Group, and here I am now for the last fifteen years. I realized that if you can't beat 'em, you really just have to join them. I laid to rest all my qualm with the organization knowing that I can do a lot more good if involved, and now, all that patience is about to pay off."

The elevator doors opened and the two walked out and continued down concrete sublevel of the tower. They went around and then came to a large locker room garage where there were various tactical security officers and some vehicles parked nearby, including two unmarked vans. Diana stood by Scot as he addressed the team.

"What's the word?" a member asked.

"The word is that the mission has been cancelled," Scot informed them. "Thanks to that idiot that was arrested, we don't have enough intel needed to confidently go in there."

Diana's ear twitched as she heard some incoming footsteps from someone in high heels. She turned to the exit that went into the sublevel corridor and saw a woman in a pink blazer, matching pink business skirt, and clipboard in her hand. She wore a scarf around her neck and had wavy dark hair that was let out. She was also of fair skin. Diana looked to her as she entered the garage, which caused Scot to look at her too.

"Damian," the woman addressed.

"Hyacinth," Scot replied. "What are you doing here? Don't you have papers to shuffle or something?"

"Very funny," Hyacinth replied in her Londoner accent like her father. "Are your men prepped and ready?"

"I just spoke with the Leader, and he cancelled the operation."

"Funny, I just spoke with him as well and he told me the exact opposite," Hyacinth replied. "He said that the Syndicate is suffering enough as it is and that this may be our last chance to retrieve that plutonium. He also expressed confidence in your abilities as a leader, saying that this would be a test to prove if you truly are capable."

Scot frowned at her. He scratched the side of his beard.

"I'd hardly wish to put the lives of my men on the line for a selfish test of *my* capabilities," Scot remarked. "Are you sure he gave the okay? I really did just talk to him."

"Are you saying that I'm lying to you?" Hyacinth responded, slightly mad. "Trust me, Damian. It's what's best for the Syndicate and the company. You wouldn't want our father to think less of you in face of his current condition, would you?"

Scot nodded. He then turned to the others.

"Alright, you heard her," Scot said. "She's technically our boss, so let's go."

Diana gave a skeptical look to the Leader's daughter. She then looked back to Scot who went over to one of the unmarked vans. She hesitated to approach him, but in the end didn't as she instead went to finish readying herself lest she fall behind and provoke him. Diana quickly put on her duty belt with all her equipment, armed herself with an assault rifle, and then stocked herself on ammunition before going over to join her teammates as they set off for the mission anyways.

"Scot, are you sure about this?" Diana questioned in private.

"Don't worry," Scot replied. "I reviewed the plan, and even with what happened, I'm confident it's safe to proceed. If anything, if she is lying, then she gives us an excuse to go ahead anyways against what Montgomery wants, which is what I want, even if she doesn't realize it."

Diana nodded to him and said, "If you're confident, then I'm confident too."

Act 1, Scene 4

"Bravo One, this is Alpha One actual," Scot projected over the radio. "Ten-Zero."

"You are Ten-Two, Alpha One," Bravo One replied.

"All units, check in," Scot then said.

"Roger," Alpha One-Two replied.

The rest of the six-person team sounded off between the two vans, finishing with Alpha Eight.

"Roger," Diana finished.

"All communications are good," Scot stated.

"Copy that, Alpha One," Bravo One responded.

Diana sat patiently in the van with her assault rifle at her side as they drove through Lincoln and towards the highway. They went north towards King Island, crossing the Marke Bridge, and then exiting into the Industrial District. The vans then drove up Steele Drive, which was riddled with potholes. Diana looked to Scot who gave her a confident smile. He then looked to the rest of the team.

"Alright, people, look alive," Scot remarked. "Paladin provides the security for this place, so if our intel from within is clear, we should have no problem following the planned route. Bravo One will have the Stewards doing some alarm testing, so they shouldn't get in our way. At the same time, the alarm systems will be down, so there won't be any alerts sent to the HPD."

The van drove past the front gates of the Harlech Nuclear Power Plant. A checkpoint at the entrance was manned by a security officer. The van continued down the road and turned right onto an alleyway just before a steel mill.

"We'll take the sewer tunnels and make our way into the maintenance tunnels underground, and from there we'll make our way to the administration offices so that we can secure the codes."

The van came to a halt and the rear door opened. The two other mercenaries with Diana hopped off, followed by her from behind. They went ahead and began to work on a manhole cover. Diana went ahead and took position up ahead. There was a mild, cold humidity in the air and the smell of garbage from the pollution. The area around them was very quiet.

"Easy there," Scot said.

The mercenary pulled the cover out. Another then lowered a rope down.

"Alright, let's head down there," Scot said, taking point.

The other two followed from behind, while Diana kept point. They were followed by another two from the other van before she dropped down with them. Diana slid down and met with the others to enter the confined space. She landed on her feet and then met with the others.

The tunnel below was small with pipes in one corner followed by neatly arranged, but thick wires. Once they were all accounted for, Scot turned to face the other side of the tunnel that went south.

"Alpha Six, stay vigilant," Scot projected over the radio. "We'll be in and out."

"Roger that," Alpha Six replied over the radio. "We'll keep an eye on things from up here."

"Copy that," Scot responded. "Alpha Seven, we're waiting on your word. Is the alarm system offline yet?"

No response came.

"Copy, Alpha One. The system has been placed offline for thirty minutes so that the grunts can do their alarm testing along the north side. You have thirty minutes to pass through the obstacles. I also have CCTV on loop footage for the path you'll be taking."

"Copy."

Scot proceeded forward through the dark tunnel. Diana observed ahead that one of their teammates, a larger man, carried a large duffel bag around his back, while another carried a smaller bag. Diana kept her head up as they went ahead into the depths of the tunnel until they found themselves at a gate. The same two mercenaries who had opened the pothole went ahead and began to cut through the iron gate. They removed the iron bars and then stepped aside for Scot to continue through. Scot stopped again at a ladder, which he climbed.

The ladder took them upstairs, but not outside, but instead to another space underground that was brighter and larger than the tunnel below. Diana followed Scot and then took position near him while the others arrived. Afterwards, they proceeded forward down a maintenance tunnel until they reached a set of double doors.

"Alpha Seven, I need access at the first panel, serial number: Three-Hotel-Four-Five-Two-Delta-One-Three-Five-Four-Golf," Scot said over the radio.

"Stand-by," Alpha Seven responded.

Diana observed as the panel went from a red light to a green light. The door also clicked open.

"You're in," Alpha Seven said.

Scot opened the door and the two entered a sort of workshop with various workbenches, tools, and other material around. They passed this area and came to a room where there were lots of loud noises. The room was dim and messy. Scot went up a set of stairs and reached the floor above. He then opened the door and came to some offices on the ground floor. Scot continued forward with the team behind him and stopped at a set of doors.

"Alright, everybody spread out and take point. Diana, keep watch from the door while I get Alpha Seven a window into the administration network."

"You got it," Diana responded, taking point near Scot while the others spread out around the administration offices.

Scot took out a device from a pocket on his belt and began to pick the lock. The door opened and he pushed against it. Diana looked inside to the small office with a computer on the desk. The window behind looked out towards the mainland, in particular, Rosalynn Provincial Park and the divergence of Harlech River and Walham River. Scot moved in and went to the computer.

"Remote uplink established," Alpha Seven reported. "I'm extracting the data... one moment, please."

Scot waited.

"Okay, I have access. I've deactivated the countermeasures in the lower plant, so you shouldn't have any trouble down there."

"Copy that," Scot responded, moving away from the computer and out of the office. "You heard him. Let's move."

The team regrouped and then followed Scot as he took them back downstairs into the workshop, and then into the maintenance tunnels. At the end of the tunnel, they reached a junction that went left and right. Scot took them down the left where the tunnels turned and then came to a large stairwell with metal grated floors and stairs. The team soon arrived at the bottom, which took them into some darker tunnels that went south.

Scot led the team along the tunnel until they could hear the sound of rushing water from afar. There was a cold chill in the tunnels. The team turned left and then continued down the right until they reached an intersection that led down a narrower hall with a dead end further along. Scot led the team through the only other way forward, which took them to a set of thick steel doors with a sign that read, 'Restricted Area' above and at the side, there were biometric sensors and a proxy panel.

"Alpha Seven, we're at the front doors," Scot remarked.

"Roger that, stand-by."

Diana waited for the panels to switch green.

"Alright, you're in."

Scot pushed against the doors and moved in. Diana looked around at the large room that they had just entered. The room was at least three-stories tall and bent around in a circular manner, following a core in the center that was inaccessible. At the sides away from this core there were platforms and catwalks, while in the main space between the core and these platforms there were large turbine engines that hummed. Scot proceeded to lead them around the room where it was quiet. The room did not complete in a full-circle, but instead stopped little more than three-quarters. At the side away from the core there was a corridor that branched off. Scot went towards this corridor and met up with a set of doors.

"The vault's just through here," Scot remarked, stacking up at the door. "Alpha Seven, we're at the second door."

"Roger."

The door opened for them to bypass the biometric sensors and proxy panel. They then entered a short corridor that led to a set of large thick doors. Diana took point at the doors that went into the corridor while Scot went to the door with two others. The rest also spread out and took point to keep watch. Diana looked to a camera that pointed into the corridor while the others worked.

"Alright, Alpha Seven, open the vault door. Let's extract that plutonium and get the hell out of here."

"Copy that," Alpha Seven replied. "Once I open the doors, you'll have five minutes until I need to lock the doors again. It's a fail-safe protocol that was set in place by the client – I have no control over it."

"There should be a package waiting for us inside."

An alarm sounded and the locks on the door began to release. The doors then slowly opened outwards while Scot and the two others with the bags waited. Diana looked over occasionally. After a minute, the doors were open for the two to enter and go inside. Scot stayed where he was.

"I... don't see the package anywhere," the mercenary inside remarked. "Wait..."

Diana lowered her head as she heard an explosion come from within the vault. She then looked over and saw that Scot had been blown over by the shockwave.

"Man down!" a mercenary reported over the radio.

"They... they set up a trap for us..." Scot remarked. "How could they have set up a trap for us?"

Diana rushed over to help Scot up, but he pushed her away.

"Boss, HPD dispatch has called for every available unit to surround the power plant," Alpha Seven reported. "Whatever's going on down there, you need to leave at once."

"Copy that," Scot replied. "Everyone..."

"ERT are at the plant!" Alpha Six reported. "I can see two police vans have pulled into the compound. Get out of there...!"

The radio then returned static followed by some gunshots and an explosion.

"Alpha Six? Alpha Six, do you copy?"

No response came.

"If ERT are here, then we better go," a merc remarked.

Scot nodded and said, "We're going to have to fight our way out of here, so get ready."

Scot picked up the large bag that was blown out from the vault. He unzipped it and picked up a rifle.

"Diana, take this and run ahead," Scot said. "We'll be behind you."

Diana took the sniper rifle and nodded. She then went ahead. The others began to follow from behind as they ran away. Diana was soon blown back as a second explosion detonated from the exit. She quickly scrambled into cover behind an engine as shots began to run through. Diana then peaked around the corner to see the Emergency Response Team (ERT, or SWAT) pour in.

"Diana, take a vantage point and give us some cover!" Scot requested.

"Roger that," Diana replied, running towards a set of stairs so that she could drop down into prone.

Diana readied her rifle and prepared the scope. She then aimed down and pointed towards the ERT as they shot into the room. Diana aimed the crosshairs, but as she tensed her finger at the trigger, she hesitated to pull all the way down.

"Man down!" a merc from below shouted. "Man down!"

"Leave him," Scot replied. "Push forward, or we'll all be down."

Diana finally shot towards the police but missed. The bullet ricocheted upwards and hit a pipe. She continued to try and assist, but her hands were shaky and there was a sweat that dripped from her face. Diana finally moved away from the scope and wiped the sweat from her head, taking a deep breath before she looked back out the scope.

"Alpha One, I'm buzzing off," Alpha Seven reported. "There's too many of them, and…"

An explosion could be heard on the other side.

Scot growled as he reloaded, "What happened to proportional response?"

Scot and the other mercenary that remained began to push back against the others. They managed to take cover at either side of the exit.

"Alpha Eight, you can come down," Scot remarked over the radio. "We're going to push in and get the hell out of here."

Diana stood up and began to make her way down. Scot continued forward with the other mercenary as they pushed back. An explosion then detonated from the corridor before she could exit. Diana looked down with horror, placing her hands on the railing before she started to rush down the stairs to check on Scot. Diana then paused as she saw twelve more ERT members walk in, scanning around the room.

"There's one!" an ERT officer remarked, pointing to Diana.

Diana flinched and ran back into cover. She took cover behind a machine and looked over to see that they were shooting at her. She held the sniper rifle in her hand and then looked around again to see that she had no line of sight from where she was. Diana tossed the rifle aside and instead retrieved a smoke grenade from her belt, breaking the pin, and then setting it down.

Diana picked up the rifle again as she ran off and hid behind a set of large tanks. She then jumped down a gap to go below and then ran towards a grate in the wall. Diana used the rifle to pry the grate open, tearing the vent cover away and popping out the screws. She put her rifle away, placing it on her back by its strap, and then lifted the cover out and held it in her hands.

"Freeze! Drop it!" an officer yelled, approaching from the smoke with a rifle pointed at Diana.

Diana turned towards him and immediately threw the grate like a frisbee, hitting him in the head. She then prepared to kneel down, but another officer approached and confronted her head on. Diana's reflexes took over as she grabbed the barrel of the rifle and then pushed the rifle down so that it hit him. She then tossed the rifle aside as it pried loose from his grip and then brought the ERT officer onto the ground in pain. Diana then took a smoke grenade from his side and set it off so that she could disappear through the vent.

"She's in the vents!" an officer yelled.

"Flush her out!"

"Grenade!"

Diana crawled through the vent and turned right to go down and reach the end where she turned right again. Once Diana reached the end, she reversed her body so that her legs were pointed forward and began to tighten her arms along the sides of the shaft as she exerted a force from her legs and tightened her abdomen. The grate on the other side began to pop out as she pressed her boots on it. Once the screws had been popped out, Diana saw two officers pass by. She adjusted herself again and crouched in front of the grate. Diana then took her hands onto the bars and gently opened the grate, setting it aside and then rushing out.

Diana made her way towards the exit and took cover. She saw only a single ERT officer ahead, but facing forward. Diana took out a knife from her vest and raised it, aiming and quickly throwing the knife to hit the man in the thigh. The man fell onto his knees. Diana rushed over and took him down. She then continued, but stopped as she saw two bodies nearby

"Scot..." Diana gasped, rushing to one of the persons.

Diana approached Scot and knelt down. He was still alive.

"Diana..." Scot spoke in a coarse voice, "I'm sorry, I was wrong about the mission. Do whatever you need to do... for the sake... of the Syndicate. Just don't... live by the sword, like I did..."

Scot tilted his head back and then just like that, his body became lifeless. Diana looked into his open eyes that stared out.

Tears formed in her eyes as she looked at him. With a fist in one hand, Diana closed Scot's eyes with the other. "You were the closest thing I ever had to a father…" Diana whispered, sniffling as she stood up. "I won't let you down."

Diana quickly continued down the corridor and made her exit. She then turned the corner and began to run down, unarmed. Diana saw the shadows of some officers up ahead at a junction. She hid beside a grate and took out her sidearm. The ERT officers went the other direction. Diana turned the corner and continued onwards.

A flash of a red light could be seen ahead as well as the ringing of a fire alarm. Diana turned the corner and began to run down, stopping at the next junction only to stop as she saw another squad of ERT officers blocking her way. They opened fire at her. Diana quickly ran down the other direction, keeping low and keeping her movement inconsistent as the gunshots came towards her. Diana tossed a smoke grenade behind her.

Diana reached a three-story room where there was the sound of a rushing water that entered into large, but low cylindrical tanks or pools spread around. Diana saw some windows above from the top platform. She took cover behind one of the tanks and then eyed a ladder nearby. She moved to the ladder as the patrol reached her as she reached the top of the platform.

"Freeze!" an officer shouted.

Diana ducked at the sound of bullets. She then continued forward, staying low and using the floor grate as cover. The water below Diana had a hazed look, almost as if the water that poured in was hot. Diana could see some ERT officers close in on her position from behind as they climbed up the ladder. She quickly turned the corner and continued forward towards the window. Diana put her sidearm away, stood up and was immediately hit in the arm by a bullet that grazed through her sweater and left behind blood and torn skin as if she had just been whipped. Diana attempted to climb up onto the window, but she was forced down as the shatter of glass caused some blades to fall down on her.

Diana looked behind her as the ERT officers caught up with her and pointed their rifles at her. She span around and looked at them as they trained their guns on her. Diana looked around the room. There were more than just ERT members, but also regular forces and even some men in suits.

"End of the line," an ERT officer remarked. "Put your hands up."

Diana gently raised her hands. She then looked back down and towards the people below who were looking up towards her. Her eyes then went to the pool of water. Her body shook and she refused to raise her hands all the way up as she instead vaulted over the railing and dived into the water. Diana hit the hot water with a firm splash.

"Hold your fire!" a man shouted.

Diana struggled to stay afloat in the water. The torrent pushed her around and round until she could no longer hold her orientation and the water whisked her away, submerging her, and sending her off.

Act 2, Scene 1

Diana felt the cold touch of steel along her right cheek and the mild sensation of warm water that juxtaposed the touch on her other cheek. She opened her eyes and looked forward to the darkness around her as she laid on a metal grate with the surface of the Harlech River below her from the coast of the Industrial District.

The water from the nuclear plant poured down on her from an exit pipe that had flushed her out and sent her outdoors. Diana felt around and looked down to the icy water below. Her sniper rifle was not too far from her. Her clothing was warm and wet. The wound on her arm was fresh but cleaned out. She began to stand up and took her rifle, which was nearby, so that she could come away from the rush of the water. The nature of the floor that she was on, which was not so much a floor nor was it a surface, was difficult to stand on, so she ended up crawling her way to the edge. She then climbed up and came onto a grated ledge. From here, Diana looked around at the coastline she was at. The water below was the only immediate path to take, but the clumps of ice around the coast forced her to look for another way.

Diana eyed a ladder ahead that went up the side of the coast. She climbed down the ledge she was on and touched her feet onto a thin ledge against the concrete seawall. She then began to shimmy her way towards the ladder. Diana suddenly stopped as she heard footsteps above and the sudden beam of flashlights from above. She hugged the wall and breathed gently. The lights soon passed. Diana came to the crusty ladder, covered in barnacles, and began to climb up, stopping at the very top so that she could peak out.

Over the edge, Diana saw the flash of sirens and the wreckage of the two unmarked vans that were charred chassis. Diana lowered herself and began to remove all of her equipment, including her belt, vest, and all of the accessories she had. She simply dropped them into the ocean, watching them plop into the sea. Diana took her vest, which read the words 'Security' on the back and threw it towards the grate. She removed all of her uniform until she was only in her boots, black cargo trousers, and undershirt. Diana kept her sidearm and rifle and took them with her as she finally surfaced and quickly went around the rear of a structure.

Diana took the rifle and hid it underneath a nearby dumpster alongside her pistol. She soon began to grow pale as the coldness overwhelmed her. She chattered her teeth as she quickly left and went away from the crime scene. Diana went around the alleyway and soon found herself on Steele Drive, going around towards Keswick. She stopped in front of a bus stop and quickly boarded a bus as it arrived. Diana ignored the bus driver as he cursed at her for not paying her fare or wearing a face mask.

Instead, Diana went and sat quietly at the back of the bus where she heated up and looked out the window as the bus drove through the Industrial District but went the opposite-direction from towards her home and instead went towards Bromley. Instead of going underneath the highway, the bus continued along onto the extension of Steele Drive, which was W Stuart Street at the south end of Keswick. Diana remained on the bus and went into Central Harlech though.

Diana sat on the bus with fresh tears that fell from her eyes. Once the bus turned onto Durham Street, Diana got off and began to wander the cold streets. She soon came onto Campbell Street, turning east and then stopping before Cabernet Tower. At this hour, the front doors of the tower were locked with no way in, except through the parkade. Diana continued down Campbell Street and turned on Earle Street. She then went down and around to enter the parkade from outside and through a door that was unlockable via a pin. Diana inserted the only pin code that she knew, 1921, which caused the door to unlock.

Diana entered into the parkade and made her way over to the elevator. She then called for an elevator and entered, inserting the pin code again so that she could travel to the top-most floor where the penthouse was. Diana put her back against the wall of the elevator and slid down, sitting down as she continued to shiver despite being indoors and away from the outdoor chill. Once the elevator arrived at the 98th floor, Diana exited and went towards the front door of the penthouse. She then banged her head against the door, before pushing herself back to hit against the door again, causing a loud knock to echo. After the second knock, Diana hit the door frame and slid down again. She waited for a response, but none immediately came. She continued to shiver in place, closing her eyes until she heard some footsteps and the removal of a chain from the door and then the lock.

Allodia opened the door and looked down to Diana.

"Oh my God!" Allodia remarked, stepping back. "Diana?!"

Diana looked up to Allodia who was dressed in a silk pink robe. She knelt down and brought a hand to Diana's cheek. She observed her red eyes and a wetness at her cheeks. She also felt the coldness in her body temperature.

"What happened to you?" Allodia questioned. "Come inside, please."

Allodia helped Diana onto her feet and then brought her into the apartment. The door closed behind them, slamming shut. Allodia took Diana and sat her down in the living room.

"You're going to catch pneumonia in this condition," Allodia said. "Here, I'll go and get you a blanket and a towel."

Allodia left while Diana remained seated on the couch. She continued to shiver. Allodia soon returned and gave Diana the towel, bringing it over her wet t-shirt and then wrapping the blanket around. She also went and turned on the gas fireplace nearby to give some warmth.

"Tell me, Diana, what on Earth happened to you?"

"They- they killed them all," Diana emotionlessly answered. "All of them... even Scot."

"What? Who's Scot? What are you talking about?"

"The people I worked with. They killed them. The police killed them. I almost died."

Allodia gave a sigh.

"Nobody is making any sense these days..." Allodia muttered, bringing a hand over Diana's back. "There, there... you're safe now. Can you please explain to me in better detail what happened so that I can understand? Let me get you some tea."

Allodia left and went to turn on the kettle. Diana stopped shivering and seemed a little livelier than she was several minutes ago. Allodia returned with a mug and gave it to Diana to hold.

"Please explain to me what happened," Allodia asked again.

Diana nodded. She explained to Allodia a brief synopsis of the fallout she had with Tristan where he cheated on her. Diana did not name Helene Köhlen, nor did she discuss the events that occurred with Iustina Vaduva and Cardinal Mario Calavera at Aegis Castle. She instead jumped to her desire to move on with her life where she left off before meeting Tristan, her return to Keswick, and her meeting with Scot that led to her joining

Paladin Group's special weapons and tactics team. Diana avoided mentioning the Harlech Syndicate though.

"We had a job tonight," Diana explained. "We had to go to the nuclear power plant and retrieve a package, but we were set up. We were ambushed. I don't know how, or who, but somebody ratted us out. I'm not too sure at the moment, but my coworkers and my... best friend died because of what happened. I lost them all. I just... I can't wrap my head around all of it, but I'm alone now because of it," she said, beginning to cry again. "Scot was all that I had left..."

"Hey, easy," Allodia replied, comforting her. "It's over..."

"No," Diana quickly replied with cold eyes. "It's not over. It's far from over."

Allodia was silent at Diana's words. Diana stared across the room while Allodia stood up and turned off the fireplace. She then sat down in an armchair. Allodia gave a sympathetic look to Diana who then looked at her.

"It was her," Diana remarked. "Hyacinth."

"Hyacinth?" Allodia questioned. "Wait... Hyacinth Dulles?"

"That woman... she set us up," Diana stated. "She set us up..."

"What are you talking about now, Diana?" Allodia asked.

"Hyacinth Dulles is Oswald Montgomery's biological daughter. She's been in charge of Paladin Group ever since Mr. Montgomery's health declined in the last month. Today, Mr. Montgomery told me and Scot that he intended to step down and let Scot takeover, and I thought that she wouldn't take that well. It wouldn't surprise me if she knew already, and did what she did to... Of course."

"What?"

Diana stood up and placed the mug of tea on the coffee table. She then began to leave. Allodia immediately stood up and blocked her.

"Where are you going?"

"I need to find her," Diana responded. "She needs to pay."

"No, no, no," Allodia remarked. "You're not going anywhere. You've just been through a hell of a lot. You need to stay here and rest. You've just been through a traumatic situation."

"I'm fine."

"You may believe yourself to be, but that doesn't mean it is true. I'm not letting you go out there all alone. Normally, I'd tell you to call the police, but… it doesn't seem like that's a viable choice right now."

Diana looked at her as she brought her hands to her temples.

"Oh God," Allodia murmured. "Am I housing a fugitive in my own home?"

"I will make her pay…"

"Oh yeah? How?"

Diana looked aside and avoided looking back at Allodia. She then looked to the ceiling.

"Justice," Diana stated. "I am going to make her face justice."

"If you want justice, then you're going to have to take a moment to sit down and think rationally. You can't simply assume Mrs. Dulles to be guilty based on a hunch. If I understand the Montgomery family, this man (Scot) was her brother, wasn't he? Damian Sutherland? Why would she do such a cold-hearted act as to eliminate her own brother for the sake of inherency? She was the Chief Executive Officer of Zimmerman Corporation and currently a major shareholder in that company.

Why would she want to be the Chief Executive Officer of Paladin Group?"

Diana didn't respond. She looked away from Allodia and then looked back her coldly into her eyes. She dropped her eyes down for a moment, took a deep breath, and then focused back on her.

"Listen, Allodia. I'm going out there either way. You may think of me as the innocent girl you've known all you want, but that isn't who I am. I've only taken that persona when I was with Tristan because for the two and half years that I was with him, under Charlemagne's care, that's who I wanted to pretend to be. A normal, healthy girl... but that simply wasn't the case. What happened between me and Tristan was a reminder of that, that I'm no ordinary girl, and that my vacation was over. I was born in Keswick, my father a negligent drunk, raised only by my mother until they both passed away so that I had to raise me by myself, fending for myself... After I was caught by the police, I was placed in Charlemagne's care, but even then... I suppose I wasn't ordinary. I've been trained by the world's most elite special forces, and also trained by one of the most disciplined martial artists in all of Japan. Recently, I've had additional training with Scot in the art of urban warfare."

Diana sighed.

"My point is, I'm not who you think I am. I've grown up – I can take care of myself. I'll be out there, doing what I feel is right whether you, or Charlemagne, or even Tristan, like it or not."

Allodia looked back at her. She then stepped aside.

"Fine," Allodia replied. "You're right, I can't stop you."

Diana nodded and began to walk to leave.

"But I can in the least help," Allodia added, causing Diana to stop. "For the sake of making sure that you don't kill yourself out there."

Diana gave a puzzled look at her. Allodia walked over to her.

"I'll help you on a number of conditions," Allodia explained, "and only if you agree to them."

"Which are?"

"You cannot kill anyone," Allodia stated. "I have no desire to let yourself exact 'vengeance' by taking another person's life. If you want to bring this woman, or whoever is actually responsible, you will do it by the books."

"Of course," Diana replied.

"Second, you cannot go out there and act with your own identity, for the sake of myself and Charles," Allodia said. "You must remove yourself from all records with this organization, erase any affiliation, and start your life as a new woman. Any actions you take, you must do so either anonymously, or under some sort of persona."

Diana didn't nod or reply to this request.

"Thirdly," Allodia went ahead and said, "if you're going out to enact this… quest of yours, then you'll be needing an alias of some sort. The police may never question or confront the daughter of Charlemagne Cabernet, nor would they a person they believe to be incapable to doing what she intends to do. Therefore, I want you to intern with me and the Cabernet Foundation, shadowing the Chief Executive Officer as she works, with intention to succeed me when it is my time to retire."

"An internship?" Diana questioned.

"To give you a public alias in the daytime," Allodia said. "You can have the nights to do whatever it is that you need to do, but in the day, you're going to be with me in a place that I think you belong in. Think about it, Diana. You could own all of this one day. You could be not only the CEO of the Cabernet Foundation, but also the CEO and Chairwoman of Cabernet Industries, and that entire empire."

Diana paused for a moment. She looked aside and then back to Allodia.

"Business has never really been my… business."

"You'll never know what you want to do unless you expose yourself to that trade," Allodia remarked. "It'll be good for you to experience… as my brother always said."

Diana sighed. She nodded.

"Fine then," Diana replied. "We have a deal."

"Good," Allodia warmly smiled. "Come, you can sleep in the guest room. In the morning, there's a lot more for us to discuss."

Diana nodded and followed Allodia upstairs to the same spare bedroom that she slept in with Tristan last September.

"Goodnight, Diana," Allodia said before she closed the door.

Diana went towards the bed and sat down. She thought to herself carefully before she laid down and passed out, falling asleep out of mere exhaustion.

Act 2, Scene 2

Tristan woke up and looked above him at the bottom of the top bunk where he could hear Finn lightly sleeping. A small trace of light poured in through the blinds and lit the room in a greyish tone. He turned onto his side and scratched his head, rubbed his eyes, and kept them closed as he looked away from the brightness pouring in from the window. At the side of Tristan's bed were various empty bottles of beer. Tristan carefully avoided them as he brought his feet out from his bed and sat up. He held a saddened expression on his face – one of depression and emptiness.

Tristan stood up and stretched his body. He then went to the washroom before returning to get dressed. Once Tristan was dressed, he put together his backpack, placing some notebooks in and then he quietly left so that Finn could continue to sleep. Tristan went to the commonplace to have some breakfast and then sit down on his own to study some physics. He occasionally looked to his phone, prancing his eyes over as though in expectation. Once it was late morning, Tristan closed his books and picked up his phone, unlocking it, and then going to his messages to scroll down to his undeleted, final messages between him and Diana from October. Tristan began to type some words, typing out a long paragraph before deleting the entire thing and then putting his phone away. He tilted his head up and took a deep breath. He then stood up and packed up his things again.

Once he was ready, Tristan left the dorm and went north towards the physics and astronomy building so that he could take a three-hour exam. After he had finished, he brought his answer booklet to the front of the lecture hall and gave it to one of the teaching assistants. He then left the lecture hall and returned to the outside of the campus where it was very quiet in the square before Harlech Manor. Tristan began to walk back to his dorm and entered to meet with Finn who was at his desk.

"Hey," Tristan said, waving to him and setting down his backpack. "Well, that's it... I'm done for the semester."

"Congratulations," Finn replied, raising a bag of trail mix over his mouth and eating it whole. "I've got two more and then I'm off, I suppose."

"That reminds me," Tristan remarked. "Since they're kicking us out for winter break, do you want to come to Allodia's penthouse with me? I didn't think you'd have any other place to hangout at, unless one of your other friends has set you up."

Finn shook his head.

"I have a plane ticket back to England for the 21st," Finn remarked.

"Wait, what?"

"I'm going to spend Christmas with my mother... Mrs. Cunningham. She'll be all alone otherwise, and I couldn't do that to her. This might be the last time I get to travel to the UK since it's getting a little intense over there as well."

"Aren't you worried about, say... getting arrested?"

"I'm not going in with my UK passport. I'm going in as a tourist with my US passport. It'll be fine."

Tristan looked unconvinced. He went over to his desk near the window and began to unpack his backpack. His eyes then wandered out the window as he caught the attention of someone with dark hair from the corner of his eyes. Tristan quickly shifted his whole attention and looked out to see who it was, but he dropped his focus when he saw that it was simply a man with really long dark-brown hair.

"Tristan?" Finn questioned. "Oy, you twat!"

Finn threw the empty, crumpled bag of trail mix at him.

"What?" Tristan replied, annoyed.

"Amanda wants to know if you're interested in going out with her friend Cheryl and us this Friday," Finn restated. "I know it's a little sudden given your breakup, Helene disappearing, but who knows. Maybe it'll be good if you went out and talked to another woman."

Tristan didn't immediately respond. He continued to do what he was doing before taking a deep breath. He looked over to Finn.

"Sure," Tristan remarked. "If you think that'd be good for me, then why not?"

"Cool," Finn responded. "We're going over to the Wellington Pub in Lincoln. Don't forget the fake ID that I got you, because they check at the door."

"Sure," Tristan replied, nodding.

"Do you still miss her?" Finn questioned.

Tristan didn't respond. He gave another sigh and then looked to his best friend.

"You do, don't you."

"What's the point of even lying anymore," Tristan instead replied. "People give me a tonne of crap because I try to be polite with them, but it doesn't matter."

"Don't be polite with me," Finn remarked. "I want you to be upfront and serious. I want you to be honest. I've never lied to you, ever... I've never had to."

"Yeah, except for when you manipulated me into staying with you in that forest," Tristan grumbled. "If you could have arranged for weapons to be dropped somehow, you sure could have let me get into contact with Charlemagne."

"You stayed of your own accord," Finn remarked. "You wanted to be with me."

Tristan was silent.

"If you don't want to meet Cheryl, then it's no big deal."

"No, it's fine," Tristan responded. "Of course I'm still hungover about Diana. From what I've heard, that's not going to change for at least a year and a bit, because they say it's the time you spent with them, divided by two before you start to feel normal again. That being said, I'm not doing myself any favors thinking we could be together again. She hates me. I feel guilty about what I did. That's that."

"It's your fault you never tried to talk to her after you woke up."

"What was I supposed to say then? Apologize? She wouldn't want to hear an apology from me. She wouldn't want to hear anything from me. She knows me too well. Anything she wanted to know, she probably already knew."

Finn shook his head. Tristan looked at his phone.

"Oh great," Tristan muttered. "Your dad wants me to give him a call."

"Dad…" Finn silently said, looking down at his notes.

"Maybe the day you muster up some courage to talk your own father is the same day that I pointlessly go and talk to Diana only for her to ignore me," Tristan remarked, leaving the room.

"Hey, I might just hold you to that," Finn yelled as Tristan left.

Tristan shook his head and then exited out into the corridor. He brought his phone to his ear and went to the common room where it was quiet. He then sat down on the couch.

"Hello, Tristan," Charlemagne greeted in slightly cheerful tone. "How did your exam go? Is that all for this semester?"

"Yeah, that's all," Tristan responded in a bored tone. "I'm done until January."

"Good, good. When will you be returning to the penthouse? I'll have the Protection Squad come over to give you a ride, help with your bags…"

"Probably not for another week," Tristan interrupted. "My roommate isn't leaving until solstice, so I want to spend some time with him. Is that okay? I don't think you'd have a problem with that… as long as you have somebody watching me… like I'm a child or something."

"The day in which I'm confident with your mental health is the day that I will no longer worry about leaving you alone," Charlemagne said in a serious tone. "This goes far beyond what happened between you and Diana, but extends to your past traumas from Finn, your parents, and your experiences with the Huntsman. I once had confidence in Diana to keep an eye on you, but she has seemingly both withdrawn to keep to that promise and is longer in your life. Now that I don't have her to rely on, I must take matters into my own hand."

"Wait… you had Diana spying on me? Why am I not surprised? I still remember eavesdropping on you two talking about my psyche back in November."

"I didn't have her 'spying' on you," Charlemagne replied. "And this isn't related to my incorrect assessment that you were experiencing delusions over your father and what happened in Allabrese on Halloween. I was wrong about that, and to that I say, I'm sorry. No, this was about her worries in regards to the trauma you experienced after your return from China. She had nobody else to talk to, to confide in, except me, so she came to me crying about her worries in your mental condition. Had I not been there to talk to her, she would have continued to suffer."

Tristan held a saddened look.

"Maybe it was for the best that we broke up then…" Tristan muttered. "I was hurting her."

"Enough," Charlemagne remarked. "I'm not telling you this so that you can wallow in self-pity and regret. I'm telling you this so that you can understand the depth of her concern for you. She loved you. She wanted to be with you."

A tear fell from Tristan's eye.

"My point is, however, that she came to me with this information, and naturally, as your guardian and a friend, I was concerned. We operated the way we did because a head-on approach would have had backlash, but that time has changed."

Tristan didn't respond. Charlemagne took a deep breath.

"Anyways," Charlemagne said. "I'm sorry if I've had to bring up any unpleasant emotion about your relationship with Diana. She has moved on with her life, and so should you."

"Right..." Tristan replied, rubbing his eye. "Anyways, are we going back to Allabrese for Christmas, or...?"

"No," Charlemagne responded. "I don't think we will. I don't think it'd be good for you to return to the manor just yet, plus I have work to complete here. Mavis is on holiday and Diana's horse is in the care of her former instructor, Mr. Cavanagh. There is no reason to return other than to bring you harm."

Tristan groaned and replied, "I can handle it."

"No," Charlemagne denied. "Instead, Allodia has invited us to spend Christmas with her at the penthouse. I believe that would be suitable, to have the family together... at least part of it."

"What? Allodia can't travel to Allabrese?" Tristan questioned in a sarcastic tone.

"We are not going to Allabrese and that is final," Charlemagne said in a stern voice.

"Can I at least have some more of my things sent for?" Tristan asked. "I don't have much winter clothing."

"If you want some items picked up, then let me know and send me an email," Charlemagne replied. "The Protection Squad can courier them… They've just been to the manor to pick up some items that Diana's requested."

"You've been in contact with Diana?" Tristan quickly questioned.

"No," Charlemagne denied. "Allodia has though. The two have been in contact. Diana's asked for some of her own clothing, so I've heard. Eventually, all of her personal belongings will have to go, I'm afraid. And such is that."

"Yeah…" Tristan muttered. "Okay, I'll send you an email. Anything else?"

"No, that is all. I'll be in contact with you. Take care."

Tristan hung up and lowered his phone from his ear. He took a deep breath and then sat back in the couch, looking up to the ceiling with a contemplative expression.

Act 2, Scene 3

Diana looked at the headline of the Harlech Herald, the major local tabloid, which read, '*Oswald Montgomery, dead at 84.*' The subheading read, '*Future of Paladin Group uncertain as calls for the organization to be investigated by the Harlech Police Department come from the public.*' She closed her laptop as she sat at the kitchen table and then sat up, walking over to the window in the living room that looked outside and down to Bennett Street. The sun had set, and it was dark out. The skies were a dark grey and a deep snow continued to cover the entire city. Diana held her arms together, crossed, and she took a deep sigh. She then turned around went into the kitchen.

Atop of the dining table there were several boxes. Diana picked up the top-most box and brought it down onto the surface of the table. She then tore at the tape and looked inside to the contents. Inside was Diana's old uniform that she had brought with her from Asia and that the Oishi Clan had given to her, which included her gauntlets, hood and mask, belt, baggy pants, and her boots. The package also included her black tunic and metal chest piece, both of which were still damaged from when Bogdan Alexandrov shot her. The chest-piece had a bullet hole through the abdomen that tore right through the metal, while the tunic had a tear with dried blood around. Diana looked at these two pieces carefully and gave a nostalgic sigh.

Diana picked up the box and went to her bedroom. She placed the box on her bed and then went to her wardrobe to fetch her leather jacket. Diana took it out and threw it on her bed as well, and then she proceeded to change into her ninja outfit, adding the leather jacket overtop. Diana lowered the hood over her face and then took a deep breath. She knelt down near the door and began to remove the floorboard where she stored her valuables. Within the floorboard was some cash and two firearms. Diana picked them up and the magazines with them. She placed each pistol into a different pocket within her leather coat and then went into the kitchen to open a cupboard where there was a box inside. Diana took the box out and opened it, looking inside to see the set of knives inside. Diana carried them at her belt.

Once Diana was ready, she left her apartment through the fire escape and went down to remove the tarp over her motorcycle parked behind a dumpster. The license plates on her motorcycle had been removed and the serial number at the side of the bike had been scraped off. Diana hopped onto her bike and then drove into the night to make her way onto the highway and then go south towards Jarsdel Island. Once she was over the Marke Bridge, Diana continued on until she reached the Lincoln exit, and she came into Lincoln.

Diana turned onto Urhan Street and then drove into an alleyway besides Calypso Tower, the nearly seventy-story neo-gothic skyscraper where Paladin Group, and by extension the Harlech Syndicate, were headquartered in. Diana parked her bike near a set of garage doors that went into the shipping and receiving area for the tower. Diana then moved down the alleyway on top of a dumpster and then jumped up to pull herself onto a canopy ledge over the garage doors. She then climbed onto the side of the building and pulled herself over a set of balustrades by a patio at the side of the building. Diana was in a small garden at the side of the building with some fountains nearby. She laid low as the garden was visible from the public eye. Diana moved through and approached a set of vines that were growing at the side of the skyscraper.

From the garden, Diana found herself on the ledge of a tall window. The ledges went up to a balcony above and the sides of the window were constructed with slightly protruding bricks. Diana grabbed hold and began to climb up the side of the building, making her way up and then pulling herself over the balustrades above that took her onto a balcony. The balcony had a set of doors that went into a rented office on the other side where the lights had been turned off for the day. Diana approached the door and attempted to open it, but the door was locked. Diana broke the glass and unlocked the door from the other side. She then opened the door and went through, going through the office, and then exiting to find herself in the corridor of an unknown floor of the Calypso Tower. Diana proceeded to move forward, following the fire exit signs to take her to a stairwell.

Diana went down the staircase and passed the ground floor to carry on down all the way to the sublevel. There, she reached a set of doors that required a proxy card to unlock. Diana took her old card and scanned it. The door then unlocked for her to enter. Diana rushed into cover as she heard footsteps up ahead. She poked her head out and watched as two men pass and stop in the middle of the corridor ahead. They wore similar uniforms like the ones worn by Diana and her former team, but without any lethal weapons and instead with the Paladin Group logo on the shoulders.

"It all sounds nuts," a tactical security officer remarked.

"Is it true though?" the other replied. "Is the Leader really dead? It can't be…"

"He's dead alright," the security officer responded, "which means our new Leader will be his daughter, who I've heard can be quite merciless."

"Great…"

"You don't think there's some sort of conspiracy, do you? Between what happened to Alpha Team at the nuclear plant and then the Leader dying?"

"Now you're starting to sound nuts," the other remarked.

"I'm serious… Nobody tells us anything. To know something, you have to either be on Alpha or Bravo Team, or within the intelligence department."

"Come on, we're not even halfway through our twelve-hour shift, and I'm already starting to get sick of you."

The security officers continued to walk down the corridor. Diana watched them turn the other corner up ahead before she continued on. She took a deep breath and then continued to venture through the sublevel of the building until she reached a set of doors that required a proxy card to unlock. Diana tapped her card and then pushed on through, entering a corridor with lockers on the left side alongside some benches. The lights in the room were dim and came from lightbulbs in the ceiling. Diana continued down and turned left to a set of doors. She tapped her card again and then entered through into the dim room on the other side.

On the other side, Diana entered into a storage room, or armory, where there was a library of shelves on the left side with an open space protected by railing in the middle, and then more shelves lined up against the right wall. Below, there were more shelves both left and right in the form of aisle likes above on the left. Diana immediately came to face two mercenaries who wore unmarked uniforms just like the ones that Diana and her team used to wear. However, both of these mercs were unarmed.

"Who the hell are you?" one of the mercs questioned. "This is private property…!"

Diana raised her arms up to assume her combat pose while the others raised his fists. One of the mercenaries began to charge towards her, which caused Diana to drop her pose and instead take a knife out, which she threw at this mercenary as he charged her. The mercenary fell to the ground, clutching his shoulder. Diana ran to him, hopped onto his back to crush him down, and then jumped over to kick the other mercenary down. She then grabbed him by the collar and finished him off with a simple punch. Diana stood up and looked around the dark room.

Below, Diana could hear chatter. She jumped over the railing and confronted two more mercenaries who raised their fists up. Diana took another knife and assumed a defensive pose. One of the mercenaries went into punch her, but she dodged out of the way and then swiped with her knife, cutting the arm of the mercenary before going in to grab his arm and then push him down. The other mercenary went in to strike Diana while she brought the other down, but she dodged down and then jumped back. At the third swing, she grabbed his arm and then flipped him over, twisting his arm to dislocate the joint. The mercenary shouted out in pain. Diana shifted her attention over to set of heavy-duty doors at the other side of the room.

Another mercenary joined the fight, kicking down the door and raising his fists as he went to approach Diana. Diana re-assumed her defensive pose with the knife in her hand. He went over to punch Diana, but she quickly jumped out of the way and then looked over to see that one of the mercenaries (the one that she had not seriously injured) stood up and rejoined the fight. Diana dodged another punch from the mercenary she was focused on and then went in to pick him up and dodged underneath to come up behind and trip him with her leg. Diana then turned around to face the other. He threw a punch, and she grabbed the arm and then threw him into a brick pillar. She then grabbed him by his head and bashed it into the pillar to cause him to back down. Diana then refocused on the final mercenary again and grabbed him by the arm. She threw him onto the ground and held his wrist in an awkward pose, holding it there as the man yelled out in pain.

"Please, let me go!" the merc cried out.

"Tell me what I want to know!" Diana shouted.

"Screw you! I won't tell you anything!"

Diana tightened her grip on his wrist, edging closer to tear his arm from its socket.

"Keep it up and you'll be in as much pain as your friend over there…" Diana threatened. "I want to know what's going on with the Syndicate and Paladin Group!"

The grunt resisted.

"What's it going to be…?"

"I'd rather take the pain…"

Diana frowned and took out her pistol.

"What about your life? Is that worth it to hold on to whatever it is that you know?"

The man's eyes widened.

"Okay… okay…!" the merc conceded. "What do you want to know?"

"The Leader is dead," Diana said. "I saw him last night and he was nowhere close to dying… What happened? Who killed him?"

"I don't know, I swear…! All I know is that Mrs. Dulles is in charge now… everybody was hoping that Damian Sutherland would take over, but… he was apparently killed in action, according to her at least."

"Scot died a hero last night!" Diana yelled. "He was betrayed by someone within this organization. There was a conspiracy against him and Mr. Montgomery."

"If there was, I wouldn't know about it. H-have a look at CCTV. All footage was archived today and is only accessible to people with the right credentials… You'd need a pass from someone higher up or on Alpha Team to get access to that. All I know other than that is that there's a civil war going on within the Syndicate. He has the support of those who work in the intelligence department, but nobody's heard of him before. Everybody who defected to work with him are being labeled as rebels by Mrs. Dulles."

"What's his name?"

"I don't remember! Please, go look at the archived footage to find what you want to know. I don't know anything."

"Hmph," Diana grunted. "Fine."

Diana took the mercenary's head and bashed into the hard ground to knock him out. She then stood up and looked over to the others that had passed out. Diana looked to the storage closet this mercenary had come out of and went towards it. She entered and began to look at all the stored explosives. She went and helped herself to some plastic explosives, C4. She also took some blasting caps and a remote detonator as well as some smoke grenades. Diana went to find a backpack so that she could stock up on a good supply of materiel that she would need.

After Diana was stocked up, she left and snuck through the corridors to find a stairwell exit. She then began to climb up sixty or so stories to where she exited and went towards the corporate office doors of Paladin Group. She swiped her card and then entered through. The office lobby was modern and consisted of the company's red-white-blue colors, and behind the main reception was the company logo: a silhouette of a horse with a lightning bolt behind it. She went down a corridor at the side of the lobby and followed it to a heavy, unmarked door at the side of the room. She tapped her card at the proxy reader and then opened the door, walking into a very dim room with a glass wall on one side that looked over to various servers on the other.

Diana took a pistol from her jacket and readied it. She then tapped at the second proxy card reader and opened the door.

Diana entered through the door and let out a shot from her pistol. The room that she entered was a communications center, set up similarly to a 911 dispatch center with various desks set up in four rows and large monitors at the front that displayed a map of Harlech alongside the locations of various cars, sites, and mobile security officers. The dispatchers in the room, who were dressed in formal-casual attire, stood up and lowered their headsets as they all turned to face Diana.

"Hands up!" Diana shouted.

"Oh my God!" a dispatcher remarked.

"Everybody out!"

The dispatchers immediately began to make their way out of the communications room. Once they were out, Diana closed the door behind her and went to one of the computers. She turned the computer on and began to sign-in to her account. On one screen, Diana brought up the CCTV for Calypso Tower so that she could keep an eye on her surroundings, while on the other, she began to sift through recorded footage. She found protected footage for the cameras outside of Montgomery's office and began to go through them to find footage for when she and Scot had left the office before returning to the garage downstairs. Once she had found that footage, she began to go through all of the footage recorded afterwards.

Diana went through each video until she stopped and found one where Dr. Bishop could be seen. He was stopped just before the door by someone off-screen. Mrs. Dulles soon appeared and confronted him before the door. They spoke. The two then entered and the footage ended. Diana played the next footage, taped several minutes later when Mrs. Dulles exited. She appeared to be slightly mad. Dr. Bishop followed soon afterwards. There were no other recordings after this moment from this point-of-view until later in the morning. Diana followed to the next camera point-of-view and tracked Mrs. Dulles as she went towards the elevator next. Dr. Bishop caught up to her and then the two spoke. They got into an argument. Mrs. Dulles then entered the elevator on her own. Diana closed the video and proceeded to export it. Diana then took a red USB drive from her pocket and inserted it into the computer hard drive. She dragged the footage from the desktop and placed it onto the drive. Above the footage on the USB drive was some old footage from 2019 with the names of camera positions at the Nattau Water Treatment Facility and above this as Moira's anti-firewall worm. Diana looked at the MP4 files and growled lightly.

"I should probably think about sending that to Moira sometime," Diana whispered.

Once the footage was saved, Diana took a headset and began to record herself on a simple computer program. She cleared her throat.

"Attention all members of the Syndicate, Oswald Montgomery is dead – murdered by his faithful daughter, Hyacinth Violet Dulles, and his humble doctor, Dr. Nash Bishop. I repeat, our Leader has been murdered by his own daughter at the hands of his personal doctor, Dr. Bishop. I speak to you, on behalf of Damian Sutherland, to abandon what remains of this organization. All members, please abandon your posts and escape while you can. A takeover has ensued, and the Syndicate has fallen. I repeat, the Syndicate has fallen."

Diana took the recording that she had made, quickly altered her voice, and then uploaded it on a loop to the radio dispatch towers across Harlech. She then signed-off and took her backpack, going towards the server room. She unlocked the door and then began to lay down C4 on all of the servers. Once she was done, she removed one of the server drives and placed it in her backpack. She then placed a blasting cap in each of the explosives and then exited, going to a corner of the dispatch center to lay down a small packet on the floor. Diana then exited to the furthest point and detonated the explosives, covering herself as it happened.

A sharp explosion blew from the server room and from the far corner of the room. The fire alarms immediately set off, blowing the water pipes in the remains of where the server room once was and causing water to spray everywhere. The same occurred from the corner of the room where a hole had been left in the floor. Diana jumped down and proceeded to make her escape as police responded to the disturbance reported at the Paladin Group office.

Act 2, Scene 4

Tristan sat on a public bus with Finn as they went from the University of Harlech all the way to Jarsdel Island. There was a hefty amount of traffic along the highway as well as an echo of sirens from up ahead that went on and on non-stop. Eventually, the bus pulled out and began to drive through Lincoln where it made its stop just before the roundabout near the Eclipse Towers. Tristan and Finn hopped off the bus and walked the remaining way to reach the Wellington Pub slightly south of Lincoln Drive.

The snow that fell around them was light. A woman with golden blonde hair and fair skin waited outside the pub with her friend who had orange-red hair and even fairer skin. Finn smiled at the blonde-haired woman and gave her a kiss on the cheek.

"There you are," Finn remarked. "Sorry we're a little late. Traffic was nuts."

"It's okay," Amanda, the blonde-haired girl, replied.

"Hi," Cheryl, the ginger-haired girl, said to Tristan.

"Hi," Tristan simply replied to her. "I guess you're Cheryl then."

"That's me," Cheryl replied. "You must be Tristan."

"Yeah…" Tristan responded.

"Come on, let's go and get a seat before it gets any busier," Amanda remarked.

"Good idea," Finn said, looking towards Tristan.

The four of them entered the pub and were seated. Tristan, Finn, and Amanda presented their IDs to their waitress. She instead ordered a non-alcoholic beverage.

"You're not going to drink?" Tristan questioned.

"I'm underage," Cheryl replied. "Also, I have to drive Mandy home."

"Sorry you had to pull that short straw," Finn remarked, "especially since Mandy might not need a drive home."

Amanda giggled. Tristan held a neutral face that turned to look over to the televisions over the bar. He looked over as an ad played for a teen drama. Coincidentally, the drama was the one that Helene Köhlen had starred in. Tristan's eyes widened and he focused on the ad to its end. He then looked over to Cheryl who had been watching it with her.

"I'm really going to miss 'Love Lost,'" Cheryl said. "It sucks that they cancelled it."

"I heard that it was because of one of the show's actresses," Mandy replied. "I can't remember her name, but they couldn't continue the show because of her."

Tristan's eyes refocused on the TV as there was a loud chime.

"Breaking News at this hour," a newscaster reported. "Mayhem in Harlech tonight as local police responded to an apparent possible terrorist attack at the historic Calypso Tower, where a blast has shaken the metropolitan center of Jarsdel Island and caused a fire midway up the tower. The source of the blast is unclear, but our sources suggest that the blast was connected to a bizarre infiltration by an unknown figure who forced various workers for the Paladin Group to exit the area before the detonation. More information to come as the situation develops. The blast comes as the company faces an uncertain future with the death of its Chief Executive Officer and President, Oswald Montgomery; more on that tonight at eleven."

Tristan looked away from the news and looked over to the waitress as she returned with their three pints of beer. Tristan took his and immediately began to indulge.

· · · ·

Meanwhile, Diana sped along the highway as she went through King Island from Keswick where she made a pit stop to drop off her newly acquired supply of equipment. She made her way across the Penultimate Bridge and continued northward, coming off only at Legion Hill where she continued north towards Mount Harlech and entered Foxwood Vale. The traffic was thick on approach, but Diana simply sped around the cars so that she could maneuver with speed to reach this high-end neighborhood that looked out towards the rest of Harlech. Diana took her motorcycle and drove towards the Mayfair, the former private home of the Leader of the Harlech Syndicate, located in the remote base of Mount Harlech down a long road.

A single pickup truck with the Paladin Group logo was parked at the front of the gates at the end of the road with two mercenaries ahead. Diana sped up and raised the wheel of her motorcycle as she made her approach, tipping up, climbing onto the hood of the car and then onto the roof so that she could gain the leverage she needed to hop over the wall and land in the courtyard on the other side.

Diana quickly hopped off her vehicle as it slid towards the front door. She then sprinted off to make her disappearance as the mercenaries became alerted to her presence, vaulting through a window and entering into a room within the mansion. Diana quickly made her exit from the room and entered a corridor.

"What the hell was that?" a voice remarked from nearby.

"Keep your eyes peeled," another voice said, but over the radio that projected from nearby mercenaries. "There's been an attack at Calypso Tower. It's most likely that inept doctor and the rebels. We're on lockdown until further notice.

"Understood," a third voice affirmed.

"I want a sweep of the entire grounds," the voice over the radio said. "Move it."

Diana crouched forward and came to an exit that went into an arcade beneath the second level of the foyer. She was near a set of stairs that faced away from the main entrance. Diana looked around and then continued forward, approaching the mercenary up ahead who was armed with an assault rifle. She kicked him in the calf and then cuffed in her arm in a tight embrace as he squirmed. The mercenary fell to the ground and Diana walked over him as she continued her way forward to the end of the arcade, and then around the corner as another came by. Diana stood up and ran towards him.

The mercenary turned around as Diana approached, but she took her hands and planted them on his face, forcing him into a cabinet at the side and causing the loudness of smashed glass to echo through the room.

"What was that?!" a mercenary remarked. "Spread out and find whoever's there!"

Diana forced the mercenary down and then continued along.

"Systems are down throughout the entire network," the voice over the radio projected. "We're currently stuck with local communications until further notice."

"Roger…"

Diana came around the corner and then went down. She looked about and then proceeded up a set of stairs at the far-side that took her to the second floor of the large foyer. Diana saw a mercenary ahead, turning from an open doorway. Diana kept back and saw him go off. She stayed where she was, looking around until she looked at the pillar she was standing at. Diana looked up and then began to climb the pillar, bringing herself onto the beams above.

Diana held her balance as she made her way over to the opposite-side of the room and then swung down behind the mercenary, approaching him from behind and asphyxiating him into unconsciousness. The mercenary fell into a deep sleep. Diana dropped him and then checked the ground floor for any remaining grunts. The foyer seemed to be clear. Diana looked around at the manor and saw that it was very much the same as it was in November.

Diana took a step back from the second floor and made her way around to the end of one of the corridors to enter a circular stairwell that went up to the rooftop above the foyer, where there was a garden around the skylights that looked down. There were various pots and squared wooden troughs with hedges and other plants. Mercenaries could be seen ahead, looking down to the courtyard on the other side. The snowfall had begun to pick up in this area, especially as they were at a higher altitude at the base of the mountain.

All eight of the mercenaries immediately turned to face Diana with their flashlights pointed at her as the door behind her slammed shut. Diana looked back at them.

"What's with the freaking ninja?" one of them remarked.

"Grab him!" another said. "Don't let him get away!"

Diana glared at them as they made their approach towards her. She then began to run towards one, kicking him down with a roundhouse kick before she went to another, picking up a pot and throwing it at him. The pot hit the merc in the head and knocked him out instantly. With seven left, Diana hopped over one as he charged towards her, pushing him over the ledge so that she could face the six remaining. Diana jumped over a hedge as a merc attempted to throw a pot towards her. She then raised her hands up in a defensive stance and began to dodge some punches from another until she was able to go in and grab him by his own fists and then take him down, bashing the side of his face into the floor. Another attempted to provoke Diana, but she quickly clapped her hands at his ears and then head-butted him down.

"Who the hell is this guy?" a grunted remarked, stepping towards Diana nervously.

"Don't just stand there," another remarked. "Stop him!"

Diana stepped forward and grabbed one of the mercs by the arm and then turned him around to smash his head into a lamppost. She then looked over to the final four. Diana paced around one of them as he approached her. She then went in and grabbed his arms, pushing him into one of the sunroofs and into the ground below.

"Come on," one of them taunted. "Come at me!"

Diana jerked her head over and tripped the grunt onto the ground, but then dodged out of the way as another tried to punch her. Diana pushed the second grunt into the third, and then readjusted her focus to the initial one as he got off from the ground. Diana kicked him in the side and then threw a pot down at him before readdressing the other two as she kicked one into the ground and then took a knife and slashed the other's thigh. Diana took the knife and stabbed it into the other leg, incapacitating him.

With everybody out of commission, Diana wiped the sweat from her forehead and then took a deep breath. She continued along and went up a set of stairs on the roof that went towards the east side of the house. She went to the very end and stopped at the side of a circular tower. She climbed up the ladder and then confronted the last mercenary that remained. He looked over at Diana and began to charge at her. Diana hopped over him and rolled onto the other side, over a skylight that looked down into the tower below. She then stood up and taunted the merc to come at her. The mercenary took the bait, and Diana grabbed him by the wrist and then tossed him into the skylight, causing it to smash and for the two of them to come down and land on the floor below.

A loud shriek greeted Diana as she looked up from where she landed to see Mrs. Dulles in the bed of her father with two strange men at either side.

"Well, well, well," Diana remarked, taking out her pistols, which caused either man to freeze as they got out of the bed.

One of the men inched to the side as he dragged a blanket to cover his groin. Diana instantly shot him in the knee and caused him to collapse onto the floor.

"Ah, you son of a bitch!" the man remarked.

"Who are you?" Mrs. Dulles questioned. "What do you think you're doing?"

"Shut up!" Diana shouted, firing a bullet indiscriminately into the air. "Get out from that bed, you whore! Your short-lived rule is over."

Diana took her pistol and shot the other man in the knee, causing him to collapse on the other side. He yelled out in pain. Diana jerked her neck behind as she began to hear sirens in the distance.

"No..." Diana muttered.

Diana instantly looked back over to Mrs. Dulles who placed a short wool robe around her. She held a frown as she looked over to Diana. A mix of red and blue lights began to flood into the room from outside. Diana held a nervous expression. Her expression turned to anger.

"You have no idea... no absolute idea how tempting it is to end this here and now..." Diana said in a nervous, cracked voice.

"Then do it," Mrs. Dulles replied. "I'm not guilty of anything and the courts will know that. If you want any real justice, then you'll have to do it yourself. If that's what this is about, then you'd know that."

Diana frowned at her. She then gave a sly smile as she released her backpack and allowed it to fall behind her. Several small packages of cocaine fell out from the bag.

"You can't honestly believe that they'll arrest me over a bit of cocaine?"

"The cocaine and else in there... the fact that your mercenaries whose butts I kicked are illegally armed to the teeth... that's just the tip of the iceberg. What really will set the ball rolling is the sudden appearance of information and footage over the web that ties you to the infamous, mythical Harlech Syndicate. All of the people of Harlech will chant for and plead that you stay in prison for a very, very long time. So, unless you have some friends like Kau Waomoni, I'd say it's just about over for you."

"You wench!" Mrs. Dulles yelled out, picking up a wine glass at her side and throwing it over to Diana.

Diana quickly raised her pistol and shot at the glass, causing it to explode like a firework in the room.

"Don't test me. You had your brother and father killed. If there's any miserable soul in the room, it'd be yours."

"If you think you have anything on me..."

"Oh, I do," Diana remarked. "I've been very busy, going to the trouble to destroy the company's servers at Calypso Tower, while keeping one for myself. I've got lots of work ahead of me, but it'll be oh, so worth it."

"Who are you? If you think your vigilantism will pay off, think again. Crown would never prosecute someone for evidence that surfaced over the webs. We have a rule of law in this country, and the law can be very picky about evidence."

"Hmph," Diana grunted. "We'll see."

"And as if you'd even be able to get out of here yourself," Mrs. Dulles warned. "The police will surely take you in too."

"We'll see…" Diana remarked, inching forward. "We'll just have to see… so get moving!"

. . . .

Tristan laughed with Finn as the pair played some pool and conversed with the girls from within the Wellington Pub. Neither of them desired to end the night and return home, especially as both of the boys, Tristan more than Finn, were clearly drunk.

"Tonight on the Harlech News Network," a newscaster said from the TV. "At this hour, our newscopter and reporter in the sky has received word of violence and mayhem from within Harlech today. Earlier, we had reports of an unconfirmed terrorist attack on the Calypso Tower in Jarsdel Island, but now we are receiving words of an attack at the Mayfair Estate in Foxwood Vale. Police are on the scene, and it seems that some sort of conflict has broken out between possible terrorists, or gangs from within…"

Tristan raised his head and kept his smile as he looked over to the TV screen, which showed aerial footage of a large mansion with various figures unconscious atop. The helicopter attempted to readjust itself as a large semi-trailer truck broke the police line and slammed its way into the mansion walls, causing the police on the ground to take cover as it backed up. The truck destroyed the walls of the manor and exposed the interior where there was a woman in a red silk robe and another mysterious figure in black on the second floor above. The figure in black pushed the woman down and then hopped down on its own.

"Police are in disarray tonight as they attempt to handle this second incident at the former home of Oswald Montgomery, the former Chief Executive Officer of Paladin Group, whose offices were targeted at an initial attack earlier this evening. Police have confirmed that various members of the Paladin Group were injured at Calypso Tower, but none killed although two are in critical condition at Harlech General. What we are now seeing from the Mayfair is some sort of black-clad ninja and what appears to be… Hyacinth Dulles, who has been taken hostage."

The truck backed up and then rammed itself into the mansion once more as armored police cars arrived on scene. The mysterious black figure did a back flip out of the way and landed on its feet as the truck attempted to run the figure over. Mrs. Dulles ran away into the manor while two mercenaries exited from the truck and began to engage the ninja in hand-to-hand combat. Tristan watched as the figure quickly disabled each of them and took them to the ground where they screamed out in agonizing pain. The figure then escaped as police began to shoot at it, going into the manor.

"Police are attempting to control the scene, but it appears that… oh!"

The woman was pushed out through the front doors and onto the ground below with her wrists tied behind her. The black figure walked over and picked up the motorcycle on the floor. A van moved from the rear of the house and towards the gate. The figure hopped onto the motorcycle and then sped off seemingly after this van. Police attempted to fire at the figure but were unsuccessful.

The footage on the TV shifted back to the newscaster, but in the corner, it began to replay footage of the ninja as it backflipped from the truck. Tristan looked at the figure in the corner of the screen with intent, especially as she made her landing and then swiftly took out the two mercenaries with ease. Diana grabbed the man by his wrists and then twisted his arm to force him into submission, disarming him and then dislocating his arm. She then swiftly moved to the other as he attempted to punch her, grabbing him and forcing him onto the floor before she then pulled his arm out of its socket. The footage then cut out.

Tristan flinched. He shook his head and looked back over to the pool table.

"Yes, it's quite a chaotic scene at Foxwood Vale at the moment. We have not received an official word from police in the area, although they have advised residents to stay indoors. Our hopes are that these attacks may be enough to call attention to the lack of action the HPD has taken when it comes to organized crime, as the death of Oswald Montgomery, who has long been suspected to be the ringleader of the Harlech Syndicate, may have caused a sort of crisis that could bring the entire organization down onto itself. Here is hoping…"

"Tristan?" Finn questioned.

"Yeah?"

"It's your turn, mate," Finn said.

"Right, sorry… I was just caught up in the news. I also think I might call a cab and call it in for a night… I'm starting to hit that level of drunkenness that's an unpleasant nausea," Tristan lied.

"Ah, piss," Finn remarked. "Alright then… if that's what you want."

"Aw, you're leaving?" Cheryl responded.

"Yeah…" Tristan replied. "Sorry about that, but I… also have an early start tomorrow. Let me pay for my share of the drinks."

"Nevermind that," Finn responded. "It's all on me. You just run along now… I'll see you tomorrow, probably."

Tristan nodded to him. He sat his pool cue down and then went to grab his coat from the booth. He looked over to the TV as it played the same footage from the Mayfair again. He looked at it with intent.

"Diana…" Tristan muttered, eyeing the ninja on the screen.

• • • •

Diana raced down Legionnaire Way on her motorcycle as she made her escape from the scene of the crime. She held a microchip within her fist and placed it into her inner jacket pocket before placing both hands on the handles of her bike as she continued forward. Diana rode along the highway, going back over the Penultimate Bridge, and then exiting in Camross to then enter Whitney Harbor as she drove along Maiden Drive. Diana soon took herself into Keswick and into the alleyway where she covered her motorcycle.

Once Diana had climbed up the fire escape by her apartment, she raised up the window and climbed into the other side. Her bed was covered in plastic explosives, canisters of smoke grenades, and blasting caps. Diana passed them and went instead to her computer where the server piece she had stolen sat on top of. Diana took the microchip in her jacket and placed it on top of her desk. She then looked at her phone and checked the time.

It was little past midnight, but Diana had a message from Allodia. Diana picked up her phone and looked at the message, which read, 'Hey Diana, wanted to know if you had plans for Christmas next week! If not, you're welcome to come and spend it with me at the penthouse. Lots of love to you!'

Diana immediately replied and said, 'Thanks a lot for the invite. I'd love to come over to the mansion to spend Christmas with you. Do you want me to bring anything?' Diana looked at this message and then sent it. She then sat her phone down and began to remove her jacket. Diana turned on her computer and as it loaded, she took off her armor and went to close the window as the bitter night chill drifted into the room. Diana went back to her computer and brought her laptop screen up so that it could boot up as well.

Some news footage online showed clips from her assault on the Mayfair. Diana played a clip from when the semi-truck attempted to run her down. She began to download as much footage as she could to watch later. By the time she was finished going through all the footage, she went back to her other computer and began to attach some cables to a second monitor and the rest to the server. She then booted up the server and waited for it to load.

Meanwhile, Diana watched some more clips from her assault, playing some slowly so that she could analyze them. She watched carefully as the semi-truck suddenly appeared on the property. She saw a separate black van come up from behind the truck and disappear to the side of the building. She played this clip over and over again, looking pensively at it. She then played some footage from later on where that same van could be seen exiting the property.

"Hm…" Diana wondered. "How did I miss that?" she whispered.

Diana sat her laptop aside and then looked over to all the equipment she now had. She left the room and went to fetch the boxes in the other room so that she could place them all in and then put them to a corner in the room. Diana then returned and sat down at her desk, picking up the microchip, and then inserting it into her hard drive. She then booted up a program and waited for it to load. The program began to decrypt the frequency on the chip. Diana raised the volume so that she could listen. She also brought a set of headphones over her ears.

The program played the looped distress signal that Diana had set to broadcast over the main channel used by the Harlech Syndicate. She cringed at her own distorted voice and quickly changed to the next channel.

"We extracted the package carefully, sir. The secondary target was arrested in the aftermath," a voice reported.

"She is of no concern to me," another, slightly familiar voice remarked. "Return to base for debriefing."

"Yes, sir."

The communications then cut out. Diana frowned and tapped her hands at her desk. She then moved her hand to the computer mouse and began to set up the program on her computer to record all incoming transmissions on this channel. Diana then removed her headset and stood up.

"I can work on the rest later..." Diana said to herself. "Where's Moira when you really need her?"

Diana finished undressing herself and went to take a shower. She then returned, dressed for the night, putting away her pistols before looking over to the box of plastic explosives and grenades to realize that it was a fruitless endeavor to conceal her weaponry. She placed her guns on her desk, close to the bed for easy access, and then pulled the covers over.

Diana laid down and looked over to the brightness that poured in from her window as the blinds had not been lowered. She looked over to the window pensively and took light breaths. She stayed like this for several minutes until she moved onto her back. She then sighed and brought a hand to her forehead.

"What was in that van?" Diana muttered. "I need to know..."

Diana closed her eyes and drifted asleep. Her mind focused on the situation at hand, just as Tristan's was as he laid down in his bed at his dorm and fell asleep.

Act 3, Scene 1

A week passed since Diana's assault on the Calypso Tower and Mayfair. She went on with her business, attempting to extract files from the server that she stole, and gradually releasing them anonymously onto the Internet. She also continued to obsessively study the footage and hypothesize what could have been in the truck that the 'rebel' faction of the New Syndicate was so desperate to recover at the Mayfair.

Diana woke up next week and grabbed her phone from her desk, looking at the time to read approximately one o'clock in the afternoon. Diana sat up and brought her legs out. She looked at the text message that she received from Allodia, wishing her a Merry Christmas and asking what time she would come to the penthouse. The message had been sent four hours ago. Diana immediately replied and said, 'I'm on my way now!' Diana then looked at the notification that was below this text message, which was a news alert from last night, detailing highlights from a Christmas Eve press conference held by the Harlech Police Department. Diana put her phone down and brought her laptop up to watch it. She skipped through the beginning where some other senior officers spoke and then went to the moment that HPD Commissioner Harris Errol Game took the podium. Diana watched.

"The revelation of certain documents and footage has brought forward new charges against Mrs. Hyacinth Dulles, and it is my hope that in exchange for her cooperation and a reduced sentence, we may uncover further information into the operations of the Harlech Syndicate that could put thousands of others behind bars and clean up our city. However, it is my belief that at the present moment, the presence of a gun-toting ninja vigilante is a larger threat to our police work and our quest to bring people like Mrs. Dulles and her associates to justice. The work of vigilantes on the street harms the ability of Crown to prosecute, and as I'm sure this vigilante desires, bring to justice these people who ought to be brought to justice."

"Commissioner," a reported pled.

"That is all, ladies and gentlemen," the commissioner said, moving away from the podium.

Diana paused the video and then began to go through the news article below. According to the Harlech Herald, various servers in the Paladin Group office were damaged and the information on them unrecoverable. A large cache of weaponry was seized from the sublevel where paramedics recovered wounded security guards. The article then finished with a critique against Game and the negligence of the Harlech Police Department in which more work had been done by this mysterious vigilante than had been done by the police force in the last forty years. Diana closed her laptop and stood up to go and take a shower.

Once Diana had returned, she went to her computer and woke it up. She then began to see if there were any new recordings from last night on the Syndicate channel. There was not. She turned the computer off and got dressed for the day. Diana put on a white t-shirt, white pants, and a dark red wool sweater atop. She then went into the kitchen to put on her motorcycle boots on, pick up her leather jacket, and then pick up a gift bag left on the kitchen counter before going over to exit the apartment building.

Diana went around to the alleyway as she left the building, but then stopped as she looked over to her unmarked motorcycle hidden under the tarp. She took a step back and then decided to continue on foot to reach Cabernet Tower.

Tristan watched security footage from around Cabernet Tower as she sat at the large computer with double monitors at the back of Charlemagne's private workshop in the depths of the tower. He looked at footage from the main lobby of Cabernet Tower and then to the parkade where he could see Diana entering the tower from the parkade entrance. He focused on her and saw her make her way across the underground parking lot above them and then go towards the elevator. Tristan sighed and stood up, looking over to Charlemagne who had a welder's mask on as he worked on the large unknown piece of machinery behind.

"Diana's here," Tristan announced, walking over to his guardian.

Tristan looked at Charlemagne and watched as he continued to work.

"I said Diana's here!" Tristan said, slightly louder.

"Hm?" Charlemagne questioned, jumping and quickly turning off his torch.

Charlemagne lifted his mask up and looked over to Tristan.

"I'm sorry, what did you say?"

"I said Diana's here," Tristan said for the third time. "Come on, we better go."

"Sorry, yes. Allodia will want us to be there before she arrives. Otherwise, she'll say something and accidentally give her an opportunity to leave."

Tristan returned to the computer and turned it off. He then began to power down the lights in the room, leaving only dim ones near the stairs and platform above on. The pair walked up to the elevator and then waited for it to arrive.

"Are you sure this is a good idea?" Tristan questioned. "For any of us?"

"It's Christmas," Charlemagne said. "If I can't enjoy Christmas with the two children that I adopted, then where's has the spirit of Christmas gone?"

"I didn't expect she'd show," Tristan muttered. "I really don't think she'd expect us to be there."

"It'll be a pleasant surprise then."

"Or unpleasant."

• • • •

Diana waited before the elevator in the parkade with the gift bag handle around her arm. She tapped her foot as she continued to wait.

"What's taking so long?" Diana muttered, looking up to see the elevator coming down from high above.

The elevator door finally opened, and Diana entered. She tapped for the 98th floor and then inserted the pin code. The door then closed and began to ascend up to the penthouse. Diana waited patiently as the elevator went up and when the door opened, she stepped forward and went to the front door of the penthouse. There was a scent of cooking that poured through from underneath the door. Diana knocked twice and then stepped back as she waited for Allodia to answer.

"The door's open!" Allodia shouted from the other side.

Diana placed her hand on the doorknob and opened the heavy door. She then stepped through and took her shoes and jacket off before she went anymore forward. The door slammed shut behind her. Diana then walked to the end, before the stairs where she looked immediately to her left and frowned as she saw Charlemagne and Tristan sitting at the couch.

Tristan immediately stood up and faced her as he noticed her, looking at her for the first time in almost two months. Charlemagne simply looked over to her and extended a warm smile. Diana looked at Tristan, seeing him for the first time since he was on the stretcher in the depths of the University of Harlech Hospital extension that was under construction. His hair was cut short since the last time they had seen each other, and he had the same mass. In fact, almost everything was the same about him, including the dull, emotionless look in his tired eyes and frown across his face. Tristan wore a thin green wool sweater and jeans.

"Hi," Tristan sheepishly greeted.

Diana didn't respond and instead her frown grew deeper at him.

"Diana!" Allodia greeted from the other side, walking over and extending her arms out to hug her. "Merry Christmas! Isn't this nice?! The four of us spending Christmas together again…!"

Diana received Allodia's hug and said, "Merry Christmas," in a quiet voice.

The two soon parted and Diana gave her the present that she had bought for her.

"Oh, you shouldn't have. Thank you… I'll go and put it by the tree to open later in the evening."

"It's no problem."

"Can I get you something to drink?" Allodia offered. "Some cider? Some wine?"

"No, I'm fine. I don't drink…"

Diana turned to the other two as Charlemagne began to carefully stand on his feet. He went over to Diana, blocking Tristan and Diana's view of each other, and extended a hand towards Diana.

"Merry Christmas, Diana," Charlemagne greeted, clasping her hand with both of his gloved hands. "I hope you've been well."

Diana sighed and then went in to hug Charlemagne.

"You don't need to shake my hand, Charles. We're still family..."

Tristan watched as Diana hugged Charlemagne.

"Oooh!" Allodia expressed. "I almost forgot to turn the radio on. What kind of atmosphere would it be without some Christmas tunes?"

Diana and Charlemagne parted. She quickly ignored looking over to Tristan who continued to stand as if he was expecting to receive the same from Diana, but instead she looked over to Allodia with both her hands before her. Allodia soon returned from the Christmas tree and walked over to Diana.

"Diana, Diana, Diana," Allodia chanted. "Come and sit down," she said, bringing her over to the living room. "Tristan, sit down. Here, you can sit down here."

Diana was sat down on a couch at the end of the living room where there was a pleasant radiation of heat from the fireplace nearby. The TV was turned off and Charlemagne was simply looking forward pensively. Tristan sat back down at the other end of the couch while Allodia sat down between him and Charlemagne.

"Isn't this nice?" Allodia said again. "Oh! I almost forget...! I left the turkey out of the oven!"

Allodia stood up again and went back towards the kitchen at the other side of the penthouse. Diana looked over to the end table next to Tristan where there was a glass of a champagne-colored liquid on a coaster. She looked at it with disgust and then looked over to Charlemagne. Charlemagne had tired eyes and an unnatural paleness to his fair skin that made his skin look almost like marble. His hair had almost turned completely white. He was dressed in an expensive knitted seater with a dress shirt underneath and grey dress pants. He wore slippers over his feet. Allodia wore a thick crème white sweater that had a plumpness around the collar. She also wore white pants like Diana and a pair of slippers her feet. Allodia turned on the radio and then went to put the turkey in the oven. She soon returned and sat down again between Tristan and Charlemagne.

"So," Allodia said, "what's with everybody being so quiet? How's everybody doing? Tristan?"

Tristan dropped his arm and turned over to Allodia. He then looked over to Diana, which caused her to turn away.

"Diana?" Allodia questioned. "How did your exams go?"

"They were all online for me," Diana replied. "I think they went okay."

"What about you Tristan? How did your exams go?"

Tristan turned to her and hesitated to answer. He then said, "Alright, I guess. I'm just glad they're over," in a plain tone.

"Good…"

The four of them sat in awkward silence. A knock at the door soon took them by surprise. Diana looked around, confused at who it could be.

"Oh, that must be Barry," Allodia said, walking off to answer the door.

Charlemagne carefully stood up and went to join her. Diana and Tristan were left with each other, which Diana immediately changed as she left to follow the others and stand at the end of the corridor to watch as Allodia opened the door.

"Hello, Barry," Allodia greeted. "How are you?"

"Hello, Barr," Charlemagne greeted.

"Merry Christmas, all," Barry replied, presenting a bottle of wine.

"Ooh, thank you," Allodia remarked, taking the bottle.

Charlemagne and Allodia parted so that Dr. Lambert could walk in. Charlemagne took his coat and hung it on the wall. The two then walked forward.

"Hello, Diana," Barry said, waving to her.

"Hello," Diana replied.

Tristan looked over to Barry as he entered the main room while Allodia went to the kitchen with the bottle of wine that he had brought as a gift. Charlemagne walked Barry into the living room and offered him a seat on the armchair across from where Diana had been sitting.

"Dinner should be ready within a couple of hours," Allodia said. "It's still a bit early... Make yourself at home, Barry. Can I get you a drink?"

"Yes, please," Barry replied.

"Cider or wine?"

"Cider, please."

Barry sat down and waved over to Tristan.

"Hello, Tristan."

"Hey," Tristan replied.

Charlemagne and Diana sat down at their seats. Allodia soon returned with a glass of cider and gave it to Barry alongside a coaster. She then sat down, and they resumed into the awkward silence they had been experiencing until Allodia took control and picked up the conversation amongst the adults. Diana and Tristan resumed to sit in silence, however. Charlemagne and Barry took the moment to catch up on their work in the last six months, the progress of the new lab in Allabrese, and the current conditions of the portables where scientists were working from out in Champion Plains. For the most part, Diana and Tristan ignored each other – Diana more than Tristan who would occasionally look over to his former girlfriend with a sad look in his face. Diana wholeheartedly ignored him especially as she noticed these glances. Charlemagne and Barry became the focus of the party as the two of them soon became steadily drunk and hearty, laughing and reminiscing in old times.

The hours soon passed and before Diana knew it, it was five o'clock and time for them to sit down for dinner. Allodia and Charlemagne each took a head of the table, while Barry sat on Charlemagne's right, next to Tristan, and Diana on the other side on her own. The conversation turned to pleasantries at the table where Charlemagne and Barry calmed down and Allodia spoke more. After the dinner had ended, Diana helped take the plates into the kitchen where they amassed all the unwashed dishes in the sink and left it there while the boys went back to the living room to sit down.

Tristan sat down in the armchair that Barry had been sitting on while Charlemagne and Barry went to sit next to each other at the large couch. Allodia went to the loveseat where Diana had been sitting and sat down there. Diana walked over to join her, removing her sweater as she became warm. She also tied her hair in a ponytail as she went back to the living room.

"Well," Allodia said, looking at her watch, "it's almost time to open presents."

Tristan looked over to Diana now that she had taken off her sweater. Across her arm there was a deep cut that had healed over and left a thin red scab. He eyed it carefully while Tristan turned on the television and began to slip through the channels. Charlemagne stopped at the news and watched for a moment.

"Look at this... pure propaganda," Charlemagne said to Barry. "They say what they want people to know..."

"It's always been like that," Barry remarked. "All media has always been propaganda, because in every story, tale, from the smallest poem to the largest series, there's something an author is attempting to address to his readers. Decades ago, these messages used to be wholesome, but now it's all more or less politics…"

"Of course, because the hands of the media have come to rest in a collective few who wish to project their message to the masses."

"Hey, wait!" Tristan remarked as Charlemagne changed the channel as the story about the vigilante was about to air. "Go back!"

"Hm? Why?" Charlemagne questioned.

"Go back!"

"No, don't," Diana pleaded. "It's all Fake News… We don't need to see that garbage."

Charlemagne went back anyways.

"What is it, Tristan? What did you want to see?"

"Look," Tristan pointed as they aired the footage of the vigilante. "Isn't that astonishing? A vigilante here in Harlech."

"Compared to the many things we have seen over the years, it's not much," Charlemagne simply remarked.

"Who do you think could be under that mask?" Tristan asked, looking over to Diana.

Diana glared at him. The pace at which her chest expanded sped up slightly as she became nervous.

"I don't know," Charlemagne grumbled. "I'm not really interested in things to do with the Syndicate or Paladin Group."

"You should be," Tristan said, continuing to look at Diana. "I mean, who do you know has had extensive training in martial arts and owns a ninja costume."

"It's not a costume," Diana muttered.

Charlemagne muted the TV and looked over to Tristan.

"What on Earth are you on about?" Charlemagne questioned.

Allodia bit her lips as she looked away. Diana's heart pace was close to a hundred beats per minute as she breathed sharply.

"We'll never know," Diana answered before Tristan could speak. "It'd be a waste to guess…"

"I don't know," Tristan remarked. "You'd think that between the get-up and the motorcycle, it'd be pretty clear who it was…"

Charlemagne looked over to Tristan with a confused expression.

"I'm sorry, I'm lost. I don't understand what you're going on about."

"Nothing," Diana deflected. "He's going on about nothing and being stupid as always. He's not thinking about what he's doing. He never thinks about what he's doing. That's Tristan's entire problem, especially when the only thing he knows to do is speak…"

"At least I can speak," Tristan jeered, "but on that topic, you haven't talked much, have you. What have you been up to, Diana? How's the job with Paladin Group? Is that how you got the cut on your arm? Were you busy last Friday night?"

Nobody responded. Diana's face was flush with anger. Allodia gave a look of concern. She then looked over to Tristan.

"Actually," Allodia said, "as a matter of fact, Diana was with me last Friday night."

"Yes, you see?" Diana replied. "I was with Allodia."

"Really?" Tristan scoffed, looking at both Allodia and Diana. "So, that wasn't you nearly getting run over by a truck and wearing those ninja clothes that I swear, look a lot like the ones you brought back with you from Asia."

"Shut up, Tristan!" Diana snapped. "That wasn't me!"

"Wait a moment…" Charlemagne said in a serious tone, extending his hands to the former couple to settle them down. "Diana, is what Tristan is saying true?"

"Of course not," Diana lied. "He's talking out of his ass, as usual."

"Tristan?" Charlemagne questioned.

"I'm not lying! How have you not made the same assessment? The movement… the motorcycle… Hell, even the jacket…! It's the same jacket hung up by the front door! How can you doubt me?!"

Charlemagne looked over to Diana and then to Allodia who held a nervous smile.

"Allodia?" Charlemagne questioned.

Allodia looked down and was silent.

"Good Lord," Charlemagne muttered, bringing a hand to his face. "How did this slip past me? I've been so caught up in my work…. I can't believe this."

"Then don't believe it," Diana replied, crossing her arms.

"What in God's name do you think you're doing out there?!" Charlemagne shouted, standing. "Have you absolutely lost your mind?! Are you mad?! For what?!"

"Hey, don't take that tone with me!" Diana deflected.

Allodia put a hand on Diana's shoulder and looked to her brother.

"Charles, calm down. Diana had a purpose to go out there. She knew what she was doing – she had my confidence, and that's not something that's so easy to come by. Even then, I tried to talk her out of it, but she was certain, and at her age, her decisions are own, not yours."

"I can't believe you knew about this! I told you to keep an eye on her so that I could be certain that this sort of suicidal behavior was not the case in her – that she was well."

"You had Allodia spy on me?" Diana questioned, looking to Diana. "You were spying on me?"

"No, clearly I wasn't if I kept this between us," Allodia replied, looking to Charlemagne next. "Don't you see? She's here with us now, safe and well. What she did last week went off without a hitch."

"Hmph," Tristan grunted. "Am I the only one that sees the scab on her arm? The danger she placed herself in...? She's clearly looking to get herself traumatized again."

"Hm, at least I can overcome my adversity and not wallow in it like a baby," Diana deflected, standing up. "And what do you care about me? Huh? You've never given a damn about me, except now when it clearly suits you."

"You don't know me," Tristan responded, standing up. "You don't know what I've been through or what has gone through my mind – the regret!"

"Yes, blame your infidelity on your traumas. As a matter of fact, blame all of your problems on your traumas because that's *exactly* what I want to hear from you. It's at least, what I'd come to *expect* from you...!"

"I'm sorry," Tristan confessed. "Okay, I'm sorry. I'm sorry. I'm sorry. I've felt terrible about what I did to you, and I *do* regret hurting you. Never have I done something to someone to garner such a backlash, but at least I've placed a value on my life – the life that you've saved so many times. At least I'm not as suicidal as people fear me to be. You on the other hand... that's a completely different case. I'm scared of what you might do to yourself out there."

"Ha!" Diana laughed. "That's laughable. If you even gave a damn about me, you would have never have slept with another woman. You would have kept me in mind when you were aware of her!"

"Leave Helene out of this," Tristan insisted. "She did nothing wrong. It was all me."

"Now you take ownership for your crime? You expect me to believe that you care about my life when you didn't even care about my emotions?" Diana said, shaking her head. "If you cared about me, it would only be because of some sort of delusion that we could be together. That's all you care about. Yourself. Your own ego. You're a sociopath."

Tristan didn't respond. Charlemagne cleared his throat and shook his head.

"And what about me?" Charlemagne questioned. "You can lambast Tristan with insults all you want, but we are family by blood and law, Diana. It is my justified concern that you may hurt yourself out there, or worse, die. You may have forgotten what your life was like before we met, but I haven't. I still remember the young, traumatized girl who ached to return to Harlech where she was free. I won't permit you to return to such a state simply for the sake of nostalgia, or whatever it is that you desire."

"What I want is none of your business," Diana snapped at him. "This isn't some thrill-seeking quest. I'm not a daredevil! I don't forget my past…! I don't long for a return to it! I also don't long to return to being with this chump either…" she said, pointing at Tristan. "I've moved on with my life, and what I'm doing now is apart of it."

"A likely story," Tristan muttered.

"Tristan," Allodia scolded. "Show some respect. Diana has been through more than enough without having you or Charlemagne treat her like this."

"Oh, definitely," Charlemagne said, shaking his head. "Let us all support the vigilante who is aiming to get herself killed.

She believes she has nothing worth living for… I've clearly been concerned about the wrong one…"

"I'm not aiming to get myself killed!" Diana shouted. "Just because I don't fear death, doesn't mean I'm suicidal! I had my reason to be out there… a good one at that!"

"Oh yeah?" Tristan questioned. "So let's hear it."

Diana paused for a moment and glared back at him. She hesitated with two fists her hand and instead of saying anything more, she left.

"Diana…" Allodia said, attempting to stop her.

"That's what I thought…" Tristan muttered, turning to her.

Diana twitched and turned to face Tristan. She grabbed him by the collar, which took him by surprise. He raised his eyes wide open as she looked at him angrily. Tristan grabbed her by her thin arms and pushed her back.

"Let go of me!" Tristan yelled.

"Easily," Diana muttered, looking back at him with hateful eyes. "You might want to pick up on that skill."

With those final words, Diana went to the front door and picked up her jacket. She also picked up her shoes and then left out the front door. Allodia went after her. Charlemagne held a hand at his forehead as he looked to the ground, pivoting on the spot. Tristan sat down and let out a deep breath. He fixed his shirt and rested his arm on the armrest, bringing a fist to his cheek as he looked out the window. Barry let out a deep breath.

"Well, this has been quite a Christmas," Barry said, hands at his lap. "I think I should get going now…"

"You don't have to leave," Charlemagne replied. "It's over."

Barry remained seated. Charlemagne sat down next to him and let out a sigh. Tristan stood up and went towards the stairs.

"Where are you going?" Charlemagne questioned.

"To my room…" Tristan replied, storming off.

"Bloody teenagers…" Charlemagne muttered, looking to Barry.

"You could have had worse," Barry remarked.

"I believe I did have worse…"

"Oh right…" Barry replied.

"What can you do though?"

"Well, you could stop her…"

"How could I do that?" Charlemagne replied. "Why would I do that? Allodia was right. She's an adult now. Her decisions are her own and I can't get involved."

"You're going to let her kill herself? You sat here in Harlech worried about Tristan, but you won't meet the same standards for Diana? Sounds like you're biased towards her."

"I couldn't do anything even if I wanted to… Even though I'm scared for her."

"Well, there is something that could be done… but we'd need the right person for it…"

Charlemagne looked at him.

"What are you thinking of?"

Act 3, Scene 2

Diana fled from Cabernet Tower and returned to her apartment. She entered through the front door and began to mull her way up the stairs to reach the top floor. She then took out her keys and entered into the darkness of her home. She stepped down the corridor and looked around at the dim room decorated in her austere style. She then went to her room and closed the door behind her. She sat her keys down at her desk and sat down, waking her computer, and placing her headset over her head. Diana then opened the program that was intercepting communications from the Syndicate.

Two audio clips had been saved between the early afternoon and recently not too long ago at about nineteen-thirty hours. Diana played the first and listened.

"What is your status?" an old voice said.

"Bishop," Diana muttered.

"We're at Zimmerman Tower," a grunt replied. "No sign of the Loyalists, so we'll get that intel as soon as possible."

"Good. Mrs. Dulles is behind bars and the Board of Directors have taken over leadership of the company. Paladin Group is in disarray while she is away."

"Of course, sir."

The audio recording finished there. Diana played the next one.

"We've got the location," a grunt said. "We're compromised though. We'll regroup and then make our way towards Dock F at Port Burnes ASAP."

"Understood," Dr. Bishop replied. "I want a team on the outside and another on the inside looking for the package. Am I clear?"

"Yes, doctor," the grunt replied.

"I want everyone to pay close attention – we all saw what happened last week, and we can expect that to happen again if you're not careful."

"Of course, sir."

Diana stood up and removed her headset. She went to one of the boxes where her uniform was stored. She then proceeded to get changed so that she could head out. Since last week, Diana had bought a better belt to hold more equipment as well as holsters for her torso to hold her pistols and magazines within her jacket. She checked the location of the docks on her computer and studied it carefully. Once Diana was ready, she climbed out her window and went down to the dumpster, moving the tarp from her motorcycle, and then started the engine.

Diana sped out from the alleyway, came onto Bennett Street, and then made her way down to W Stuart Street and then right onto Bailey Drive to go towards the highway. She turned and crossed the river, entering Jarsdel Island and going off to enter into Port Burnes district. Diana went down the entire stretch of Burnes Drive and turned onto Harthdam Way. She then slowed down behind some cars parked on the curb. To her side was a tall fence that was three-stories tall with barbed wire at the top. There was a thick snowfall that came down and blinded her visibility up to fifty feet. Diana got off her bike and started to walk down the sidewalk towards the crosswire gate blocking the entrance through the checkpoint within the perimeter walls.

Diana took out her pistols from her hand and fired at the steel lock that kept the chained gate together. The lock collapsed onto the snow for Diana to unravel the chains. She then pushed the gate open and stepped onto the compound.

Dock F of Port Burnes was a large private plot of land to the south with various shipping containers in different colors spread throughout, stacked up to four containers high. Each one was about two meters in height and width, and several meters in length. Towards the left of the area was an office above a platform that was on three-story tall struts. The platform connected to another one beside, which housed a crane. Some more cranes could be seen to the right at the far end of the compound and behind the many containers in the area.

Diana began to step forward into the quiet, but well-lit area by the bright LED lights that created an artificial daylight. She made her way to the center of the compound, putting her pistols away into her jacket and then walking over to a container. She began to open the contents doors and looked inside to see what looked to be like some sort of armored vehicle, or tank. The tank was colored in an urban camouflage mixed in a dark-purple grey and black. The turret of the tank faced directly at her and contained other turrets at the side. Diana stepped out of the container and looked above as she saw several more containers. All of them were labeled with the Zimmerman Corporation imprint at the doors. There were several rows that all looked the same. She gave a sigh.

Diana immediately twitched her sights towards the entrance as headlights shined through the front gate and people in tactical uniforms stepped out and opened the gates. She stepped back and began to run down an aisle before climbing up the lowest container at the end and making her way to the top of the tallest container in the row. Diana looked down from above as she could hear some incoherent chatter from the mercenaries. They had driven a semi-truck into the area and parked it. Approximately eight of them spread out, armed with assault rifles as they went to their designated areas. Two of the mercenaries went up the stairs towards the office house, while the others spread out around the area. Two mercenaries secured the entrance and shut the gate, while another two began to go down the aisles and two kept close around the open ground before the struts. Diana looked around and then saw one of the mercenaries go towards the crane on the other end.

Diana backed away and ducked down, out of sight from the mercenary that took point in front of the crane. She made her way down and hid around a corner to check the aisle before rushing over to the next container, hiding behind its corner and looking down to spot a merc as he obliviously came towards her. Diana glanced over to the next corner and looked down. She retreated down the back aisle and stopped as she saw the other mercenary up ahead. They were both walking at a similar pace. Diana retreated back and went down one of the empty aisles in the middle. She made her way to the end and spotted a guard having a smoke at the checkpoint booth while another stood inside the checkpoint house by the gate. The other two were by the front of the truck as they waited around. Diana went forward and came to the side of the semi-truck. She kept low and approached the merc by the front gate. She took a smoke grenade, pulled the pin, and then threw the canister at him.

"Smoke!" the merc yelled.

Diana sprinted towards him and kicked him onto the floor. She then lowered her thigh down onto his neck and choked him unconscious. Once he was out, Diana went towards the door that went into the checkpoint house and waited for it to open. The second grunt stepped out and Diana jumped him, bringing him onto the ground and choked him unconscious as well. The smoke began to clear as Diana stood up. She quickly rushed down the aisles, causing the mercenary by the truck to open fire at her as she disappeared down the aisle. Diana then jumped up the side of the containers and fled up top.

"It's that ninja!" a mercenary shouted. "You know what to do. Nobody leaves until that ninja-thing is dead. Am I clear?!"

"Yes, sir."

Diana continued down the aisle and jumped down at the rear. She went forward and began to sneak up on one of the grunts up ahead, taking a pistol out and grabbing him with one arm around the neck. Diana then hit him in the head, causing him to fall over, and then another one on the front of the face to knock him out.

"I've got him!" a grunt from the other end of the aisle shouted.

Diana looked over and then flipped out of the way as he opened fire towards her. She reached the end of the corridor and looked out to see if the two mercenaries by the truck were still there. They weren't. The mercenary atop by the crane was still in position with his rifle pointed downwards as he scanned the floor below. Diana saw one of the mercenaries at the mouths of the aisles ahead and another at the foot of the stairs where he took point.

Diana went down the mouths of the aisles and approached the grunt ahead with a smoke grenade in hand. She threw it towards him, engulfing him in smoke and then taking him down to the ground to knock him out. Diana then continued down the aisle and stopped at the end. She saw the other grunt that had been around the containers rush away from his unconscious friend and go down one of the middle aisles. Diana ran after and sprinted towards him. She kicked him down onto the ground and smashed his face into the snowy concrete.

Once the grunt was down, Diana took another smoke grenade and went to take cover behind the semi-truck. She looked around the corner and saw the final merc was still at the stairs. She threw her grenade towards him and covered him in smoke. Diana then went towards him and approached him from behind, wrapping her arms around him just as she had done previously and knocking him out.

In the last second as Diana went up the stairs, she checked the area around her to make sure she had gotten all six that were on the floor. Once she was certain, she continued up and went to the top catwalk just before the office. The blinds that looked into the office were shut. Diana went to the door and brought her hand to the handle. She then paused as she could hear some chatter from within. She took her pistol from within her jacket and readied it. Diana then kicked the door open, aiming at the mercenary's leg and shooting him.

The merc fell to the floor and dropped the radio in his hand. Diana picked up a foldable chair and brought it down to his chest. She quickly disarmed him from his sidearm and threw it aside. She also picked up the rifle and carried it with her as she went to the door on the other side. Diana peaked out the blinds and saw the other mercenary make his approach. She opened the door and shot at the man with the rifle, hitting him in the leg. Diana then tossed the rifle aside and went over to pull him out of the way before going back into the office to pull the other out.

"What are you going to do to me?!" the mercenary leader questioned. "Let go of me!"

Diana pulled him over the bridge and took her pistol. She pointed it towards him.

"You're here because of Dr. Bishop, aren't you?" Diana questioned.

"What? No! No! We're loyalists! We work for Mrs. Dulles!"

"Mrs. Dulles is in prison…! Who is your leader now?!"

"I won't say anything!"

Diana scoffed. She grabbed the man by his leg again and dragged him further towards the crane. She pulled the hook down from the chain and attached it to the back of the man by his vest.

"What are you doing?!"

The man tried to break free while Diana went to the crane control panel. She began to churn the winch and raise the chain up, raising the man up. Diana then extended the arm out so that the mercenary leader dangled over the ground.

"I'm going to ask again," Diana shouted at him. "I want to know specifics!"

"Oh God..."

"Not too long ago, Dr. Bishop had his men here. Why? What's here that's of interest to him...?"

"I-I don't know!" the mercenary replied, screaming.

"Answer me!"

"We- we were sent to secure the cargo, that's it. There was something else though... a specially marked container that Dr. Bishop was interested in, but that's all I know. I don't know what was inside...!"

"So you were here to secure a package... that's it?"

"And the cargo... all of this... Why?"

"The containers aren't ours, but they belonged to Zimmerman Corporation. We had our orders to go around and secure containers like these, but when we heard that Dr. Bishop had come to this lot, we went in to see if he took the special container. Paladin Group leases this lot to Zimmerman Corporation, but ever since Mrs. Dulles has taken over, she's had us doing a lot of work that's one and the same between them. It's understandable... She's the executive of both companies, technically... and from what I've heard, the private military company that used to do security for Zimmerman Corps is no more."

"Why? What interest does she have in what's in these containers!"

"I don't know! All I know is that there are a lot of special weapons – drones! All of these things are advanced weapons developed by Zimmerman Corporation overseas... it's a lot of fancy crap. Mrs. Dulles has been interested in it, and I thought it was because we were going to escalate the war against the doctor!"

"What about the 'package' that was secured at the Mayfair? Last week, the 'rebels' launched a desperate attack while police had closed in on the mansion to extract something that must have been extremely valuable to them. What was that?"

"It was…"

Diana jerked her head over before the mercenary could finish his sentence. A mysterious figure ran down the bridge that connected the two platforms and stopped at the end, taking out a modified modern bow and firing at Diana, which caused her to cover her face with her gauntlets at the arrow hit above her. She then looked back at the figure as she intercepted an oncoming punch. The mysterious figure pushed back at her and she attempted to punch back at the man, but her punch was intercepted, and they were caught in a struggle.

The mysterious figure pulled Diana around and threw her back onto the bridge. He then pulled at the crane and brought the arm back so that the man hung over the platform. The mysterious figure then shot an arrow, breaking the chain, and causing him to fall to the floor. Diana took out her pistol and looked over to the man. The mysterious figure wore a dark urban camouflaged advanced exoskeleton robotic suit with a head-shaped helmet that was completely dark, covering the figure's face. The man was armed with sidearms, but at his thighs, and had a belt with various accessories, including an item that looked a lot like a stun gun. The mysterious figure pulled another arrow towards Diana. Diana pointed her pistol at him and shot at him. The mysterious figure ducked out of the way behind the body of the crane.

Diana's pistol then began to click as she was out of bullet. The mysterious figure came out from his cover and quickly shot an arrow towards Diana, disarming her as it hit her other pistol and causing it to fall over. Diana growled at him and threw the other one onto the ground before she went to face him head-on. The mysterious figure put his bow away and raised his fists up as Diana went towards him.

The mysterious figure went quickly towards Diana and attempted to wrap his arms around her torso. He exerted a tremendous amount of force, more than she could ever hope to exert. Diana took a knife from within her jacket and attempted to stab him in the visor with it, but instead scratched it and caused him to back up and let go. Diana then jabbed him in the side and ran off. She picked up pistol on the floor and placed it in her holster. She then jumped over the railing and hopped down onto a container below, jumping down onto the ground and then going to grab her other pistol as she made her escape. The mysterious figure looked down towards her from atop and took out the stun device at his side, climbed over the railing and then shot at the side of the platform to cause a thick wire and claw to extend out. He then grappled down and made a safe landing below while Diana looked at him from the other side.

Diana took steps back and proceeded to make her way down the aisle of the shipping yard. The mysterious figure took out his bow and shot towards her, causing her to duck her head as she ran. Once she was out of his sight, the figure ran forward and took his grapple gun and shot it towards the top of a container, zipping up to the top and then continuing from above as Diana had just climbed up a container at the end. Diana looked over to him as he pulled out his bow and shot towards her. Diana jumped to the container next door and then began to climb up to get a higher ground.

The mysterious figure continued to shoot at her until she came out of his sight. He took his grapple gun and jumped over to the next container, eyeing her ahead. He shot towards her and zipped over, extending his arm out to grab her and slam her onto the ground as he caught up with her. The two fell overboard and landed on the ground below in the thick blanket of snow. Diana hit him in the side of the head and then rolled out of the way. She took out two knives that were left in her jacket and proceeded to run off. The mysterious figure stood up and went after her.

Diana stopped ahead and threw the knives at him. The mysterious figure blocked it as he raised his gauntlets up to cover his mask. He then took the grapple gun and shot at her, causing the claw to attach onto Diana's armor. The man pulled her towards him, causing her to slip and land before him. Diana quickly jumped up and ran to punch him. The figure blocked the punch and grabbed her arm. Diana kicked him back. She then raised her hands up in a defensive stance.

The unknown figure went in to grab at her, which she responded to by grabbing him at his own arm. The man took her by the other side and kicked up his leg to force her up and then pick her up. Diana quickly responded as she was lifted up, bringing her leg and kicking him in the helmet. The man dropped her, and she fell to the ground. She then quickly ran away and began to climb up the container again so that she could make her escape. The unknown figure adjusted his helmet and then looked over to her as she ran.

Diana climbed up another container and continued upwards. He took his grapple gun and launched it towards her, pulling her back so that he could climb up after her. Diana quickly recovered and continued up the container. Once he was at the top, she took a smoke grenade and dropped it where she was. Diana then jumped onto the other side and looked around as the mysterious man had disappeared. She looked around and then saw the grapple gun attach to the side of the container she was on and the man zip over. She kicked him as he climbed over. Diana then hopped down to make her escape.

The mysterious, unknown figure climbed up and looked down towards her. He then hopped down and gave chase to her to the other side of the row of containers, all of which were high up. Diana attempted to climb up at the end, but the man took his grapple gun, hooked onto her, and pulled her back again. He then went towards her, but she threw a punch at him. The figure raised his arms up, blocking his helmet with his gauntlets.

Diana shook her fist as she hit the hard pieces of armor, and she continued to run off. She climbed over and took another piece of equipment from her belt, readying it as she knelt down. The mysterious figure climbed to the top of the container and looked over to Diana. Diana stood up and jumped over to the other. She then took the detonator in her hand and blew the piece of C4 that she had placed. The mysterious figure was blown back by the blast and thrown over. He rolled his landing below, but then looked up as she saw the container above come towards him. Diana watched with fearful eyes as he was nearly crushed by the heavy container. The impact caused the container she was on to shake and fall over. Diana jumped out of the way and landed on the one next to it, which was safe.

The mysterious man shot his grapple up towards Diana, which prompted her to run to the next, especially as the container shook from the impact of the other container. Diana landed on the other side and pulled herself up. She then looked behind her and took a knife, throwing it at the mysterious figure as he jumped after her. The knife hit the visor, which broke his momentum. He hit the side of the container and missed his opportunity to grab hold, falling over instead and down onto the floor below. The masked man's mask was cracked and displayed a sort of static on the other side that faced Diana, especially as sparks flew out. The mysterious figure rolled onto his side and then came onto both hands as he looked down.

Diana watched as the mask fell off. She squinted towards the man but was unable to see him clearly until he stood up and saw the side of his face. Tristan looked up to her.

"I should have known…" Diana muttered, shaking her head.

Tristan looked up to her as she looked down at him. His nose was bloodied and the impact from the mask scratched the side of his cheek.

"Why?!" Diana yelled from atop, raising her arms up as she lowered her own mas. "Why did you have to interrupt?! I was getting the information that I needed! Why did you have to interfere?!"

Tristan scowled at her and replied, "You don't know what you're doing here, Diana! Somebody has to stop you before you get yourself killed!"

"Are you honestly so arrogant?" Diana shouted at him. "I had everything under control – I was not under any threat until you came around… and even then, you're still no threat to me! Stay out of my way!"

"Either you stop now, or I take you into the police," Tristan remarked. "Either way, I just want this madness to end before you make a regrettable move!"

"Stay out of my way!" Diana repeated.

Diana ran off. Tristan took his grapple gun and shot it up so that he could chase her. He then pointed it back towards her and pulled her towards him. He raised his fists up and dodged the kick that Diana tried to hit him with. He then attempted to grab her by the arms, but she broke out from one of them and fell to the floor instead. Diana then kicked Tristan with her feet and forced him back. She then continued to run away from him and make her escape.

Tristan spat out some blood and then looked back towards Diana as she climbed up a container and almost made her escape over the fence. He took out his bow and prepared it. He let it fly and it ripped past Diana, grazing her arm. She knelt down and grasped the wound before continuing forward, but Tristan took his grapple gun, grabbed her by the back again and pulled her over. He then ran towards her and attempted to subdue her, but Diana kicked him off and nearly caused him to fall over. Tristan grabbed the edge of the container and pulled himself up. She grabbed him by the arms, but Tristan overpowered her and picked her up, bringing her onto the ground again. Tristan attempted to subdue her again.

Diana head-butted him and then forced him onto his back. She punched him across the face, but before she could punch him again, he grabbed her wrist and maintained control of her. Diana brought her feet onto Tristan's abdomen as she attempted to pull off. She then stamped at his face which finally got him off. Tristan attempted to grab her again, but Diana instead jumped away and faced him. Diana then charged towards him, grabbing his hands as she attempted to push him back.

Tristan grunted and overpowered her again, raising her up. Diana kicked back at him. Tristan grabbed her leg, but he lost his balance on the edge of the container and fell backwards. Diana grabbed the side as she nearly fell down with him. Tristan crashed onto the snow below and rolled onto his side. He spat out some more blood and then looked up to Diana as she climbed over the side and then jumped over the fence to make her escape. Tristan growled and punched the snow at his side. He then fell onto his back and took a moment to pant as he caught his breath. Tristan closed his eyes out of exhaustion while Diana rolled her landing on the other side.

Diana scrambled to pick herself up and then quickly ran through Dock E to leave through the main entrance. Tristan leaned over and hacked some blood out. He then heard some sirens and picked himself up, using his grapple gun to return up and then make his leave. Diana returned to her motorcycle and instantly fled the scene before police arrived.

Act 4, Scene 1

Allodia sighed as she looked underneath Diana's front door and saw the trail of blood that followed from downstairs lead underneath her door. The door was slightly open, requiring Allodia to simply push the door so that she could enter. Allodia carried with her a tray with a coffee on one corner and a small takeout bag from a local coffee shop. She walked through the old apartment's entrance and looked around the living space that Diana called her home. Allodia went to some of the curtains and opened them, allowing some daylight to enter in, and then she went to the bedroom door, which was left ajar too. Allodia walked through.

The trail of blood continued in and all the way to the bed inside where Diana was dressed in a bloodied white t-shirt with her back to the door. Allodia set the tray on Diana's messy desk and then looked at her arm where she had been wounded. She placed a hand on Diana's head, which caused her to immediately wake up and grab Allodia's hand in a panic. Allodia let out a minor shriek, but her panic subsided with Diana's as she lowered her attention as she realized that it was only Allodia behind her. Allodia took a deep breath.

Diana closed her eyes as she sat up. She then took her own deep breath.

"You startled me," Diana said.

"You left your front door open..." Allodia replied. "Not a safe idea if you expect police to be looking for you."

"I don't expect the police to be looking for me..."

"Well, you should. You left a trail of blood worthy of a murder from the front door."

"Did I? I was really tired when I returned home last night.... What time is it?"

"It's one o'clock," Allodia answered. "Time to get up. We have work to do."

"Huh? It's the day after Christmas... doesn't the company take a break until the new year?"

"Not the Cabernet Foundation," Allodia remarked. "Come on, I have to introduce you to the board of directors at Cabernet Tower."

Allodia sighed as she looked at Diana's bloodied sheets. Diana looked at her and saw that she was dressed in a pink blouse, white blazer, and white skirt. She also wore a coat and had earmuffs around her head.

"You do know blood is hard, if not nearly impossible, to get out of sheets, right?" Allodia remarked. "You're going to have to get yourself some new sheets... and what happened to your arm?"

Diana looked at the wound with tired and uninterested eyes and then lied back down.

"I was hit with an arrow," Diana simply said. "It didn't penetrate, but the speed of the arrow tore my skin like a bullet."

"What the hell did you get up to last night?" Allodia questioned. "You know, these kinds of results are exactly the kind of results that Charlemagne and Tristan were worried about."

"Please don't say his name," Diana requested.

Allodia looked at Diana with disbelief and then closed her eyes. She then opened them.

"Sorry... come on, sit up. Let me set it."

"You don't have to," Diana replied, sitting up again.

"Yes, I do. You can't let a wound stay exposed like that... it'll never heal. Besides, I won't let the board of directors (my bosses) see you with a massive gash on your arm. Where's your first aid kit?"

"In the bathroom, under the sink."

Allodia left to retrieve the kit. She then returned, put on her reading glasses, and then began to suture the wound.

"I was down at Port Burnes," Diana began to explain. "I received some intel that one of the two people who was responsible for Scot, and by extension, Oswald Montgomery's death, was doing something over there, but when I got there, they had already left. Instead, the people still loyal to Mrs. Dulles arrived and began to scope the place for the container they had already taken. I'm nowhere closer than I was before yesterday into figuring out what is going on..."

"What about the archer? I didn't realize private security, especially Paladin, was famed for its skilled archers. Where does that come in to play?"

Diana didn't respond.

"Well, you only need to have this doctor arrested now, don't you? I suppose you're halfway complete."

"Ow!" Diana yelled.

"Easy," Allodia replied.

"Be careful then," Diana bickered.

"I'm not a doctor," Allodia remarked. "I'm a vet, so be grateful it's not you instead. Otherwise, you'd bleed out and the doctors in this country... they've got quite the nose, so they'll call the police before you leave out the door."

Allodia finished up the stitches on Diana's arm and then looked to the floor at Diana's chest-piece on the floor.

"Is that the armor you're wearing? It looks medieval," Allodia remarked, removing her glasses.

"It's the armor that was given to me by the Oishi Clan in Japan," Diana replied. "It's durable, but a bit heavy."

"There's a bullet hole through it."

"That's not recent..."

Allodia sighed.

"If you want, I could look and see if Charlemagne has some prototype exoskeleton suits that you could use."

"I'd rather not wear anything that Charlemagne's built – not after the support he gave me last night. For all I'd know, it'd restrain me."

"Well, how about some regular Cabernet bulletproof armor? It can be your Christmas present – it should provide more protection than what you're wearing."

"Thanks," Diana replied, looking at her stitched wound. "Also thanks for all of this help, you defending me yesterday, and this job you've done here."

"You'll have to limit your motion for the next couple of days to let it heal," Allodia said. "I'll take it off later, but now, you need to get ready for the day ahead of you… or what's left of it. It's already past noon."

Allodia stood up and looked at the mess around her.

"Also think about hiding your gear in a better place, maybe? If the police came here right now, even the tightest of alibis would bust you."

"I'll think about it."

"No, you're going to do it, missy," Allodia warned. "I'm a part of this too. I'm an accomplice to whatever it is you get yourself into from now on, so with that you need to take my own wellbeing into consideration. Am I understood?"

"Sorry," Diana apologized. "Yes."

"Here," Allodia said, handing her the coffee. "Also here are some donuts. Get dressed… we have an appointment at a tailor in Stoneridge to get fitted for a business suit."

"A suit? I don't wear suits…"

"You will if you'll be meeting with the Cabernet Board," Allodia replied in a stern voice. "The meeting is at four o'clock, so please hurry."

"Right..." Diana replied.

Allodia began to pick up some of the mess around while Diana picked up some clothes and went to take a shower. She got dressed in a plain shirt, some jeans, and a zip hoodie before she came out to see that Allodia had done some serious work in tidying up the room.

Once Diana was ready, the pair left her apartment, and she closed the door behind. They walked downstairs and went to Allodia's red convertible parked nearby. She unlocked the car and Diana got into the passenger seat while Allodia went around to get into the driver's seat.

"You'll need two outfits," Allodia said. "One for this evening so that you look sharp and affirmative, and another for the New Year's Gala next Friday."

"New Year's Gala?" Diana questioned. "Do I need a suit for that?"

"No, you'll be needing a dress for that. It's a fundraiser, and the nicer and more beautiful you can make yourself, the better success it is for us to secure donations."

"You mean... we have to dress nice, basically prostitute ourselves, so that we can secure money for the Foundation?"

Allodia sighed as she turned on the car engine.

"If that's the way you want to put it, then yes. You don't have to sleep with anyone though, unless you want to. You only need to work your womanly charm for these men..."

Allodia drove off and began to make her way towards Bailey Drive from Keswick.

"We'll need to get your size," Allodia said. "I know this place in Stoneridge – there's a man there that does an excellent job with suits and dresses. I've gone to him for the last ten years."

"Okay…" Diana replied.

Allodia drove into Stoneridge and parked her car on the curb. She then took Diana and went to get her fitted for a business suit and a dress. Diana took off her hoodie as the well-dressed male with a thin white beard, dressed in a pink dress shirt and silver vest took her measurements.

"Hold your breath," the man said in his flamboyant voice.

Diana inhaled and attempted to suck in her stomach, but she wasn't able to fully take it in all that much. She looked depressingly at her stomach and sighed.

Once the man was done taking her measurements, Diana and Allodia went to the front counter.

"How long will it take?" Allodia questioned.

"The dress will take a couple weeks, but the suit can be finished at the earliest on Monday."

"Monday?" Allodia remarked. "Alonzo, please, I need this suit to be ready now… preferably for this evening."

"Hm, I'm sorry, but that's the best I can do… these things take time, you know? You can't rush perfection…"

"What if I pay so that you can rush perfection? You've allowed me to rush suits… It's not like it's a man's suit. It's a woman's suit. All you need to do is hem the blazer and skirt."

"It'll take me more than two hours," the man replied. "I'm sorry."

"What about the dress? I need that by next week."

"If you want me to rush that, I can have it done by Thursday for triple the cost."

Allodia took a deep breath and then smiled.

"Fine. What do you have in Diana's size so that she can wear tonight?"

"Come and take a look."

Diana went back into the store and looked at all the different skirts, blazers, and blouses. Alonzo helped pick her out and a set. Diana put on the black blazer, the Giza cotton blouse that felt like silk, and the black shirt. She sucked in her stomach and looked at herself in the mirror. Alonzo then helped her set up her hair in a bun that fit the style. She was then fitted into a pair of Italian leather high heels. Diana then returned to the front of the store where Allodia was waiting.

"She looks gorgeous," Alonzo remarked. "How does it feel?"

"I feel... professional," Diana simply said.

"Excellent," Alonzo replied. "Okay, the dress will be done on Thursday, but for now, your total comes to... one-thousand six-hundred, including the two-hundred-dollar deposit for the dress. Will that be on debit or credit?"

"Credit," Allodia responded, taking out her credit card from her purse to pay.

Diana wore her suit as she left the tailor ship with Allodia. They then returned to Allodia's care as the sun began to set. Allodia drove up Earle Street and turned into the parkade of Cabernet Tower. She drove into her parking space and the two of them exited to make their way to the elevator.

"Alright, here's the rundown. First, we have to meet with the board of directors. These are the people who have investments in the company, decide Cabernet Industries' budget for all of the subsidiaries, including the Cabernet Foundation. It's important to make a good impression on them, especially in regards to the public work we do which brightens the company's image. The only other man who you need to dazzle with our good work is Mr. Gilbert, the Chief Communications Officer and a personal friend of Charlemagne. There are twelve directors, many of whom you probably already know. I'm one of them. Charlemagne is the Chairman of the board, being the majority shareholder. Really, while the board represents the investors, they don't have much power since Charlemagne has the final say on all decisions, but they can influence him by withdrawing their funding of certain projects. It is ideal to keep them all happy with what they want from Cabernet Industries. Over the years, the people in that board has changed hands a lot, especially since Charles can be a bit of an autocrat. However, since Charles has stepped out of the limelight recently, I've taken hold and really just allowed them to manage things as I sign off on them. Thankfully, Mr. Huxley and Mr. Bowman has been a big help, but in general the rest of the investors are smart people who know what's best for the company, so it's been okay to trust them... so far."

The elevator door opened, and the pair found themselves in the main lobby of Cabernet Tower. Allodia continued to explain to Diana the way of the company as they walked through and made their way towards an escalator to the second floor.

"Second, after we meet with the board of directors, we are going to meet some of the department heads that work here in Harlech. You've already met most of the ones, I'm sure, who work in Allabrese, but these are the ones that work from Harlech. They include our Head of Finances, Head of Human Resources, and other department that the manpower in Allabrese can't suffice to fill. There are also the individual subsidiaries that work from here, such as Cabernet Airlines, Cabernet Extraction, Cabernet Construction... all of them are housed here for the most part. We'll be meeting each of the CEOs that are here for you to meet. You should have met Mr. McGarrick by now since he's Charles' friend. He's the Vice-President of Cabernet Industries and on the Board of Directors. He's also the Chief

Executive Officer of Cabernet Airline. His office is on the thirty-third floor."

Allodia stopped before a set of elevators on the second floor. Diana looked at them and saw that they only went up.

"There are different elevators for the business tower?" Diana questioned.

"Of course," Allodia replied. "Security has become pretty strict ever since what happened to you guys in France. The Protection Squad restricted traffic into the towers since last year out of a lockdown protocol which was never really lifted. Speaking of which, we also have to meet Mr. Heavner and his team. They're on the twenty-fifth floor."

"So, what happens if you try to go to any of the floors from the other elevators?"

"They don't go up…" Allodia simply replied. "Except to the penthouse. Everything else is only through these doors. Even the fire escapes have been placed on restricted access. The doors are only supposed to open if the fire alarms go off."

"Interesting…"

Allodia and Diana waited for the elevator doors to open. She looked down and looked below towards the lobby doors. She saw a man and a woman enter, arms locked. The man was none other than Tristan with snow in his strawberry-blonde hair. He was dressed in a grey coat, jeans, and boots. The other woman was unknown to Diana but made her gut turn as she saw him. She had orange-red hair and fair skin. Allodia saw Diana's glance focus ahead and saw that she was focused on Tristan.

"Try not to get into a fight, please," Allodia warned as the elevator doors arrived.

Diana tensed her hands over the brass rail guard of the glass railing before her. Allodia walked into the elevator as Diana let go of the railing and followed her. The doors then closed, and they were taken up to the eighty-eighth floor. The doors then opened, and they walked out into a corridor with its brown carpet and crème walls with dark wooden crown moldings and baseboards. There was a retro atmosphere about the corridors of Cabernet Tower. The lights were incandescent and hung from jade glass lamps. Diana took a deep breath and smelt a cleanliness in the halls of the office.

Allodia took Diana down the corridor and into a conference room. From the outside, the conference room had a glass wall with frost on the window that blocked view up to seven feet. Diana walked through the door and entered a large meeting room with a polished wooden table in the center. At the back and front of the room there were projector screens, and on the walls, there were picture frames with vintage pictures from the Cabernet Industries' personal history. At the sides of this wall there were windows that looked outdoors.

"Four years ago… my brother almost made a stupid decision in this room. God, how we all feared for him. Here we are now though…."

"Where is everyone?" Diana questioned.

"We're a little bit early," Allodia remarked. "Why don't I take you to Charlemagne's office?"

"He has an office?" Diana remarked. "I thought his office was in Allabrese."

"This is his Harlech office, which he hardly uses," Allodia remarked, leaving the room. "It's technically the official office of the Chairman, but since Charles never comes over here, it hasn't really been used. In the past, this used to be the office my dad, his dad, and his dad's dad worked from."

Allodia led Diana down a corridor and then around to a set of double doors. She opened through them and walked into an extremely large room, almost as large as a high school gymnasium, which contained a large open space in the center. The floor of the office was made of dark brown wood. The walls consisted of dark carved wooden panels. The ceiling also consisted of panels with lights above that were turned off. The room was at least two-stories tall, and it had large windows at the far-side where light poured in. The curtains at the window were open. On the wall on the right, there was a fireplace with an old, but large portrait of Charlemagne when he was noticeably younger by his light-blonde hair and youthful face. His blue eyes and serious stare looked down at Diana. Around the fireplace there were regal couches with turquoise floral cushions, wooden coffee tables and end tables, and brass lamps. A set of doors at either side of the fireplace went elsewhere. Over the doors, there were the coat of arms of the Cabernet family molded in gold. Next to the doors that Diana and Allodia walked through were two brass lamps against the wall. Next to these lamps on eithers side, were two paintings on each side, left and right. Directly ahead from the doors was a heavy table with no chairs, but lamps on either side. On the left-side was Charlemagne's desk, a large desk with various items neatly placed around. Before the desk there were armchairs spread apart. Behind the desk was a large armchair with arm rests. The desk and chairs sat atop of a regal dark magenta rug with tassels at the end. On the wall behind the desk, there was a large, but beautiful portrait with doors at the side that went elsewhere into the tower. Allodia looked around and then looked to Diana who marvelled at the size of the office.

"This… this is the kind of office I'd expect the chairman of a company like Cabernet Industries to have," Diana said. "Not the office in Allabrese, or even the one in the manor."

"That just goes to show, I suppose," Allodia replied, "how humble Charlemagne is. He doesn't make himself to be like a king… if he did, he would have had a castle built for himself… just like his grandfather. The only reason Cabernet Manor is the size that it is, is because our grandfather (from what Charles has told me) did not want anything extravagant. The former family property in Lennox I've heard was around the same size, as was the home in Westford. That aside, imagine though… this could be yours one day…"

Diana looked back to Allodia. She then looked back to the office with a tame smile.

"Maybe…" Diana muttered.

Act 4, Scene 2

Six days later, Diana remained silent at her apartment, going out only to join Allodia at Cabernet Tower during the daytime for at least four hours. At night, she would monitor the airwaves but hear little to nothing. Diana leaked the remainder of the documents that associated Hyacinth Dulles with the Harlech Syndicate, while at the same time, exposed Oswald Montgomery and even Damian Sutherland, post-mortem, for crimes that dated from 1969 to the present. The information became the most-shared trend among the Harlech area and thousands of users online spoke out for justice. When that justice wouldn't come, Diana leaked information that indicted the Harlech Police Department and their own police commissioner, Errol Game.

Meanwhile, Tristan was unable to keep track of Diana in the same manner that he had done so on Christmas. Diana's cellphone never left her apartment except in the day when it went to Cabernet Tower. Tristan took the extra time that he had to practice using his new tools and weapons. In Charlemagne's private workshop, his exoskeleton stood in a glass cabinet near Barry's workspace in the right corner of the room. The helmet, which included a heads-up display (HUD), included a targeting mechanism that Tristan practiced with as he aimed the grapple gun and shot at targets in a simulation room nearby. The HUD provided a thermal setting that allowed him to see through thick smoke and a night-vision setting that allowed him to see in the darkest of corridors. Charlemagne and Barry also prepared Tristan an upgrade that extended his grapnel gun, various EMP pulse chips to disable electronics, and some small sticky explosives. Tristan familiarized himself with these weapons and maintained his fitness as much as he could in preparation of another encounter with Diana.

Diana on the other hand, was less prepared. She maintained a fair stock of smoke grenades, plastic explosives, and knives, as well as semi-automatic pistol magazines. She also received her new ballistic torso-piece which was lighter and more flexible than the metal chest piece she was wearing before. She also put together her own two-way communications radio, inserting the communications chip that was in her computer to be able to intercept all communications as long as she was within radius of a local radio antenna. Paladin Group installed radio antennas at most of the high-profile sites they were contracted to provide security to, which was most of Harlech. She didn't have much, but it was enough for her.

Diana spent occasional nights, on her motorcycle in regular clothes, riding around town in a hoodie to listen in on intercepted communications as she attempted to scan for the Syndicate. However, she was unable to close in on them, even as she searched the entire island chain and mainland. It was almost as if the Syndicate and New Syndicate had vanished or gone dark. By the sixth day, Diana had resigned to the fact that they probably changed their encryption algorithm.

Diana stood from her desk and went to her wardrobe. She opened it and looked inside. Alonzo, the tailor in Stoneridge, had crafted her a dazzling sparkling champagne-colored dress that covered her up to the breasts and included a slit at the legs. Diana changed into it and sucked in her stomach at the mirror. She gave a smile as she looked at herself. She then set off to work on her make-up and hair for the party tonight. Diana then returned to her room so she could put on the high heels that went with the dress.

At the last second, Diana's phone went and sounded off. She looked at the unknown foreign number at the top and at the characters in Kanji. She quickly picked up the phone and went to the window, barefoot, and climbed out to climb up to the roof. She looked around and saw only the roof access from the main stairwell via a ladder that extended downwards from a hatch in the ceiling. Nearby, there was a large rectangular machine where Diana hid a duffel bag with her uniform underneath. The side of the machine said that it was an air-conditioning unit, but Diana hadn't heard it run since she was a little girl. Diana looked around and then turned around as she suddenly felt the presence of a black clad ninja jump up from behind.

Diana looked at the character before her, who wore a mask that showed the face of a Japanese demon. The man removed the mask and looked over to Diana with a sly smile. Shinji straightened up and put his sword away.

"Diana-kun," Shinji greeted. "You look... like you're ready to go to a ball..."

"I am about to, actually," Diana replied in English. "I didn't think my message got through... How have you been, Shinji-kun?"

"I've been better," Shinji replied. "I don't have long to talk. My uncle told me to deliver this message to you personally. He said that he's received your intel and that he will treat it very seriously. He expresses his thanks, but in the meantime, wishes you good fortune in your own quest."

"He sent you across the Pacific just for that?"

"No," Shinji denied. "He also says that he has sensed a shift in world tension in the last year and had suspected that something may occur. He never realized something to the extent of what you suggested, but we're trying to locate all of the containers in Japan with the insignia of the Zimmerman Corporation so that we can keep a tab on them. However, we don't believe these machines to have been made in Japan..."

"What?"

"Our own intel suggests that these containers arrived to Japan, and not the other way around..."

"I don't understand... I thought they'd be used to wage war against Dr. Bishop, but if that's not it then..."

"Japan has many ports. Our search is not yet complete. We will continue to search for more of them."

"Of course," Diana responded.

"Here," Shinji said, taking out something from his belt. "I retrieved the caltrops you requested. I also have these for you..."

Shinji handed Diana a velvet bag with sharp caltrops inside. He also gave her a box of throwing knives.

"Thank you," Diana replied, bowing.

"Try to be a little... conservative with them. They're good quality and aren't disposable."

"I will," Diana responded. "Thanks again."

"Good luck on your quest," Shinji simply said, putting on his mask.

Diana watched as he ran off and jumped onto the other roof. She watched him disappear into the skyline before she went to the duffel bag under the air-conditioning machine to put the caltrops in with the throwing knives. She then picked up the duffel bag and took it with her downstairs where she continued to ready herself for the gala tonight.

• • • •

Tristan patiently waited in the elevator as he was taken down from the penthouse and into the sublevel that went to Charlemagne's private workshop. The elevator doors opened, and Tristan exited to look down and over to Barry and Charlemagne who were at work. Charlemagne was on the central platform, working on his unknown project, while Barry was at his workbench, working on Tristan's helmet. Tristan went around and down the stairs so he could join them.

Charlemagne worked diligently on his mysterious project, tightening screws on the top of the machine that was hidden underneath a tarp. Tristan watched him as he worked, scratching his head as he looked at the bizarre rectangular shape of the object underneath, almost shaped and sized like a telephone booth, but slightly larger. He then went away and over to the cabinet where the exoskeleton was kept, looking over to another display case where the amulets worn by the psychics were on display via a string. This display case was next to one that had Alexander the Great's staff with the other stone. Charlemagne finished what he was doing and then climbed down the side of the machine to join Tristan.

"Hey," Tristan greeted, turning to him.

"Tristan," Charlemagne replied.

"You know, I'm still waiting for you to tell me what it is that you're doing down here all the time," Tristan remarked, looking at the tarp.

"One day I'll share that with you," Charlemagne replied. "Not just yet though… it's almost done."

"You wouldn't believe him if he told you what it is right now," Barry added. "You'll just have to see and experience it when it's ready."

"Hm, I don't know," Tristan replied with doubt. "I've seen and been through a lot of weird crap ever since I was adopted for the third time in my life. Then again, I wouldn't want to ruin the surprise."

"Speaking of ruin," Barry retaliated, looking over to Tristan with vengeful eyes. "Could you stop breaking this helmet? I'm not going to fix it again! You just need to be more careful – and stop landing on your face!"

"I haven't landed on my face," Tristan deflected. "I just keep getting hit in the face. It's not my fault this thing is so damn fragile."

"Then be more careful," Barry scolded. "It's a prototype. It's not easily replaceable."

"Yeah, well, make it more durable then," Tristan replied, looking over into a corner of the workshop as he noticed something under a tarp. "Hey, what's that over there? Charles wouldn't tell me what it was…"

Barry looked over to the corner. He then smiled.

"Don't touch that," Barry pleaded. "It's also a prototype. Just something I cooked up when I was bored… A little project of mine that could never land itself on the market except as an incredibly niche item."

"Another prototype? So, it'll break if it falls over?" Tristan jeered. "You got to let me know what it is."

"Funny," Barry sarcastically replied, standing up and removing his lab coat. "I'm going home."

"You're not going to the party?"

"Good God, no," Barry replied, putting on his blazer. "I've got better things to do than be surrounded by obnoxious rich people. Besides, my cheque is in the mail. I already give money to Allodia. God knows she has better use for it than I do."

Barry walked towards the stairs and waved to Charlemagne who had gone back to working on his project.

"I'll see you tomorrow, Charles," Barry said. "Happy New Year, you two."

"Happy New Year," Charlemagne responded, standing up and waving to him.

Charlemagne walked over to Tristan again.

"Speaking of the fundraiser, I think it's time we wrap up here. I have to get my speech ready, get my suit ready, and… perhaps shower as well."

Tristan looked at him. Charlemagne was as dirty as he had ever seen him. He was like a child coming indoors from playing outside.

"Yeah, you're right," Tristan said in a quiet voice. "Cheryl is meeting me at the gala. I don't want to keep her waiting."

"Right," Charlemagne replied, patting his hands. "Let's go."

Act 4, Scene 3

Allodia's red convertible pulled up to the red carpet that extended out from the Bradford International Hotel along the corner of the waterfront at Whitney Harbor, connected to the Expo Center. A valet took care of the car as Diana and Allodia exited from the vehicle and began to walk down the red carpet towards the entrance of the hotel. Allodia wore a designer white dress with a diamond necklace at her chest and clutch in her hands, while Diana wore her sparkling dress. Allodia's hair was beautiful - styled for the night, while Diana's was straightened out and made to fall before one shoulder.

Various journalists could be seen behind the velvet lines, taking photographs as people from all over Harlech and beyond arrived for the party. Diana held a nervous expression as she walked behind Allodia towards the front doors. The flashing of cameras blinded her slightly, but she got through it as she arrived at the other side. Diana took a deep breath and then looked back towards the reporters before turning over to Allodia. She then began to look around at the inside of the hotel, which had a warm glow from the holiday season with all the Christmas decorations still hung around.

Diana caught up with Allodia as she walked over to the ballroom where the party was being held.

"So, this is what high society is like then," Diana murmured to her.

"Come on now," Allodia expressed. "You don't have to be so upset to be here. I know it may sting a little, but it's necessary work to secure funding for our charitable operations. Here, let me introduce you to some of Harlech's notables."

Diana was taken to the ballroom where they entered through to a large space where there were various people dancing in the center while others conversed from the side. At the end of the room there were a set of stairs that went up to a second floor above. To the right there was an exit that went down a corridor where there was a bar. Likewise, to the left there was a corridor that went to another space where people had amassed to chat amongst each other. Diana looked around and then to Allodia.

"If you're going to make your stay with the Cabernet Foundation, then you need to learn how to schmooze and be welcoming. You need to know how to socialize with people, get to know them quickly, and then speak around what they desire and how that connects with the dream of the Cabernet Foundation."

"You mean manipulate them?" Diana remarked.

"It's not manipulation. It's being clever for the good of the charity; persuasion. Here, let's start with the curator of the Harlech Art Gallery. Let me find him…" Allodia said, looking around. "Where is that damned Morris?"

Diana watched as Allodia went off on her own. She slipped out of the way and ran into a handsome young man before her. He was tall, had dark hair and fair skin, and blue eyes. She blushed as she saw him, and she had caught his attention. The man approached Diana.

"Well, hello there," the man greeted in an eloquent Londoner accent. "The name's Prospero."

"Wait," Diana replied with a shy smile. "You mean, like Prospero from *The Tempest*?" she questioned with doubt.

"Yes," the boy responded.

Diana laughed and muttered, "Oh boy…" She then said, "My name's Diana."

"Pleasure," the boy replied. "So, what's a young lady like you doing here? Parents?"

"Yeah, something like that," Diana replied with a light laugh.

"Would you perhaps care to dance?" the boy offered.

Diana looked to the side and saw her former boyfriend walking down the set of stairs ahead with that woman in his arms. Charlemagne was behind. The two boys wore tuxedos, while the woman with Tristan wore a red dress. Diana scowled at Tristan and then looked back at the boy.

"Yeah, I don't think so," Diana rejected. "To be honest, I have my heart set on only one man, and that is Christ."

The boy's face dropped. Diana turned away from him and went back into the crowd in search of Allodia. She eyed Tristan ahead. The two made eye contact. Diana attempted to move away from him. Tristan whispered something into Cheryl's ear and then saw her off. He then proceeded to make his way through, catching Diana by the wrist as she was about to go into the left space. Diana attempted to rid Tristan's grasp, but he held on tight to her. She growled and turned around.

"What do you want?" Diana asked as Tristan moved in closer to her.

"Can I offer you a dance?" Tristan replied.

Diana gave a sarcastic laugh. Tristan didn't smile and instead looked at her apologetically. She looked back at him with a smile though.

"You don't dance," Diana said, "and besides, I've thought long and hard about it, and I decided that I'm going to consecrate myself to God and take my vows. I'm going to become a nun."

"Well, then we have to dance," Tristan replied, "while you still can."

Tristan took Diana by the other hand began to guide her into the crowd of people who danced a slow dance. Diana allowed him to have his way, eyeing around the many people around.

Tristan gently moved about with her and soon enough, Diana came to rest her head on Tristan's shoulder.

"Do you remember the last time we danced like this?" Tristan questioned in a soft voice.

"Not too long ago," Diana replied in a whisper. "For our prom. It took me a lot to get you to dance…"

"Have I surprised you then?"

"No," Diana responded, "but you did surprise me to see that you've already got another girl in your arms. Seems to me that a girl becomes more tempting when you're locked in with someone. Was that the way it was with me all these years ago, when I was the forbidden fruit when you were technically supposed to be with Vivian?"

"It's never been like that," Tristan deflected. "I was never Vivian's. I don't have a commitment issue."

"I'll have to place my doubt on that."

"I'm sorry, okay," Tristan whispered. "I'll always say it… I'll say it to the end, because I truly am, deeply sorry for hurting you. I have no excuses for my actions anymore."

"Your apology has been noted for the umpteenth time," Diana replied, "but Tristan, your debt to me is forgiven."

"Why did you save me after what I did to you?" Tristan questioned, changing the topic.

"Does there have to be a reason?"

"I cheated on you," Tristan replied, "you should have left me to die."

"Is that what you wanted?"

"It's what I would have preferred."

"Then you don't understand why I did what I did."

"No, that's the point."

"You can wrap around your head that maybe, just maybe, I did something for you out of the kindness of my own heart. Possibly because, such a concept is lost on you."

Diana and Tristan parted. Tristan looked at Diana and into her eyes. The couple stopped to dance.

"What a pity…" Diana whispered. "To have a soul that has no concept of love…"

"Please don't say that," Tristan said in sad voice, shaking his head. "I'm not like that."

Tristan looked as though he was about to cry. Diana continued to dance with him. They went quiet for a moment.

"It was a sign that I forgave you," Diana whispered, "because people deserve to be forgiven so long as they seek to be forgiven."

"But I didn't ask to be forgiven," Tristan replied.

"You did just now."

"That's not the same."

"Well, what can I say, but you're welcome then," Diana replied in a soft voice. "I didn't expect to ever see you again… When I saw you at the penthouse… it was a lot for me. Even now…"

Tristan looked deeply into Diana's eyes again. She looked back at him.

"Seeing you here now, with that girl…" Diana said in a quiet voice. "It's as if I really did run away with the Syndicate all these years ago. It's as if you never rode to my rescue and hopped onto that plane, stopping me from coming back to Harlech…"

"But the attraction still burns," Tristan responded. "All these years, because had that been true, I would have never have stopped thinking about you."

"Oh, please…" Diana replied in disbelief.

"It's true," Tristan insisted.

"No, in this scenario, you never truly gave a damn about me," Diana laughed.

"So, does that mean, in reality, I really do care about you?"

Diana's face went flat. She looked slightly embarrassed.

"You're an asshole," Diana deflected.

"Would any other boy go to the extent he did to stop you at that port?"

"You have a problem," Diana remarked.

"Maybe I do."

"You really do have a problem."

"Do you regret it?"

"Regret what?"

"Regret not staying on that plane," Tristan questioned.

The couple stopped again, and Tristan gave a light smile to her.

"Please don't ask me that," Diana replied, her right eye watering as a tear fell.

"Sorry," Tristan apologized, continuing to dance with her.

The two drifted into a silence for a moment.

"What are you trying to achieve out there, Diana?" Tristan then suddenly questioned.

"Vengeance," Diana simply responded, "and justice. It's not like what you think, Tristan. The Syndicate isn't what it was anymore. Oswald Montgomery had a vision to achieve stability in Harlech by means other than politics. The Syndicate consists of three components, components of which have always been loyal to the mission, even if all three groups may have different desires. In basic terms, these groups are the mayor's office, the police department, and Paladin Group. Ironically, the mayor's office is the less important of the two, although its control is still important. The main component has always been the police as it's public security and allows the Syndicate to control crime while avoiding to prosecute key figures in the system, such as Montgomery himself. Paladin Group works in a way that the HPD can't. They're private security and operate almost everywhere within the city. Paladin Group and the HPD have always had a strong liaison that has allowed them to work together, but the changing times has seen the HPD drift away as well as the mayor's office and city council. Within Paladin Group is a division that does all the legwork. My friend, Scot… Damian Sutherland, led this sphere, and they were responsible for the direction of organized crime so that they could prevent the sprout of criminal organizations by suppressing and cracking down on them, essentially holding all of Harlech as their territory with the secret support of the police. This is the very essence of the Syndicate as a criminal organization, but in reality… it was nothing more a façade to keep crime in check. It was also imperfect, especially these days where crime has risen not because of organized crime, but because of the people within Harlech. To that extent, there was not much the Syndicate could do, but Paladin Group certainly profited from it as the demand for private security rose through the roof. Nonetheless, for the last forty years, the system worked because compared to other major cities of similar demographics, per capita, Harlech has significantly less crime. It worked… especially since what people didn't know, didn't hurt them."

"What does any of that have to do with your desire to seek revenge?" Tristan questioned.

"Two weeks ago, there was a takeover. Oswald Montgomery was murdered, and my team was set up… I… I barely made out alive that night. My friend Scot though… the one that spared your life and told you to protect me. He died."

"I'm sorry."

Diana shook her head and continued to explain, "Could you imagine the amount of power in the hands of people unlike Oswald Montgomery? The amount of damage they could do? Even then, these two people, Mrs. Dulles and Dr. Bishop, were responsible for the deaths of Mr. Montgomery and Scot. I'm less interested in what motives they had, but I'm certain they're nefarious. All I really care about, and I admit it, is to see them fall... I've already supressed that woman, but the other is still out there... the doctor. I don't know where's he's hiding, and I don't know what he's planning, but I'm going to find him and take him down."

Tristan lowered his head and parted from Diana.

"Diana, this... this isn't you. This fighting. This anger. This isn't the girl that I fell in love with. No, the girl I fell in love with was tenacious and fierce, meek like a horse, but never wrathful. She was never afraid to get into a fight, but she was never actively seeking to make fights. Sure, she didn't really care about the law, but she had principles... good moral principles..."

"Hmph," Diana grunted. "The same is with you. Everyday... for the past year, I've looked at you and seen someone other than the boy I fell for. You were such a happy boy... and everyday, especially when we broke up, I missed that boy."

"That's not the same," Tristan deflected. "What happened to me, changed me... How could I be happy about life when it's nothing but misery and rot?"

Diana frowned at him.

"You're better than me though," Tristan encouraged. "You're stronger than me. Let the police handle the crime, just stop! Please?"

"You don't understand," Diana responded in a quiet voice. "You're not from here. I know this city better than I know

Allabrese because I've lived here for three times as many years. The police are in a power struggle between aiding Mrs. Dulles and having her prosecuted. Anyone of these decisions could set the entire department aflame in revolt. The city would be in chaos."

Tristan shook his head and replied, "I don't believe you."

"Ladies and Gentlemen," an announcer on a PA began to introduce. "Allow me to introduce to you, Mayor Hershel Simpson."

Diana and Tristan looked over to the top of the stairs as the mayor appeared with his wife in his arms. He was an older, handsome man with grey hair that looked a bit like Ronald Reagan. His wife had golden blonde hair and looked a little like a movie star or former model. They both appeared to be in their late-fifties or early sixties.

"Look at these chumps," Diana said with a sigh. "Do you think they truly express the desires of any ordinary citizen? They have the whole of the media, banks, real estate, and other businesses behind them. They're oligarchs. Luckily, this fool was also supportive of Oswald's vision to control crime. Who wouldn't be if they're already corrupted enough to receive the money of big banks, big pharma, and big media companies? It's the same story everywhere else."

Tristan looked back at Diana.

"You can't do anything to change the system," Tristan remarked. "It's pointless to even try… All of these people, and their connections… it's deeper than you think it is. The network runs deep. You know that. These people... they'll never face justice, because they define justice."

"No," Diana denied, "good will always triumph. The bad will always collapse, because God wills it."

Tristan looked at her with doubt and uncertainty. Diana eyed Commissioner Game approach the mayor ahead and whisper something into his ear. The commission was being followed by two others who went with him as they went towards the exit. Diana's eyes tracked them, and Tristan tracked both them and Diana.

"Whatever you do," Tristan began to say to her, "please don't get involved."

Diana looked to Tristan and into his eyes.

"Please..." Tristan muttered.

Diana gave a saddened look to him and placed a hand on his cheek. She brought him closer and the two kissed. Tristan didn't hesitate to part. He instead closed his eyes and brought his hands around Diana's waist. Diana soon separated the two of them and began to step aside. She looked apologetically to him.

"Please, understand me, Tristan. Please," Diana requested to him, moving away. "Please don't follow me."

Tristan stepped forward to her.

"If you leave this hotel right now, then I won't be following you as the dazed idiot that's in love with you, but as your enemy."

Diana paused and looked back at him.

"Then I'll see you later then," Diana politely responded before turning around and walking off.

Tristan watched Diana make her exit and then let out a sigh. He held his hands in fists and gave a deep frown.

"Damn..." Tristan muttered, turning and looking ahead to see Cheryl atop of the steps that went to the bar on the right.

Cheryl wiped the tear from her eye and then ran off. Tristan let out another sigh and simply continued forward, going into the bar where he met with Charlemagne who was drinking wine on his own and watching television from the TVs above the bar as they played soccer matches from the other side of the country.

"Ah, Tristan," Charlemagne said with a slight slur. "Come and sit down.

"Are you drunk?"

"No," Charlemagne remarked. "I've only had about two drinks so far... Come though... come and sit down."

"No thanks," Tristan rejected. "Not tonight..."

Tristan looked to the TVs as one of them shifted to commercials. Charlemagne placed hand on Tristan's shoulder.

"Did you speak with Diana just now? How is the lass?"

"Yeah, we spoke," Tristan replied, "but she left..."

"Oh, where to?"

"She's gone out," Tristan explained. "Apparently, there's some sort of ruckus that needs to be seen to, and it might involve her quest for 'vengeance,' whatever that means."

Tristan stared at the TV as it ran a promo for a local news channel. The advert used a clip from the assault on the Mayfair when Diana flipped out of the way of the semi-truck. He looked at it with intent and fearful eyes and then shook his head, looking aside.

"And what are you going to do about it, my dear boy?" Charlemagne asked.

Tristan looked to him in his drunken state. He took a step back and held his head high.

"Are you going to stop her?" Charlemagne questioned.

"Of course," Tristan answered. "It's the only thing that I can do to stop her from getting herself killed."

"Atta' boy," Charlemagne cheered, toasting his wine glass. "Go get 'er then."

Act 5, Scene 1

Diana left the Bradford Hotel and made her way towards the outskirts of International Plaza at the end of the seawall at Whitney Harbor to flag down a taxicab. She then quickly asked for the driver to take her home to her apartment. She paid the driver with the little money that she had hidden in her dress and then went up to her apartment so that she could pull the duffel bag out from under her bed and get changed. Diana put on her tunic, trousers, and boots. She then put on the ballistic armor and the holster vest. Diana also put on her leather jacket, raising the hood from her tunic and then covering her face in the mask veil, but not before putting her earpiece into her ear and attaching it to her radio on her belt.

Once Diana was set, she exited out the window and climbed up to the top of the roof so that she fiddled with the radio and intercept any nearby radio signals from the Syndicate. The airwaves were silent. Diana growled and put her radio back on her belt. She took out her phone and saw that she had some news alerts. According to the Harlech Herald and Harlech News Network, a protest against Hyacinth Dulles and the Harlech Police Department turned into a riot in Westford after shots were fired at 'peaceful protesters.' The article went on to suggest that charges may be dropped against Mrs. Dulles due to the unlawful acquisition of evidence against her by anonymous sources. The Harlech News Network stated that Mrs. Dulles may receive a reasonable bail and suggested that she was a victim of the works of her father who was 'abusive' towards her. A news alert from not too long ago from social media sources on the ground stated that an armored convoy had left the HPD Westford Division where Mrs. Dulles was rumored to be kept in. Diana immediately put her phone on airplane mode and then put it away.

Diana went to the air conditioning unit and pulled out a case from underneath. She opened the case and looked at her sniper rifle inside. She closed the case again and brought it around her shoulders. She then took it with her down the fire escape as she went to her motorcycle and sped off. She made her way towards Bromley before realizing that Hunter Street, which ran east-west from Bailey Drive was cordoned off. Coincidentally, Hunter Street was the street that crossed over Bailey Drive to go down a lane that went to the coast. On the other side, the Harlech Police Department HQ was stationed. Diana continued down and turned onto Tracey Street, looking up Hunter Street to see that each of the intersections had been blocked off. Diana went down Price Street, around Price Park, and then continued down Tracey Street until she reached Hardwicke Street.

Diana stopped in an alleyway nearby and took out her phone. She began to trace a possible route on a map application from the Penultimate Bridge to the HPD Precinct. Diana traced her finger from the offshoot from the highway at Turnour Street, which went down and connected to Hunter Street. Hunter Street then went straight to the precinct. Diana put her phone away and returned onto Tracey Street to go down to Turnour Street. She stopped and looked north to see that the intersection with Hunter Street was under control by the police. Diana quietly turned around and went back to the alleyway to park her motorbike and continue on foot.

With the case behind her, Diana climbed up a fire escape in the alleyway and came onto the rooftops. She went towards Hunter Street and looked down to see that the road was entirely clear with police at checkpoints at the intersections at Hardwicke and Durham controlling traffic. Diana looked further ahead and could see a police sniper positioned ahead down the street on the rooftop. This was no ordinary police officer, but a member of the ERT. Diana removed her sniper rifle case and placed it against the ledge where she was, near her motorcycle. She then removed her hood and veil and climbed down to go onto Tracey Street where Diana began to casually walk down the street and make her approach to Sayward Street. Diana turned right onto Sayward Street and then came into an alleyway between Tracey Street and Hunter Street to climb up onto the roof. The fire escape that Diana had climbed up did not take her to the exact roof she needed to be on, but a low one approximately three-stories high. She went towards the end and climbed up to a neighboring roof that was slightly higher and then over to another where there was a ladder. Diana then began to sneak up behind the ERT officer, kicking him in the back of the leg, and then choking him from behind until he was unconscious.

Diana lowered his body behind the ledge and then removed the sniper rifle. She took the ammunition that the officer had to spare as well as a set of binoculars. Diana looked out and looked around for more ERT. There were several more officers lined down all of Hunter Street on both sides. Diana growled and lowered the binoculars. She then looked over to the officer that she had knocked out and his uniform. Diana began to strip him of his uniform, leaving the officer in the cold. She took his body over to a pipe against a brick wall next to the roof to the east and handcuffed him to it. She also gagged him and then began to get changed into his uniform. Diana kept her tunic and vest on but removed her jacket and trousers to wear the man's trousers. However, the waist of the man was significantly larger than hers. Diana put on the tactical belt worn by the officer and then put on his coat. She also put on his hat and then took some of the C4 from her belt and placed it into a pouch on the belt she had stolen. She also took some blasting caps as well as the flash grenades that the ERT officer had.

With these items, Diana made her way down to Hunter Street and began to walk casually down the street, looking around at first before eyeing some points around. She looked over to some of the snipers and saw that they were ignoring her. She made her pass across Durham Street and looked as the regular officers looked to her as if she was one of their own. Diana continued down the street and began to lay down some C4 at the side of cars parked on the curb. Diana continued down and reached a skywalk bridge between two structures near Hardwicke Street. Diana took some C4 and planted it on the pillars of the bridge that touched down at the curb of the road and at the side of the building. She did both sides and then began to make her way back down Durham Street.

"Crossing Penultimate Bridge," a voice said.

Diana suddenly stopped and looked at the radio on this belt where the voice had projected from. She attached her earpiece jack into the radio and brought the earpiece into her ear. The radio was silent. She continued to walk and continued to place some more C4, exhausting her supplies slowly. Diana crossed Durham Street and stopped up ahead to looked around. She scanned the area and then took her last two small packages and began to cross the street, planting them on the ground and pretending to tie her shoe as she left them behind. At the first one, Diana looked about to see if the snipers had noticed her yet, but they were focused on maintaining their sights down the road. She then went ahead to drop the other before she began to speed up and return up to change back into her own clothes.

"Convoy has reached King Island," a voice suddenly projected over the radio. "Coming down Turnour Street. Stay frosty, fellas."

"Roger."

Diana looked around as she was about to disappear into the alleyway. She proceeded to run and climb up the fire escape. The ERT officer that she had knocked out was still asleep. Diana pulled off the jacket, removed the belt, and detached the radio. She also removed the trousers and boots, and changed back into her own trousers, putting on her boots again, and then putting on her leather jacket. Diana took with her some of the flash grenades, the binoculars, rifle magazines, and the radio that belonged to the ERT grunt.

Diana climbed down the fire escape and made her way back down Tracey Street, casually with a bit of haste, and then entered into the alleyway where her bike was parked to climb back up to her vantage point. She then looked down the street and eyed where she had planted the C4 on the road with the binoculars. The snipers ahead were more attentive than they were beforehand, looking down their scopes. Diana began to prepare her rifle as she raised her hood up and covered her mouth.

"We've just passed Campbell Street," the radio projected aloud.

Diana turned down the volume. She also took her phone out and set it on the ledge. She also took the detonator and sat it down next to her phone. She looked down the crosshairs and aimed towards the snipers ahead, lining up a shot at them, but holding her finger away from the trigger. She then looked back down to the street, looking at where she had placed the C4 on the road and by the cars. Diana then looked to her phone as it vibrated. Her eyes widened.

Diana picked up her phone and immediately set it back to airplane mode. Her face grew red, especially as she read the reason why her phone had been set off because of a text message from Tristan. Diana read the message, which said, 'This is your final warning. Please get down from there and stop this once and for all.' Diana's face grew even more red and angry. She turned her phone off and returned to looking back down the street through the rifle. Diana looked towards the C4 and then over to the snipers.

"Coming onto Hunter Street."

Diana's eyes widened as he realized that the sniper ahead had disappeared. She looked towards the one further ahead and the same was true. They had vanished as if they were never there at all. Diana kept focused and shook her head. Her heart pounced from her chest and a drop of sweat came down from her forehead. She could begin to see the convoy driving slowly as they arrived from Turnour Street. They were still slightly far ahead, and they drove at less than a speed of forty kilometers per hour. She aimed down towards the car at the front, which was a standard cruiser with sirens flashing, but no noise. Behind there were two armored cars. Even further ahead there were two motorbikes. Diana watched them carefully.

The convoy made their way down Hunter Street and the motorcycles crossed Durham Street as the police on the ground blocked traffic while they made their pass. Diana waited for another moment longer as the motorbikes went further ahead, eyeing the convoys in the back through the scope of the rifle and waiting for them to get closer. Diana picked up the detonator on the ledge and held it in one hand. The motorcycles made their pass under the skybridge, but Diana was not focused on them. The convoy inched forward and finally the rear-most armored car drove over the C4 on the road.

Diana set off the C4 and felt the vibration as all of the plastic explosives set off at the same time, causing the cars on the road to explode, the rear-most armored car to rise up with a bolt of fire that rose up, and the bridge to collapse and block the pass down Hunter Street. The motorcycles were cut off. The other vehicles that were part of the convoy had been blown over by the blast of the parked cars, causing even the parked police cars that belonged to the officers at Durham Street to explode and knock them over by the blast. Diana covered herself as she felt the heat from the fire all the way from where she was.

When all the explosions had set, a red glow emanated from below, affecting the area around the Durham-Hunter intersection slightly towards the west where a small fire lit the street and inwards towards the east up to where the skybridge was, which was where most of the flames radiated. One of the regular police officers was on the ground near the checkpoint with a rod through his leg. Another had been blown over, either unconscious or dead. An officer quickly escaped the cruiser that was part of the convoy and fell over on the street. Diana quickly raised her sniper rifle up as she saw one of the two armored cars open their rear door and for two ERT officers to jump out and fall over in disarray, coughing heavily. These men had exited from the rear armored car which was stopped just before Durham Street – the one that was most affected by the blast. From the front armored car, which was over Durham Street, the doors opened and two more ERT members stepped out and pulled out a woman in a clean pair of clothes.

Diana eyed this woman down and raised her rifle. She lined up a shot and brought her finger around the trigger. She took in a deep breath and tensed her trigger finger. She then pulled it and felt the kickback from the rifle as the bullet shot out and made its way over. Diana looked up with eager eyes, but instead watched as Tristan appeared from Durham Street and shot his grapple gun, pulling Mrs. Dulles over and caused the high-caliber bullet to miss.

The ERT on the ground immediately reacted to Tristan presence, but he quickly approached them and took them on. Diana watched as Tristan kicked one of the officers down and then faced the other to pull his assault rifle off him and grab him by the thigh to slam him down onto the ground. Tristan then brought his knee down onto his neck in a brutal manner, knocking him out and then going to the other to knock him down as he tried to stand up. The other ERT officers began to open fire at Tristan. He dodged out of the way. Diana saw that Mrs. Dulles was still on the ground, panicking over the chaos around her.

Diana threw her rifle onto the ground in anger before taking her pistols out and moving to exit off the roof to go and join the party. Tristan ran behind the flaming chasses of the cruiser that was part of the convoy. He then took his grapple gun and shot up onto the roof, climbing over as the police shot at him. He then began to continue up the roof next to him so that he could come up to the roof where Diana had taken her vantage point with a wall that blocked the east face and looked west. Tristan looked over to the ERT police officer chained to the pipe with her clothes scattered next to him. He also looked at the rifle on the ground, but also the detonator on the ledge alongside Diana's cellphone. Tristan picked up the phone and put it into a pocket in his trousers.

"Freeze!" an officer shouted from below.

Tristan looked down and saw as more police were about to arrive and Diana faced the two ERT officers that he had just managed to avoid. Diana took a flash grenade from her belt and tossed it over. She then went over to confront the officers head on. Tristan jumped over the ledge and landed below, rolling his landing, and running over to subdue Diana.

Diana took one of the officers down and dislocated his arm. She then kicked his assault rifle before looking to the other. The

ERT officer pointed his rifle towards Diana. Tristan shot his grapple gun at him and pulled him over, causing him to lose grip of his rifle and fall over. Diana looked over to Tristan as he ran towards her and then to Mrs. Dulles behind as she attempted to make an escape down Hunter Street. She went around the wrecked armored car and cruiser to avoid Tristan, but Tristan turned and chased after her, tackling her onto the ground. Diana elbowed Tristan in the helmet as he took out his grapple gun and shot at Mrs. Dulles to pull her back.

Diana hit Tristan harder, causing his HUD to produce a brief static feed. She broke loose and hit Tristan again.

"You idiot!" Diana yelled at him.

"I'm the idiot?!" Tristan replied. "You nearly murdered somebody!"

"Shut up!" Diana shouted. "You're getting in the way of everything! First, my life! Now, my business?! She needs to pay!"

Diana took her pistol and pointed it towards Mrs. Dulles. Tristan instantly reacted and hooked onto her, pulling her back and onto the ground. Diana lost grip of her pistol as it fell on the ground nearby. The police sirens drew closer. Tristan turned around as heard some ERT officers nearby, including the one they had left conscious.

"Freeze!" ERT shouted.

Tristan jumped into cover behind the wrecked cruiser at the head of the convoy. He took out his bow and fired at the cops before they could open fire on Diana. Instead, they fired at him, allowing Diana to run into cover behind some wreckage of the cars on the curb. She took out a smoke grenade and dropped it down. She then went and took her pistol into hand, going over to where Mrs. Dulles was to realize that she had disappeared. Tristan saw Mrs. Dulles run towards the police down the sidewalk. She held a piece of debris in her hand. Diana ran after her as Tristan took care of the police. He turned around the other corner and took out the last one by shooting him in the thigh with an arrow, and then went to handle Diana. Tristan saw the flashing red-blue lights on the west-side of Hunter Street behind the fire where the C4 detonated on the road.

Tristan's HUD warned him of an impending explosion from front-most armored car over Durham Street. He rushed towards Diana who had crossed Durham Street in pursuit of Mrs. Dulles. Mrs. Dulles had fallen over at the intersection where people on the sidelines shouted obscenities at her. Diana took out her last two flash grenades and threw them over to the police cruisers as they arrived ahead on the other side. Cars were stalled and abandoned both north and south of Durham Street. Some people had come out and began to film what was going on. Diana stopped before Mrs. Dulles and pointed her pistol at her. Before Tristan could react, the armored car detonated and blew them back. Tristan's HUD began to glitch as he attempted to recover.

Diana looked up and slowly sat up as she began to hear helicopters nearby. She looked up and saw some men in suits hop down and take position on the roofs. These men wore ballistic vests over their blazers and were armed with assault rifles. They began to shoot down towards them, which forced Diana to produce some smoke and cover the whole intersection. Tristan's HUD soon recovered and switched to thermal. Mrs. Dulles was still on the ground, shaking and panicking. He could hear gunshots coming from the westside of Hunter Street as police and ERT began to shoot back at hostiles on the roof. He quickly looked around for Diana and saw that she was on her knee, taking it slow to stand up. Diana grunted as she attempted to stand on her leg.

Tristan ran over to her and grabbed her, pulling her down onto the ground. Diana struggled with him. Meanwhile, a rocket projectile shot from somewhere incinerated the helicopter above, causing it to spin out and hit a building nearby. The civilians around shrieked, and many ran away. Tristan continued to try and keep Diana down, attempting to bring her hands behind her back so that he could tie her. However, he quickly turned his attention over to where Mrs. Dulles was as he saw her stand up and ran off. Tristan took his grapple gun out to try and stop her, but as he did, he saw the sudden appearance of men that he did not recognize. These mercenaries wore a uniform that was unfamiliar to him with scopes before their eyes. Tristan watched as they secured Mrs. Dulles and she ran off with them willingly, up north of Durham Street.

Diana could see Mrs. Dulles run off with the outline of boots on the ground through the smoke. She grunted and broke off from Tristan's grip. Tristan fell over. Diana took a knife and attempted to stab at his visor through the smoke, cracking the helmet and causing the sensors to glitch. The smoke began to clear. Tristan exerted his force against Diana's arm as she continued to attempt to stab Tristan in the visor, but he held her back.

"Over there!" Commissioner Game shouted, pointing over to Diana and Tristan as the smoke cleared. "Arrest them!"

Diana and Tristan looked over to them. Diana pulled her knife back and threw it towards the police, which caused them to open fire towards her as she ran into the stalled traffic at the south of the street. Tristan was left on the ground and covered his face with his gauntlets, feeling a bullet impact him on the wrist, denting the gauntlet. He grunted. Diana tossed a smoke grenade behind her, shrouding him in a cloud of smoke. Tristan realized this and quickly stood up to go after her. Diana turned around the corner into the alleyway and went towards her motorcycle.

Tristan fell over as he was blown by a sudden blast near the intersection. He looked behind him and saw through the cloud of smoke as a police vehicle must have detonated at the police line. Tristan only looked for a brief moment before he stood up and followed Diana into the alleyway. He stopped at the entrance and looked over to her. Diana was atop of her motorbike and looked straight at him. Tristan raised his visor and looked straight at her.

"Stop right there!" Tristan shouted. "I'm taking you back with me!"

Diana shook her head and kicked off the kickstand to drive towards him. Tristan attempted to stop her as he attempted to grab the bike, but she simply brushed against him and forced him back. Tristan fell onto his side as Diana drove off onto the sidewalk of Durham Street to make her escape. Tristan picked himself up and took out his grapple gun. He shot up and climbed onto the roof, looking over towards her as she drove away. Tristan shook his head and growled, running off across the rooftops as he made his own pursuit, knowing full well that the night was far from over for them.

Act 5, Scene 2

Diana made her way down Durham Street and south towards Stoneridge and Matilpi Street. She came off the sidewalk once she reached Matilpi Street, but continued down, passing traffic so that she could arrive at Bailey Drive and then make her way around. Diana heard police sirens behind her as she drove on as the police were now hot on her tail. She got ahead of them by driving through traffic, taking advantage of the maneuverability of the bicycle over their police cruisers. Diana was able to get a fair distance between herself and the police as she came to the intersection with Turnour Street but continued ahead on a red light to go northwards.

Backup turned from Turnour Street to join the pursuit against Diana as she made her way past King George VI Park and into the outskirts of Camross. The traffic was lighter in this area, which made it difficult to separate herself from the police who closed in towards her. Diana ducked her head down slightly as they began to open fire towards her. She passed a large pond on her left at the outskirt of King George Park VI where on her right there was an exit ramp from the highway where more police joined the chase. Diana sped up as she went to the north of the island and came onto the entrance ramp that merged onto the highway.

Diana made her way onto the highway, but quickly stopped as she was about cross onto Penultimate Bridge as she realized that there was a police blockade already set up with cruisers in the way. The police officers behind the line took cover behind their cars and had their weapons drawn. Diana turned her bike away from them and readjusted to go against traffic the opposite-direction.

"Freeze!" police shouted from a megaphone. "Turn off your vehicle and put your hands up!"

Diana ignored them and went off the other direction, dodging the police that came up the ramp and attempted to block her from going the other way. She turned again and came down the exit ramp and returned into Camross, where in the hectic nature of her dare to go against traffic, she was able to lose police... for now. Diana made her way onto Maiden Drive and began to drive past Josephine Whitney Park next to the seawall path on the Walham River. When Diana saw the police cruisers ahead by their sirens, she shifted to the left and drove into the park, dodging the pedestrians as she came onto the seawall and continued eastward by the riverside. People froze as they heard the bike come for them and Diana carefully avoided them. However, there were some who were so slow and unsure as to what to do, that they began to panic, requiring Diana to be on top of her reflexes as she avoided to impact into them. Diana continued down the seawall and soon found herself in International Plaza by the Bradford International Hotel and the Expo Center. She drove over and came back onto Maiden Drive.

By the time that Diana was back on Maiden Drive, the squad of cruisers had blocked her path from going any further along. They opened fire at her as she turned around and began to go back onto Durham Street and then right onto W Stuart Street. Diana sped up down the street and looked into the side-view mirror to see a motorcade of motorcycles move in behind her. The police opened fire on her, requiring her to use nearby traffic as cover and get them to settle down. The end of W Stuart Street on the westside merged onto the highway at an intersection with Turnour ahead, but because of the awkward curve of the road to merge with the street, it only went northward. Diana maneuvered herself to go against the traffic rules and head southbound, cutting off traffic as she made the sharp turn around.

The police on motorcycles stopped at the end of W Stuart Street and continued to fire at her as traffic was clear. A bullet grazed Diana at the thigh.

"Dammit!" Diana cursed, clenching her thigh.

Diana took a pistol from its holster and returned fire back at them. She then continued down and got a lead away from them as they took their time to come after her due to the traffic. They soon caught up but stopped shooting at her. A motorcycle instead went right up to her and hit her in the back, attempting to run her off the road. Diana quickly drove in front of a car before it slowed down to the sirens, and then went around to the side of a semi-truck's trailer.

Diana continued down the highway and soon spotted a gap in the concrete barrier as she drove along the trench. She looked ahead at the immediate lack of oncoming traffic and then deked left as she feinted that she would continue right. Instead of turning around to chase directly behind her, the police on their motorcycles and those in their cruiser behind continued along the right direction, not daring to enter the suicidal direction that Diana was driving on. The police took some shots at her but stopped as Diana came into oncoming traffic and maneuvered around them.

Diana kept herself on the middle lane as two sedans passed by followed by a mini-van and another pickup truck. She then sped up as they came to a tunnel before the ramp that went upwards where the highway transformed from a trench to an overpass on the way to Marke Bridge and Jarsdel Island. She came around the bend and saw that the exits off of the highway were cordoned off and police ahead were in the process of setting up a blockade on the right-side of the highway, which she wasn't even on. A spotlight from the Harlech PD precinct next to the entrance of the bridge shined down and lit the area. Diana's attention focused on the entrance ramp from Bromley as she saw an advanced type of motorcycle zoom onto the highway Diana looked at the vehicle and driver with disbelief.

"Oh, of course…" Diana muttered as she saw Tristan on the vehicle.

Diana swerved out of the way of the traffic as she went towards Marke Bridge. Tristan dodged the police blockade as she drove through a narrow gap between police cruisers. The vehicles behind that were chasing Diana stalled as they stopped before the blockade, some of them crashing behind each other. Tristan soon caught up to Diana and began to drive at her side, but from the other side of the highway. He looked over to Diana with concern as she drove the wrong direction. He also looked behind him as he noticed a police helicopter swoop in with a spotlight that fixed their location. Diana could hear the spin-up of turrets at the side of the helicopter as it soon began to fire towards them. She slowed down so that she could dodge the bullets, while Tristan swerved right out of the way. The helicopter soon stopped firing as Tristan hid himself amongst traffic. Diana slowed down for the sake of avoiding being in the open.

"Pull over!" a voice from a megaphone projected from the helicopter.

"How about no," Diana muttered under her breath, grunting.

Tristan kept his focus on the road.

"Tristan," Charlemagne suddenly spoke through Tristan's helmet. "Sorry I'm late, I… I believe I had a little too much to drink at the party. I had to leave before my speech… Allodia was not too happy about that and seemed quite upset already. Anyhow, what's going on?"

"Not now," Tristan replied, growling as the police helicopter began to fire at them again.

The traffic that Tristan had been hiding in slowed down and stopped, and since police were hot on their tail again, he couldn't slow down, and so both him and Diana sped up.

"What's that noise?" Charlemagne questioned. "Are those sirens?"

"We'll talk later, okay?"

Tristan moved in random directions on the highway as the helicopter continued to fire towards them. Charlemagne went silent for a moment but could still be heard over the speakers. Tristan clenched his teeth as she avoided the rain of bullets but saw some vehicles ahead for him to hide amongst. He sped up even more, going faster and further ahead than Diana.

"Good Lord," Charlemagne expressed. "You're on national television…! The entirety of the Harlech Police Department must be behind you."

"Yeah, I kinda figured that one," Tristan replied, maneuvering his bike as he ran atop of a sedan. "I have to stop Diana – she's out of control!"

"I've reviewing the latest news… There are rumors that Commissioner Game was assassinated tonight… MSM have blamed, or at least suspect, Diana to be responsible. What in blazes is going on out there?"

"Just need to keep Diana safe… I can't let her hurt herself…" Tristan muttered. "Do me a favor, huh?"

"Hm," Charlemagne responded, "I'll see what I can do about getting you some intel. What direction are you going?"

"At this rate, probably Cliffe Island. We've just passed Lincoln intersection, and I think she's trying to go towards Lennox."

"How foolish of her…" Charlemagne remarked. "She'll only anger the Lennox Police Department. I'm going to see what municipal CCTV has to offer. I'll let you know what I can see."

"Thanks," Tristan responded.

The police helicopter began to fire towards them again.

"Dammit…" Tristan muttered, taking evasive maneuvers.

"Okay," Charlemagne said. "I'm looking at a live feed of the Durham Bridge… Police have set up protective walls on the side of incoming traffic, but they're in the process of doing the same for outcoming traffic…"

"Forget about that," Tristan replied, watching Diana go down an exit ramp. 'Diana seems to know what she's doing…"

"That'll lose 'em," Diana muttered as she came off the exit ramp and went towards Riverside Drive. "All of them."

Tristan came off the exit ramp on his side and stopped at the intersection at the end. He looked left in anticipation that Diana may come his way. He could see the headlights of her motorcycle ahead. Tristan revved his engine and took an EMP device as a cruiser stopped behind him. Tristan threw it and watched as the headlights of the car flashed and then the car shut off. Diana passed him. Tristan sped up and went after her with the exit ramp blocked behind him.

The pair were given a brief silence and with traffic around them, the helicopter above didn't dare to fire towards them lest they hit a civilian. They made their way down the westside of Riverside Drive, which was a commercial street with bright lights from the grungy businesses at the side. Their moment of silence came to an end as police rejoined them from the Boundary Drive intersection where Diana crossed on a red light at the upset of traffic which honked back at her and stalled. Tristan raced behind her. The pair drove close to each other.

"I've got her, Charles," Tristan said as they reached another major intersection. "We're going to cross Thames Bridge."

"Yes, I've pulled up your GPS location," Charlemagne replied. "There's no blockade there so you should have an easy time. I'll see what Grafton Bridge is like. If you continue down Thames Street, you'll run by the Cliffe Division of the police department."

"We'll have to chance it," Tristan responded. "I'm not making the decisions on what route to take. She is."

Tristan sped up so that he could drive closer to Diana. Diana noticed and took a shot at him. Tristan clenched his teeth and backed off. He shook his head and kept behind her as they came to the end of Thames Bridge. They drove past traffic and sped along to make their way towards SW Marshall Drive. However, as they passed through, Tristan could see a blockade ahead on Sinfold Street. Tristan pulled back, trying to find a way around as they entered into Southton.

Diana took the initiative before him, crossing the street and driving up onto a sedan and over a fence to land into the playground of Premier Island Elementary School. Diana drove through a sandpit and exited out on the other side to continue down Sinfold Street.

"Clever girl," Tristan remarked, turning his bike and quickly gaining speed to do the same.

The police helicopter drifted over them as they made their way into suburbs. Tristan sped up and made a sharp turn on the intersection with Lipton Street, turning right and then going down towards SW Marshall Drive where Diana turned left on a red light. Diana drove down the remainder of the road and then split off on the entrance ramp that went towards Grafton Bridge. The police helicopter took some shots at them and then flew over the highway to the other side.

Diana took a smoke grenade from her cache but put it away as she turned her neck as Tristan's motorbike fired its front cannons at a concrete barrier ahead. Diana dropped the smoke grenade without taking out the pin and drove into the other side of the highway where traffic was clear due to the blockade on the other side. Tristan followed from behind and made a sharp turn so that they could go down the wrong direction of the bridge. He sped past Diana and fired his cannon again into the barrier between the two sides of the bridge, going back onto the right direction to avoid the blockade ahead as well. Diana joined him and the two exited the city together.

The police at the blockade got into their cruisers and chased after them. The helicopter simply shined its spotlight towards them as they came to the end of the bridge and drove towards Lennox.

"I see that you've crossed Grafton Bridge," Charlemagne remarked. "Has the police chase weaned off?"

"No," Tristan responded. "I'm going to keep going ahead with her until we get to a good stretch further along. We'll have to hide somewhere for the night and then try to return in the morning."

"Chances are, if you disappear out there, there could be a manhunt looking for you…" Charlemagne replied.

"I'll take my chances. I can handle a couple of days in the woods without anything than what I or Diana have."

Diana turned her neck and saw that Tristan was behind her. She revved her engine and sped up in an effort to lose him, but his bike outpaced hers. They continued down the highway together with the police behind them. At their side was nothing but tall evergreen trees that composed a surrounding forest. Diana saw a sign ahead that advertised the Lennox Provincial Park nearby at an upcoming exit. She looked over to Tristan who was adamant on driving near her, especially in her blind spot where he lurked. Diana then looked over to see all the police cruisers behind them.

Tristan saw another blockade up ahead. He readied the cannon to blow the police cruiser so that he could pave a way for them to continue through. He then looked over to Diana. Tristan brought a hand to the side of his helmet to raise the front visor.

Diana looked over to him.

"I'm going to blow past for us to continue to Lennox!" Tristan shouted. "We'll then go through and stop when we get a chance to hide out in the woods. Okay?"

Diana scowled at him. She then raised a manipulative smile through her visor. Tristan couldn't see. Diana raised her hand up and made an okay sign. Tristan lowered his visor and brought both hands onto the handles, ready to fire his cannon. Diana pulled back and moved around Tristan so that she was on his right instead of his left. She took a bag from out of her pockets and held it. She then emptied the bag, dropping the caltrops onto the road, and then she suddenly diverged off the road and came onto the exit ramp that went down.

"Good luck, Trist," Diana muttered under her breath.

"What the hell!" Tristan shouted through his helmet as Diana left him.

"What happened?" Charlemagne asked.

Tristan quickly looked over to her as she left and then ducked his head as he heard an explosion from behind. He looked behind and saw some cars flip as their tires were ripped through by the caltrops. Tristan refocused and looked ahead of him.

"She just ditched me," Tristan remarked. "I thought we were on the same understanding?!"

"What are you waiting for?" Charlemagne questioned. "Turn around."

"I can't," Tristan replied, tipping his motorcycle up and then driving over the police blockade. "Dammit! I've lost her!"

Diana came to the dirt road beneath the highway and then turned left onto the underpass. She drove down the road and turned around with a look of fright as she made her way impulsively towards a possible dead-end with the bulk of the Harlech Police Department still behind her, although they were not immediately behind her, and she had a moment of liberty to get away. She continued to drive, coming onto a turn and a slope downwards. She continued along, but the road started to become too much for her dirt bike, especially as the snow around had turned the road into mud.

Many exits along the path presented themselves, but Diana didn't have the time to read where they went and chose to stick to the main road. She turned around as she thought she noticed the glow of the red-light police light sirens behind her. The sound of the sirens never left her, but they hadn't changed their proximity.

Diana continued to drive forward until she had to turn around at a sharp bend. The dirt ground started to become too much for her as her motorcycle tires lacked the traction for her to properly turn. She fell over, landed on the ground, and slipped downhill as she was still sat on her bike. Diana's right leg was left underneath the half-tonne weight of her bike. Diana held on for her life.

The side of the hill was steep. Diana held her hands over her head to protect them from any sudden blows that could knock her out. Suddenly, she was torn from her bicycle by a tree trunk. Diana continued to fall apart from it. She rolled through the thick thorns and dense foliage before coming to the bottom of a dirt road below, probably the same dirt road she was on, but a later segment, or even an earlier segment. Diana's bike had stopped tumbling too and laid on its side at the other side.

Diana laid on the ground for a moment, rushing her hand to her head. Her face was bloodied and gashed. Her mask had been torn in half and her hood pulled back. Her hair was amess and was sucked into the mud her head laid on. Diana pushed herself up and fell onto her back to face the sky above. She kept a hand at her abdomen and took deep breaths. Diana looked over to her bike.

Smoke floated above the motorcycle. Diana began to slowly pick herself up and stand. She kept a hand at her head and groaned in pain. She tried to walk over to her bike in the coldness of the forest where her breath appeared before her. She then cringed at the sudden appearance of a bright light a head. The lights came from the headlights of a car that was approaching towards her. The car let out a minor whoop of its siren towards her, frightening her and causing her to run into the forest at the side and abandon her motorcycle. As a result, the police cruiser shined its red-blue lights, but did not raise its sirens.

Diana ran into the darkness of the forest with a limp. She rushed through the ferns and then tripped on an exposed root. She quickly stood up and continued onwards. The police cruiser halted at a screech of the brake. The door then opened, and a police officer dressed in a brown blazer and dress pants stepped out and shined a flashlight into the woods. Diana hid behind a tree and saw the beam of the light pass her.

A lone drop of sweat rode down Diana's cheek as she he behind the tree. The light turned off. Diana began to try and climb up the tree, but the side of the trunk was too wet. She eventually got a hold of a space, but her arms shook as she tried to climb up. Diana gave up and instead hugged the trunk with her back. She took a deep breath and continued forward on foot, causing a rustle of ferns at her feet and crunch of snow where there was snow. Diana tripped again and her head landed onto some branches, scraping her forehead. She quickly picked herself up in a scramble. Her fright overwhelmed her. The officer behind was alerted to her presence and shined his light again.

Diana hurried behind a thick tree and pressed her back against it. She breathed quietly and placed her hands into her jacket, taking out her firearms, one into each hand. A tear fell down Diana's bloodied cheek.

"Forgive me, Father," Diana muttered. "For what I must do again…"

The police officer came forward with his flashlight and stopped. He looked around and couldn't see the person he had thought he had seen. He continued to walk forward with careful steps. Diana listened as the police officer moved quietly. Her heart beat harshly. She closed her eyes and continued to mutter to herself. Another tear rolled down her bloodied cheek. She gave a gentle sniffle and then wiped the tear, taking on a determined and confident face. Her grip tightened around the grips of her pistols. She kept her finger away from the trigger.

Suddenly, the brightness of the police officer flashlight hit down on her. The officer raised his pistol in his other hand and pointed it at her, seeing the firearms at Diana's side.

"Freeze!" the officer commanded.

Diana turned her neck away from the bright light, squinting before she pointed both her pistols towards him.

"Drop the weapon!" the officer requested.

Diana looked over to him. She couldn't see the face of the man behind the flashlight as the bulb was too bright. She continued to squint, but her fingers wouldn't move to the trigger.

The police officer looked at Diana and looked at her carefully. He looked at her bloodied face, her long hair, and her youth. Her eyes were a tired blue, but also bloodshot. Her hair was amess. She looked as though she was in distress and in a poor way. The officer looked at her with intent.

"You..." the officer remarked. "You're a girl... and just a kid!"

Diana didn't respond. She held her weapons where they were. The officer continued to look at Diana with his own firearm pointed. She looked back at him and began to see through the brightness of the lamp to see that the man behind the gun had curled short black hair and fair skin. He had minor freckles over his face and brown eyes. He also didn't have a serious look on his face, but one of empathy. Diana's eyes widened. Her hands began to shake. Diana looked at him with familiarity.

"I know you," the man said.

Diana lowered her pistols and dropped them at her feet. In response, the man lowered his own pistol and turned down the brightness on his flashlight.

"You probably don't recognize me," the officer expressed, moving the beam of his light to her armored torso. "Do you?"

"Officer Macdonald," Diana muttered.

"Actually, it's Senior Detective Macdonald now," Macdonald replied. "Or Sergeant Macdonald," he added, examining her. "What happened to you? What are you doing out here? I thought I sent you to be adopted, not turned into a criminal or a vigilante. What are you doing back on the streets?"

"Did you really trust the foster system to pump out a model citizen?" Diana replied in a callous manner.

Diana dropped a saddened expression.

"Although, you were right. I was adopted," Diana admitted. "I'm one of the Cabernet kids… I was adopted by Charlemagne Cabernet."

"Why the hell are you on the streets then? I thought I was doing you a favor when I turned you into Child Services… What happened to you?"

"You did do me a favor," Diana replied. "Sure, the first couple of foster homes sucked, but when I was adopted by Charlemagne… it changed my life for the better. Thank you for that."

"Then what happened to you?" Macdonald questioned.

Diana sighed and replied, "Life… life happened. I'm eighteen now. I… I tried to make my own life, but… obviously it hasn't turned out really well."

"Oh man…" Macdonald remarked. "You're in a lot of trouble…"

"I didn't do anything wrong."

"You led half of the police force on a goose chase through Harlech, blew up half of downtown, and killed the police commissioner, but not before beating up most of the ERT. You're looking at a life sentence for sure."

"I- I didn't kill him. I- I haven't… I didn't try to kill him," Diana reasoned, stepping towards him.

Sergeant Macdonald kept his distance from her and stepped back.

"I've just been trying to do some good for this city and avenge the death of my old friend," Diana explained. "To end the Harlech Syndicate – to end Hyacinth Dulles and Nash Bishop."

"Because of your escapades, Mrs. Dulles is going to be released, or was released…"

"She should have been brought to justice."

"I know," the sergeant sighed, "but that's the way it is in this city," he said with another sigh. "We have to follow the laws, and police are not exempt from the laws. In fact, there are laws against what the police can and cannot do in order to bring justice nowadays, and how evidence is acquired is one of them. The Charter of Rights and Freedoms changed a lot of that. All of that evidence that's been turning up online… it's useless."

"But it's all true, every last bit of it," Diana insisted. "How could the courts not use any of it… it spells out the truth… that's she's guilty."

The sergeant shook his shoulders.

"That's the way that Crown rolls," Macdonald simply replied. "It's not concerned about what's true. It's concerned about what is presented as truth."

"The Syndicate should have concerned itself with the courts, not the police force…" Diana muttered.

"Is that true? Is the Harlech Police Department a part of the Syndicate?"

"Yes!" Diana replied. "It is!"

Diana went on to explain the purpose and origins of the Harlech Syndicate. She then recapped the last month from Montgomery's sudden illness and then his sudden death, the incident at the nuclear plant, her raid on Calypso Towers and the Mayfair, and her work at Port Burnes.

"All I wanted to do was to bring it all down," Diana remarked, "but new obstacles keep springing up, and right now… it seems hopeless."

"Yeah, at times it does," Macdonald replied. "I'm sorry it had to end for you this way. You had a good run, but I've got to take you in."

"Yeah, I get it," Diana responded, looking back at him. "Aren't you going to call of the search for me?"

"My radio's back in the car," Macdonald replied. "Come on, I'll get you back to my car. For now, I'm going to have to ask that you place your hands on your head for me."

Diana complied and put her hands on her head.

"Sometimes, it seems like criminals get more protection under the law than they should," Macdonald remarked. "It's almost as if our society has become shaped into one that protects criminals, and people still complain about police brutality and a need to defund the police."

"My... my ex-boyfriend comes from a pedigree of police officers," Diana said. "He told me that his uncle told him that the first job of police is to protect the people around him before worrying about the law. The law of which should be designed to protect the community and the people. When I told what police were like in Harlech, that they don't give a damn about community or people, he couldn't believe me. I wonder what he thinks of them now... or if he believes me."

"It's hard to care about people in a place like this," Macdonald replied, handcuffing Diana, "but we do care... some of us at the least. We shouldn't have to live like this though."

Sergeant Macdonald finished handcuffing Diana.

"We shouldn't..." he muttered again. "Come on, let me get you patched up with these cuts and nicks, perhaps take you to the nearest hospital, and then I'm going to have to book you."

"Hmph," Diana grunted. "I bet you'll get a medal for this catch, huh?"

"Probably not," Macdonald replied.

The two casually walked through the forest. Sergeant Macdonald steered Diana as he held a hand on her shoulder and shined the flashlight with his other hand. They returned to his car, which was not a standard police cruiser, but an unmarked one. He opened the back door and allowed her to sit down. He then went to the trunk and got a first aid kit to patch her up.

"What would you have done?" Diana asked. "If you had the power to bring it all down?"

Macdonald looked back at her as he finished tying a bandage around her thigh.

"Evidence," Macdonald simply stated. "You need evidence to prosecute. People are innocent until proven guilty. I'm sure you understand that as much since you've been concerned about evidence. With the right court orders, suspicions, we could have gotten all this from Paladin Group with ease…"

"But you wouldn't have gotten the permissions from your higher ups, because they're in on it," Diana reminded him.

"I'd still keep on the case, but then again… that'd paint a target on my back, especially if I went after my own supervisors," Macdonald said with a sigh. "I suppose, one positive aspect of all that you're doing is that it's really rattled the cage. Public opinion has its power, and I don't see the mayor getting re-elected. There'll certainly be an investigation of some kind in the New Year, and if not… who knows… I know some people who have had a similar vision, but when it comes down to it… not much can be done. You need connections, that's for sure, and maybe not pouring your resources into leaking documents online."

"I could have done it then," Diana murmured. "If I had the right connections… If I had a bit of clarity."

"I'll tell you what," Macdonald said to her. "I don't know what to believe from you, especially with what happened to the commissioner, but I have to hand it to you; you really stirred up the hornet's nest when it came to the police department."

"Do you think they fear me? Because I tried to uncover the truth? Seems like the police put more effort into catching me today than they have in trying to end the Syndicate. Of course, that's obviously the case since the Syndicate benefits the HPD by controlling crime. Now though… it's a dangerous rocket in the hands of those two psychos. Who knows what'll happen next."

Macdonald nodded. A police cruiser began to drive down the road from where Macdonald came from, shining its lights at them as it approached slowly. Macdonald looked at Diana intently, paying close attention to her. He gave a sigh and closed the first aid kit, tossing it inside. Macdonald then stood up, stepped back, and placed a hand on the car door.

"Get down, quickly," Macdonald warned.

"What?"

"I said, hide," Macdonald commanded.

Diana didn't hesitate to pull her legs in and drop down as Macdonald shut the car door. She fell into the gap before the seats, on top of the first aid kit, and looked up out the window.

"Any sight of the vigilante?" a police officer questioned.

"None around here," Macdonald replied, moving around to the front of his car to open the door. "We'll have to keep looking."

"We'll be at it all night," the police officer remarked. "He's probably gone into the woods. Is that his motorcycle?"

"Yes, it is," Macdonald replied. "He's probably gone on foot. He couldn't have gone far."

"Alright then."

The police cruiser drove off while Sergeant Macdonald got into the driver's seat. He looked before him and then into the rear-view mirror. Diana sat up and brushed her hair behind her as she jerked her head.

"Well, that was unexpected," Diana remarked.

"Are you okay?"

"Yeah... I'm fine," Diana replied, "but why...?"

"I'm going to give you this last chance. I'm more tired than you with what's wrong with the system," Macdonald expressed. "I've had to live with it since I joined the police force. It shattered my hopes of what it meant to be a cop. We don't protect people anymore... we protect politicians and their laws. I don't know how much of what you're telling me is true, but I've seen you since before what happened at the Mayfair. You're the one that got away at the nuclear plant... the one that fell into the vat. I believe that you were in the Syndicate. I believe that you've been leaking all that information to try and take down the Syndicate now that Montgomery is dead. I don't agree with what the Syndicate stood for before by 'controlling crime,' or in who Montgomery was as a person, but regardless of that, there's a power struggle going on right now, especially now that Game is dead."

"I didn't kill him."

"I... I don't know if that's true or not, but you don't seem like someone who assassinates people. It doesn't make sense, so for now, I believe you. A lot is at stake now..."

Sergeant Macdonald shifted gears and began to drive off.

"Listen, I'm going to get you out of here, but you need to keep your head down and stay out of sight until we're in the clear. Got it?"

"Yeah, I got it. Thank you."

"Don't thank me just yet," Macdonald replied. "You have your reasons. I have my reasons. When I let you go last time, it was so that you could have a chance at a normal life. So when this is over, can you please promise me that you retire from this vigilantism?"

"I never wanted to stay out there forever," Diana replied. "I hoped that I'd get to stay with the Syndicate for a while, but now that it's about to come to an end. I've had to think about what I want to do, and I'm between two ideas… one of them more unlikely than the other."

"What are they?"

"I don't know about it yet, but last year I met a group of religious nuns that struck a chord with me. I've been thinking about joining them now that the Syndicate is over for me."

"As long as you're not on the streets anymore causing chaos, I don't care. It's your life."

"Doesn't seem to be my life when people try and stop me because they're afraid of what could happen to me and my life."

"Your life affects other people. You can't isolate yourself. Even if you were to join a group of nuns, you'd still be in their social circle. Your life would affect yours. You can't stop that… it's human nature."

Diana didn't respond.

"Alright, get down. We're about to pass a checkpoint."

Diana lowered herself into the gap between the seats. She huddled there and limited her movement. Sergeant Macdonald drove slowly towards the checkpoint. Diana could hear dogs barking at the car from outside. The car stopped. Macdonald opened the window. Diana's ear twitched and she listened.

"Something upsetting your pooches?" Macdonald questioned.

"Who knows what's up with them," the police officer responded. "The captain wants everybody on the ground looking for these vigilantes though. Where do you think you're going?"

"Seems a little excessive for two people. I've had my search," Macdonald responded. "I've got to head back to the station… lots of paperwork to do."

"These two people killed the commissioner."

"Allegedly," Macdonald replied. "I'll let you guys take care of it. I'm out."

Macdonald raised his window and then drove off. He began to speed up and then sped up again as the road became smoother.

"Alright, you can come out now," Macdonald said, looking into the rear-view mirror. "We're clear."

Diana picked herself up again and sat down.

"Wait, if you're the one that was at the Mayfair, then who's this other guy that was with you? The cyborg?"

"I have no idea," Diana replied. "I'm not affiliated with him. He was trying to stop me."

"Is he with the Syndicate?"

"Somehow, I doubt it," Diana answered, looking through the window as they drove down the highway. "He's the least of my concerns. Anyways, where are we going?"

"Where do you want me to take you?" Macdonald asked. "Do you have a secret hideout? A secret hideaway somewhere around here?"

"No…' Diana replied. "I've just been operating in Keswick from my apartment."

"Oh…"

Macdonald continued to drive down the highway and soon enough they were at the Grafton Bridge that returned them to Cliffe Island. He drove down and made his way over into Jarsdel and then King Island.

"Well, this was not how I wanted to spend my New Year's Eve," Macdonald remarked as he drove off the highway and came into Bromley. "I was supposed to punch out hours ago."

"Sorry…"

"Comes with the job," Macdonald responded, going right onto Bailey Drive. "What street am I going to in Keswick?"

"Bennett Street," Diana replied. "Just past Mackenzie."

Diana looked around as they passed Pentateuch Cathedral and then the major intersection with Main Street. The city appeared to be as normal as it was when she left with no chaos in sight. Diana watched as they turned onto W Stuart Street and then Bennet Street, and finally they came to a stop at the curb across from Diana's home.

Sergeant Macdonald looked to Diana through the rear-view mirror as he brought the car to a halt and shifted gears.

"Are you alright for bandages?" he asked.

"Yeah, I think I'll be alright," Diana replied.

"So, what can you tell me about the Syndicate before we part? Anything an investigator should know?"

"You're going to investigate them?"

"Well, without Game in play, I think there'll be less fear. I know a couple of other investigators who were against the Syndicate and suspicious of those that have connections with them. I didn't really bail you out on a whim… You could be useful to a resolution against this entire conspiracy."

"Right…" Diana replied in a quiet voice, "well, I don't know much about the role of police except to keep their noses out from Syndicate affairs. Paladin Group manages most of the brute force and muscle, but that was when they had a crack team of mercenaries. Nowadays, that looks a little short since there's been a split between loyalties. Dr. Bishop has the loyalty to the intelligence division of Paladin Group, who were mostly private investigators… and a lot of former NSA, CIA, CSIS, FBI, and even Mossad people. Meanwhile, the special weapons division, which I was a part of… Alpha Team, are your Green Berets, Delta Force, Joint Task Force, and SAS. The rest is split between tactical division and regular forces, the Stewards. They're just your regular security officers with a slightly more elite group who take on high-profile tasks. Combined, Paladin Group provides security for a lot of public and private spaces across Harlech… the universities, banks, movie studios, ports, and even all municipal buildings, heck even most shopping malls and hospitals."

"Any idea where each faction operates from?" Macdonald asked.

"No," Diana answered. "I've been trying to figure that one out, but been unsuccessful. I've been looking for Dr. Bishop recently, but now I've got look for both of them since… Mrs. Dulles has been let free. There's also these special packages that I have no idea in what they contain. At Dock F, the loyalists (Mrs. Dulles faction) were looking for a container that had something that the rebels had taken. There was also a shipment of drones that she was interested in, and which I thought would be used to wage war against the rebels, but I don't know about that now."

"Interesting…" Macdonald responded. "Alright then. Anything else?"

"Not on the top of my mind."

"Then we'll be in touch. What's the best way to get into contact with you?"

"I'd say text me, but… dammit… I lost my phone."

"What were you doing at Hunter Street today? What was your objective there?"

"I don't even know…"

Macdonald raised an eyebrow.

"Look, how about we stay old-fashioned… until we figure something out, talk to me in person. My apartment is #12 of the building over there and I want to minimize the trace between us for both of our sake. If you want to talk in person, just come to my place. It should be fine for now."

"Alright then."

"Thanks again."

"I'll get the handcuffs off you and then you're free to go."

"Thank you."

Act 5, Scene 3

"Dammit!" Tristan shouted as he hid in an alleyway in Lennox. "Where is she? She could be anywhere?"

"Yes," Charlemagne simply confirmed. "I don't have a signal on her cellphone. She was smart enough to turn it back off when she realized you were tracking her with it."

"Don't bother with her phone. I collected it after she left it behind at Hunter Street," Tristan replied. "At least she'll be caught, and this'll be over... I only worry about the fight she'll put up before she allows them to take her alive."

"She won't dare to use excessive force."

"She tried to kill Mrs. Dulles today..."

"Even then," Charlemagne insisted. "She has a good moral conscience, unlike another one of my children."

"I'm going to pretend like you meant Finn there."

"I've managed to hack into police scanners and heard that they're still looking for her... they've found her motorbike. A manhunt will be initiated..."

"She doesn't have the same skills as me..." Tristan said. "She'll die out there just like those two kids in Manitoba."

"Don't be so certain..." Charlemagne insisted. "You've done all that you could. Please return to the tower."

"Police have the entire way back on lockdown probably..." Tristan replied. "I have no idea how I'm going to return in this thing..."

"Do you want me to send the Protection Squad to pick you up?" Charlemagne questioned.

"I'd rather you send the Protection Squad to go out and look for her."

"You know they can't interfere in a police investigation," Charlemagne replied. "It'll call too much attention on Cabernet Industries."

Tristan didn't respond. He continued to hide in the dark alleyway.

"Wait a minute… I've got a signal from… her computer in her apartment…!"

"What?" Tristan questioned. "Impossible? How? Is it the police? Have they seized her apartment?"

"I'm not sure…" Charlemagne replied.

"That has to be someone else," Tristan remarked. "There's no way that's her… She must have a roommate, or a… boyfriend, or something!"

"Our intel says that she's been solidary since the start of the month," Charlemagne replied, "so unless there's been a recent change, or…"

"I have to get over there…" Tristan remarked. "There could be someone with the Syndicate there."

"Nevermind that," Charlemagne responded. "I'm going to send the Protection Squad to respond. You need to focus on returning to Harlech without the entire police force behind you."

Tristan growled, but submitted, "Fine."

"See if you can make your way back to Cliffe Island," Charlemagne said. "I'll have another team from the Protection Squad meet you at the location I'm sending you. Understood?"

"Yes," Tristan replied.

Tristan came out of hiding and drove through Lennox with discretion. He made his way through and went towards the coastal freeway, driving down and making his way to Grafton Bridge before going into Leicester to the location sent to him by Charlemagne. Tristan met with a small team from Charlemagne's private guard at a facility owned by Cabernet

Industries. The motorbike was hidden there, and Tristan removed his helmet to join the team in the armored car that took him back to Cabernet Tower, into the parkade, and then led him out. Tristan split from them and went directly to the elevator on his own, entering and going down to meet with Charlemagne in the sublevel.

Tristan stormed into the workshop and looked over to Charlemagne at the computer ahead. He went down the platform and down the set of stairs to join him while Charlemagne span his chair around and looked to him. Tristan dropped his helmet at the side of the computer and then looked to the computer screen. Sure enough, Diana's computer was online recently.

"How?" Tristan questioned. "How is this possible? Have the P.S. been there?"

"They have and when they went to the door to knock, she answered it," Charlemagne replied. "The embarrassment on my behalf, that I sent my protection detail to 'check up on her,' is paid. She appeared to be tired, but also in a bad shape with cuts on her face."

"Do you have the video from their bodycams?"

"Yes," Charlemagne admitted. "I'm not lying to you. You can watch the playback."

"No, that's alright," Tristan responded in a saddened face, pacing the room. "How did she do it? How did she seemingly teleport from one place to another?"

Tristan stopped before the cabinet with the amulets. He then looked away and back to the computer screen.

"She's been trained in the art of disappearing and reappearing," Charlemagne remarked.

"That doesn't make her a magician, or... a psychic," Tristan responded. "We need to be better next time. We can't let her return out there..."

"I've been listening to the police frequencies, and they've collected her motorcycle. Luckily, she was removed the license plates and scratched out the serial number, so there will be no way for them to trace possession of that bicycle back to her."

"You care about her not being arrested, but all I care about is that she doesn't kill herself."

"You gave me a hard time when I wanted to ensure the same from you, and yet you do the same towards her as if you were still with her."

"What are you complaining about? She's your cousin and your adoptive-daughter," Tristan remarked. "You get a good deal out of it. What do you care about my motives?"

"I'm beginning to fear for you as well," Charlemagne simply said.

"I'm not suicidal," Tristan clarified, looking at him and straightening up. "Do you think I could disrespect my life…? After the countless times that she poured her soul into trying to keep me alive? In Russia. In the States. Here."

"Without her bike, she may well stay off the streets," Charlemagne remarked.

Tristan shook her head and replied, "She'll buy a new one. A nicer one. She's tenacious and persistent."

"Has she really turned to murder?" Charlemagne asked.

"No… I don't think she has," Tristan responded, lying. "I must have misunderstood what was going on at Hunter and Durham."

"The police commissioner is dead," Charlemagne stated. "Mrs. Dulles is nowhere to be seen. People at International Plaza and Dominion Square are up in arms celebrating the death of Commission Game."

Tristan didn't respond. Charlemagne sighed.

"Perhaps it's time that we retire, Tristan," Charlemagne admitted. "I wanted to ensure that Diana could escape and make the best of her life without spending it in a prison – the same results I provided to you in the United Kingdom. However, if she has gone to this extent of madness, then perhaps we send the police to her home and have her arrested. If she indicts you, then my lawyers can bail you both out on good terms and have you flee the country, but at least that'll be the end of this carnage."

"No," Tristan firmly denied, moving over to the computer, causing Charlemagne to roll out of the way. "This isn't over until Diana is safe."

"Diana is safe," Charlemagne reasoned. "She's at home. Most likely in bed."

Tristan put on a headset and began to scan police frequencies.

"I said no," Tristan firmly stated again.

Charlemagne frowned at him and stood up. He then went over and turned off the monitor and pointed Tristan over to the other above Barry's bench.

"What the hell!" Tristan reacted.

"Listen to me, Tristan," Charlemagne declared, "and look at the TV."

Tristan looked and saw footage from the Harlech News Network from last night, the cellphone footage from pedestrians at Durham Street, helicopter footage of the street chase, and footage of the aftermath at Hunter Street. Afterwards, there was footage of people celebrating in downtown.

"Look at this destruction," Charlemagne said. "Look at this chaos. Ever since you got involved in Diana's business, things have not gotten better, but worse. You're a step behind her. You're not an infiltrator like she is. She is in her element in all this. You were trained to be a soldier and use brute tactics. She can take care of herself. You don't belong out there. You can't stop her… you'll only hurt both of yourselves."

"I didn't blow up a city street today…" Tristan muttered, "but even if costs me everything I have, so long as she isn't dead, I'll try and stop her. It was a risk I was willing to take."

"Listen to yourself, Tristan…" Charlemagne insisted in disbelief.

"I love her!" Tristan shouted. "Everybody's been on my case that I've never done anything to show that I love her, and now that I pour my soul into it, I'm being told to back off! I swear to God that I'll lay down my life if it means she's safe! I don't want to see anything happen to her… It's my fault she's even out there…"

"Diana made her decisions when she joined the Syndicate."

"It was my fault that she even approached them in the first place," Tristan remarked. "Because I cheated on her. Because I tore her from my life."

Charlemagne shook his head and replied, "This isn't some brave crusade," he realized. "You feel responsible for all of this. You feel responsible for what she's putting herself through, and if she dies, you will feel guilty that you did that to her – that you led her to that point…"

Tristan didn't respond.

"I don't believe it… Diana isn't the irresponsible vigilante on the streets. It is you – you and your attempt to set things 'right' because she saved your life. My God, what would Diana think of this?"

"She'd call me an idiot," Tristan whispered with a sad face, "but I will make sure she's safe," he said, picking up his volume. "You're the one that told me to be selfless, to sacrifice what I have for those that you love, because that's what love is. It is a selfless sacrifice, and I'll live up to that. Please understand me,

Charles. You can't stop my involvement in this as long as she's still out on the streets. I need to be out there... it's my responsibility."

Charlemagne shook his head at him and stepped away. He went to the staircase but stopped just at the base. He looked over to Tristan.

"Then do it," Charlemagne permitted, "but I will have no further part in this."

Tristan watched as Charlemagne went up the stairs and to the elevator. He then left. Tristan looked back over to the TV and picked up the remote to turn it off. He the grabbed his helmet and sat down in the chair that Charlemagne had been sitting in. He looked at his reflection through the visor and touched his forehead against it. Tristan then stood up and went to the cabinet to place the helmet inside. He looked back at it with a pensive expression and then sighed.

Act 6, Scene 1

Tristan doodled in his notebook as his biology lecture droned on and on. Another week had passed since New Year's, and little had occurred since then. Tristan had no reason to don the exoskeleton and helmet and neither did Diana as she hadn't heard from Sergeant Macdonald nor the Syndicate. Life, in a way, was going back to normal, but Tristan didn't want it to. He left his lecture early and left the biology building to the north of the university and began to make his way back to the dormitory. Tristan had a sunken expression on his face as he walked.

Tristan entered Building 2A and went upstairs to the fourth floor and to his room, which was empty as Finn was out. Tristan went to his desk and opened a wide drawer above the chair. He took out a pink envelope and sat down, opening the envelope and putting it into his backpack. The door into the dorm began to unlock and open. Finn walked in. Tristan sat his backpack down and looked over.

"What's the matter with you?" Finn questioned, going over to his desk as he looked at Tristan suspiciously.

"Nothing," Tristan replied. "I've been… thinking about a lot lately. Diana in particular."

"What about her? I heard what happened with Cheryl… Mandy was not too happy about that. She said that she saw you kissing another woman."

"Yeah…" Tristan admitted.

Finn shook his head.

"You damn dog," Finn remarked. "You really can't keep your hands off of just one woman, can you?"

"It wasn't just any woman," Tristan said. "It was Diana."

"Wait, what? Really?"

"Yeah," Tristan replied. "First time our lips met since we last had a date in September. There was nothing like it… it felt like ecstasy…"

"So, you're with her again then?"

"Not exactly," Tristan remarked. "Diana… she's been doing some dangerous things lately, and as a result, I've been doing some dangerous things lately."

"What kind of dangerous things?" Finn questioned, looking at him suspiciously.

"Oil plant sabotage level of dangerous," Tristan answered.

"What the hell?" Finn replied. "You've been doing some ecoterrorism without me?" he sarcastically inquired.

"No," Tristan responded. "Haven't you heard the news? Diana is that masked vigilante and I'm the idiot that's been chasing after her."

"Oh, right," Finn said. "Sorry, ah… it's starting to make sense then," he went on, sitting down on Tristan's bed. "You've got to stop chasing after maniacs, Tristan. I mean, this is like when you went after me when I went after Aidan."

"What should I do?" Tristan asked.

"What are you trying to do exactly?"

"I want her to stop risking her life over a petty quest of revenge," Tristan answered. "I want her to go on with her life without trying to kill herself."

"Oh, you pair of suicidal doves," Finn remarked. "Okay, here's what you do. You go out and buy her some flowers, and you go and propose to her."

"I'm being serious," Tristan snapped back. "What do I do?"

"I'm being serious," Finn affirmed. "Tristan, you're not going to find anyone who's as crazy as you. I mean, all women are pretty damn crazy, but this is your bird and heart. Lock her down and then she'll settle."

"Diana doesn't want to ever lay eyes on me again," Tristan remarked. "Even if I were to miraculously woo her, she's hell bent on revenge against the people that killed an old friend of hers. Until she has that, she won't rest."

"Then I don't know," Finn replied. "Give her want she wants. And I mean, what she *really* wants. She's obviously in emotional distress over the whole being cheated on and her friend being murdered. Let her know that this isn't about you and that you do care about her... tame her down and get her to back down the way you had her. She doesn't want to kill anyone, or get revenge. She wants to feel better about herself because she wants answers. It's what all women ever want – a response to meet their emotional demands."

"Okay, shut up," Tristan responded.

"Get her to forget about the whole vengeance and do what you should have done like two months ago... apologize to her."

"I already apologized to her."

"Then take the next step."

"She doesn't want to be with me," Tristan repeated.

"Are you sure about that? I don't know about you, but if a girl kissed me, I'd take it as a clear sign that she wants to be with me. Sounds like she's divided... Like I said, show her you care. Why did Diana leave you other than the whole infidelity?"

"Because I made her suffer? Because I was weak... and not who I used to be."

"Then be who she wants you to be," Finn remarked. "If she's worth it, you'll do it."

"She is worth it," Tristan muttered. "She'll always be worth it. I'll never forget that."

Tristan picked up his backpack. He took out the envelope and hid it into his sweater.

"I'm… I'm going to her apartment to talk to her," Tristan said, fetching his coat. "I need to sort this out with her like two humans instead of two psychos."

"Good luck," Finn simply replied.

"I'll see you later tonight," Tristan said before he parted.

Tristan left the dorm and went downstairs to go out towards Barcote Street near the Student Union and Aquatics Center where there were some shops. He went to a florist and picked up some flowers. He then went and got a taxi to drive him from the university all the way to Keswick – to Bennett Street where Diana's apartment was. The taxi came to a halt on the other side of the apartment building and Tristan paid the man almost fifty dollars before he came out. The taxi left and Tristan stood on the opposite-side of the street, on the sidewalk, with a dozen roses in hand and a letter in the other. Tristan took a deep breath and then began to cross the street.

Tristan approached Diana's childhood home and entered through the front doors. He then walked upstairs the stairwell in the center and came to the top, stopping before Unit #12 and muttering under his breath some words.

"Diana… I know I said I'm sorry, but… No," Tristan whispered. "No, that's not good enough. Diana, I'm sorry – Diana, I miss you. Too pathetic."

Tristan sighed and brought his hand up to the front door of Diana's apartment. He knocked hard and waited patiently for Diana to answer, but no answer came. He knocked again, but no answer came. Tristan sighed and turned around. He walked over to the railing that went down to the ground floor and opened the envelope, taking out the card inside.

The greeting card was white and had a cartoonish picture on the front of two dogs. They had their paws together and had a heart between them. The comic text above them read, 'You make my tail wag…' Tristan opened the card and looked inside, and it had a picture of the dog with a heart in hand, presenting it to the female dog that held a coy face. A speech bubble above came from the male dog and read, 'Will you be mine, Valentine?' in all capital letters. Below the cartoon were some of Tristan's sincere words that read, '*I'm sorry for all the distress I've caused you, but over the last few weeks, I've had sleepless nights worrying about you. There is no more just punishment for me than to be separated from you and in this hellish state, but I'll live like this as long as it is necessary as much as I'll fight for your life… Our last kiss reminded me that there's only you out there for me and we've given each other everything over the years, so would it be too much to ask for this one instance of forgiveness…? Even if you say no however, I'll understand. I'll love you to the ends of the Earth will prove it until you know it. Love, Tristan.*"

Tristan put the card back into the envelope. He then took both the envelope and the flowers and sat them down in front of the Diana's front door. Tristan then left down the stairwell and came to the front door of the building. Tristan's phone vibrated. He picked it up from his pocket and looked at the front screen. Tristan had an incoming text message from someone who had been silent for the last two months to him.

"Hey, Tristan!" Helene said over text. "I'm in town and wanted to see you."

Tristan raised an eyebrow as he was uncertain whether Helene Köhlen really messaged him. He unlocked his phone and replied, 'Where the heck have you been?' He then said, 'I'm free right now if you want to meet.'

"Perfect," Helene replied. "Come over to the Windsor Hotel downtown and let's have a chat," followed by a heart emote.

Tristan put his phone away and looked around. He instantly made his way down the street and began to walk down Bennett Street to reach the Windsor Hotel near the Cabernet Tower.

Act 6, Scene 2

Diana came down the elevator at Cabernet Tower with a duffel bag around her back. She looked ahead as the door opened to a sublevel beneath the parkade. She stepped forward and the lights in the room automatically switched on by her motion. She looked around and saw a large box below her on a platform and a long desk that stretched the wall ahead. Immediately across from her was a large double-screen computer with a large black chair. At the right side there was another computer with a monitor above. Next to this corner desk were some display cases. Diana came around and went over to this area to get a better look.

In an alcove to the left from where she was, hidden away was Tristan's motorcycle. Diana walked over to it and got a better look at the motorbike. It had a futuristic design to it with two large wheels, one at the front and back that blended into a dark black-grey chassis. At the sides were the cannons that shot through concrete barriers. From over the wheel, the black-tinted windscreen transitioned upwards to cover the face of the driver. The handles were hidden within the armor plating of the vehicle and the seat was hard to see, but had the driver seemingly lie down while they drove. The chrome double-exhaust transitioned outwards from the rear where there was a small compartment for items. Diana admired the bike and then looked back over the space where the computers and display cases were.

Diana walked over to the case where the Scepter of Alexander the Great was kept. She noticed that the stone had been taken out from where she had previously seen it in the mouth of the eagle at the head of the staff. Incidentally, the display case next to this one was empty. Diana ignored this detail and walked across the floor to the other side where Tristan's suit was kept. She looked at in greater detail, the dark grey paint over the robotic exoskeleton suit. There were still a few scratches on the helmet from their engagement on New Year's Eve. In the case next to the suit, there was a variety of Tristan's equipment and tools, including his grapple gun at the bottom. The other equipment included small chip-like items, smoke pellets, the bow, quail and arrows, and another gun-like object (the plastic explosive cannon). Diana gently opened the cabinet door and took out the grapple gun. She held it in her hands and then began to put it into her duffel bag.

When Diana was finished at the cabinet, she closed it and walked over to the workbench with the computer in the corner. There was a picture frame of Barry and Judith at their wedding nearby. At the side, there some grenade-like canisters stretched out – four in total. Diana looked at them and picked them up. She read what they said on the side, 'Electromagnetic Impulse Grenade,' with a stamp below that read, 'Prototype.' Diana quickly bagged all four of these before going to the desk in the center. There, Diana saw a picture frame of Charlemagne's mother, Vienna, and another that had a picture of Charlemagne with Allodia, his father, and Diana and Tristan when they were at Isla Paraiso. Diana picked up this picture and focused her eyes at the couple in the photo. She noticed that Tristan had a mild smile in the picture, or in the least, he was not upset or frowning. Diana let out a nostalgic sigh and then put the picture back where she found it.

Atop the keyboard of the computer was an envelope with Diana's name written in Charlemagne's handwriting. She picked it up and opened it. Inside were a set of a keys. Diana took the keys into her hand and then walked over to the motorcycle in the hidden alcove to the left from where she was. She set her bag down and began to get changed into her outfit. She removed her civilian clothes, including her leather jacket, and then pulled up the trousers, pulled down the tunic, and brought the ballistic armor over her chest. She put on her boots and put on her belt. She then put on her holster vest with her sidearms loaded in, attached some of her new equipment over herself, including the grapple gun and EMP grenades, and put her radio earpiece into her ear.

Once Diana was ready, she raised over her mouth her stitched veil and over her head her hood. She then hopped onto the motorbike with her duffel bag around her torso by a strap. On a dashboard behind the handles were some buttons and a lock for the keys. Diana inserted the keys and then pressed one of the top-right corner buttons that was blinking. She then looked ahead as a door began to open ahead for Diana to ride on through. She kicked the kickstand and shot off from the platform she was on, riding through the tunnel that looped around and then exited out into the parkade. Diana escaped the parkade and came out onto Earle Street, and then began to drive north towards Maiden Drive where she turned left and went westbound. The night was calm, and no snow fell, although the city was still considerably snowy. The sun had set, and it was early twilight. Diana slowed down at a quiet intersection on a red light and brought her hand to her earpiece.

"Alpha Eight here," Diana communicated over the radio. "Ten-Zero."

No immediate response came. The light turned green, and Diana continued down Maiden Drive, driving underneath Penultimate Bridge and wrapping around along the outskirts of Camross.

"Alpha Eight, you're Ten-Two," Macdonald responded. "We had a major incident in Camross as per our last conversation. Subject was DOA. I haven't been able to take a look as access is limited for obvious reasons. I've been able to determine the circumstances to be suspicious. The location is the Olympus Tower. You should be able to find the rest."

"Copy that," Diana replied. "I'm on my way."

Diana continued to drive and turned left onto Goya Street. She then turned left again onto a one-way street and stopped before a glass tower near the highway. She looked up to the multi-story tower, which was circular with glass windows covering almost every face. She then turned the bike around, driving up the pathway to the front door of the condo building and then over the front lawn to head around to some bushes nearby. She parked the bike here and then hopped over to head towards some hedges behind a chain-link fence. Diana climbed atop of the fence and hopped over to drop down into a paddock where there was a covered pool with snow atop.

Diana made her way over to the glass doors that went into a fitness center on the other side. She attempted to open the door, but it was locked. She then took out some pins from a pouch and set off to unlocking the door manually before repeating trying to open it. The door opened and she walked in. She passed through the small gym and came out into the wide corridor of the condo building where the floor was mixed between grey stone tiles at the side and pinkish-beige tiles in the center. The walls were made of a dark wood. The architecture was modernist as was some of the furniture in the lobby. Diana passed a row of mailboxes and then went around to some elevators.

The apartment building was quiet. Diana called for an elevator and the third elevator door on her left opened. Diana walked over and entered. She then attempted to have the elevator go up to the second floor, but the doors would not close. Diana sighed and then looked up to the ceiling where there was a hatch that went out of the elevator. She kicked off the wall, jumped, and hit the hatch open. She then jumped again and climbed out, coming into the elevator shaft for all three elevators. Diana looked up and saw one of the elevators to be high up above, while the other was parked at the ground floor. Ahead, Diana could see a ladder at the side that went up the whole shaft. Diana went towards the ladder and grabbed hold. She then climbed up and went to the second-floor shaft door and began to try and pry it open. The door was too tight for her to open. Diana looked around from where she was stood at a narrow ledge. She then saw an emergency release button and hit it. The doors opened. Diana stepped through and came onto the second floor. She quickly lowered her veil and hood and zipped up her coat.

"Okay…" Diana muttered to herself. "Let's find that crime scene."

Diana looked around the entire second floor for a possible clue into where the crime scene was, but when she didn't find it, she entered a fire escape and went up to the third floor. Unfortunately, Diana repeated this method for almost every floor until she reached the thirty-eighth floor of the tower and finally found a front door where there was some police tape over the front. Diana brought her hand to the door and attempted to open it. The door was locked. She knelt down and began to work on prying the lock open.

Once the door was unlocked, Diana pushed through and entered the other side, closing the door behind her. The condo suite was dark and cold. Diana walked forward down the grey-tiled floor of the entrance corridor and then came onto a light-wooded paneled floor to see police markers about the violent scene with an outline of a body in the middle of the area. Nearby the outline was a pistol on the floor and blood stain that went from the head.

"What the hell…" Diana muttered.

Diana looked at the room she was in more closely. She was in a small living room where the body was in front of a couch near a short table with a flat screen TV above. Behind the living room were some countertops and stools, and behind that was an enclosed small kitchen. At the side of the living room was a door that went into a room on the other side. Diana looked and saw that it was a bedroom that was slightly untidy as though someone had been rummaging through the personal belongings. Diana saw a bathroom extend from the left wall. She returned to the main area and went to a desk on her left. She picked up the wallet and opened it to look at the driver's license inside. Diana read the name on the license, which said, 'Daryl Vincent Moore.' She then rummaged through the wallet to find a press pass distributed by the Harlech Herald. Diana put everything back where it was and began to rummage through the desk. She produced a folder that had some newspaper clippings of articles written by Daryl Moore, most of which were on municipal politics and the Harlech Syndicate. Another folder had some printed-out documents that Diana had released online and were now publicly available. Diana looked through them and then put them back.

"What do you want me to find, Brandon…" Diana muttered, looking underneath the desk and seeing nothing there.

Diana resumed to search the rest of the apartment, going into the bedroom to have a look through, but the apartment had very little furniture and most things that were not already taken apart had very little personal effects. Diana searched underneath the bed but found nothing. She looked through the end tables and saw very little. Diana looked through a closet in the entrance corridor and then returned to the kitchen, but did not spend too much time there. Finally, Diana came to the outline of the corpse and went to pickup the pistol. She examined it carefully and looked at the brand – the brand was slightly unfamiliar, SIG Sauer, but the serial number at the side had been scratched out. Diana unloaded the magazine and checked the bullets. There were approximately six missing from the ten-round magazine. She put each of them back and then placed the pistol as it was when she found it. Diana looked around the entire area and took a deep breath.

Diana's eyes fixated on the kitchen towards a blender at the corner of the room. Inside the blender was some fruit, unpeeled and ready to be blended. Diana walked over and took a closer look around. She took a flashlight from her belt and shined it, seeing some stains of blood near the edge of the counter going down to the floor. Diana stood up and shined the light around to see if she could see more blood. Instead, she saw something lodged in the drain of the sink. Diana reached over to pull it out and saw that it was a matchbook with the name of a local bar on the front, the same bar that used to be frequented by Scot and some other people who work on the special weapons division. Diana put the matchbook back where she found it and then continued to look around. She walked into the living room and over to the couch. Diana raised the cushions but saw nothing underneath. Diana's eyes then fixated on the bedroom again. She walked over and began to push the mattress over and onto the floor.

Diana took a knife out from her belt and stabbed it into the box spring underneath, tearing the fabric and revealing a small trove of treasure within stored from underneath the bed as the sides of the fabric had become lose with age. Diana looked through and picked out a laptop as well as a folder. She sat down opened the folder. Inside were some papers and the title of a draft of a report titled, 'Corruption within the Harlech Police Department.' Diana read through it and the journalist basically spoke on evidence he had collected that connected certain police officers with the Syndicate. She then went to the back of the papers to find a spreadsheet the detailed the summary of a cost card (credit card). The paper was slightly crumpled and dirty as though it had been through some rough times. The name on the account was Harris Errol Game. Diana looked through and saw that an entry was highlighted for a reservation at the Windsor Hotel. Below was a sticky note with some dates and the current date, January 8th, 2021, circled. Diana looked through some other papers and found a handwritten note that basically read that the victim was of sound mind and did not have suicidal thoughts, but that he feared for his life because of what he was looking into. The note ended with a remark that the corruption within the police could not be tolerated. Diana closed the folder and sat it on the end table. She buried the laptop back into the mattress and then put everything back where it was, except the folder which she took with her as she made her exit.

Diana put the folder into her duffel bag and then went back down to the ground floor. She quietly avoided the two police officers at the front entrance of the apartment complex and went the way she had come in, through the patio and over the fence. Diana then quickly returned to her apartment where she dropped off the folder and her duffel bag and hid the motorbike under the tarp. Diana then went on foot to find a nearby payphone that continued to function. She dialed a number and then waited for an answer.

"Hello?" a voice questioned.

"It's me," Diana replied. "I just finished looking around at the place you told me to go to."

"What did you find?" Macdonald asked.

"Well, for a start, oddly enough, I found a matchbox to the Wet Work, a bar here in Keswick. It was lodged in the drain of the kitchen sink."

"Hm, that's a bar that some cops usually go to," Macdonald replied. "Weird."

"Well, not too weird," Diana responded. "This person is a journalist and he's been investigating the Syndicate for quite some time. I couldn't find anything else out in the open except for his ID. His name is Daryl Vincent Moore in case you want to look a little deeper."

"Yeah, I've had a peak at the police report, and they've ruled his death as a suicide."

"Suicide?"

"Unfortunately, yes. The next of kin were contacted and after receiving the police report, they don't want the coroner to look deeper, but go on…"

"I don't think this was a suicide. He didn't look like the type to own a gun, nor did he have a PAL on him. The gun that was at the scene isn't something that you easily come across and there were six missing bullets from the magazine, which meant that whoever owned that gun had been firing the shot was made."

"What make of gun was it?"

"SIG Sauer," Diana replied. "Why?"

"Hm, weird," Macdonald remarked in a calm tone. "That's the same make that the force uses."

"Wait until you hear this," Diana said. "I managed to find some hidden objects under his mattress. Hidden within the false mattress people put under their beds to make their beds higher. Inside were some documents, including a draft for a piece I guess he was working on which names some of your buddies in the HPD as being a part of the Syndicate."

"Really?" Macdonald questioned in an unsurprised tone.

"Yes," Diana replied. "The list included Commissioner Game and had some personal documents of his that he must have somehow gotten. At the back of them was a cost card statement that had a reservation at the Windsor Hotel highlighted and a sticky note that had today's date on it."

"Hm," Macdonald responded. "I wouldn't know anything about that. Okay... well, whoever this person was, they were clearly barking up the wrong tree. What did you do with the documents?"

"I have them in a safe place," Diana replied. "I'm going to upload them later tonight when I get a chance."

"Hold on that," Macdonald responded. "If you upload any of that, don't forget that you're gambling with whether or not that could be accepted evidence in court. Remember, we want to prosecute these people, so please hold off on doing that until I have a look."

"Okay..." Diana submitted.

"From what it sounds like... it seems like this person was murdered, and the perpetrator(s) may have been police officers. The matchbox could have easily been his, picked up while he's scoping these bars for information from drunk cops, but the gun... that's too close to home for me. Do you know what pistol the Syndicate uses?"

"Yeah, we don't use Sauer," Diana replied. "We used Smith & Wesson."

"That's what I thought..." Macdonald responded in a slightly tired voice, pausing for a moment. "Alright, thanks for looking into this for me. You've been a big help."

"No problem," Diana replied. "I'm going to go to the Windsor Hotel and see what I can find there. If this reporter was interested in this place because the commissioner had a reservation for a suite there, and he anticipated something going on today, then I have to check that out."

"Okay," Macdonald responded. "Please be careful though."

"I will. I'll be in touch."

Diana hung up and walked back down the sidewalk to return to her apartment. Instead of going back up to the fire escape, she went straight to the motorcycle and removed the tarp. She brought her hood over her head and covered her face, and the hopped onto the bike, turning it on, and then racing off to get back out there.

Act 6, Scene 3

Diana passed by the Windsor Hotel, an old chateauesque hotel with a large pointed rusted copper roof and stone walls built on steel frames. There was a strong presence of the Harlech Police Department ERT in front of the hotel, providing access control, and across the street from certain vantage points, such as at the Royal Harlech Museum. Diana made her pass around the entire perimeter before she shot down Durham Street and turned right onto a parkade behind the hotel on the south face. The main entrance into the hotel was on the north face and from the east and west face there was a tunnel that ran underneath towards the rear where taxis and other cabs could briefly park to load and unload guests to the luxurious hotel. Diana drove up a ramp in the parkade and came to the top-most floor (the fifth floor). She then left the bike in a stall towards the corner, in close quarters to the rooftop of the rear of the hotel. At the corner of the Windsor Hotel were gargoyles stretched out and verandas just before the top floor. The design was slightly similar to Cabernet Tower in retrospect, although Cabernet Tower was much larger and consisted of a darker stone on the exterior. Cabernet Tower was also much wider with a grey-steel panel roof instead of a copper one.

Diana looked over to the rear of the building and the rooftop over the tunnel where the causeway was. From the parkade, it was a simple jump to gain access onto this rooftop, but Diana did not go ahead so soon. She instead went around and looked down to where there was an alleyway behind the rear of the building. This alleyway had a few trucks that were parked with their rear under cover. At the side was a door where cargo could be taken into the hotel. Atop of the platform where trucks parked their rear towards, there were half a dozen dumpsters. At the delivery door, two ERT officers could be seen stationed there. Diana's eyes then looked down at a gap where the causeway tunnel branched out and delved beneath the parkade Diana was at. Diana moved back around and took her grapple gun. She shot at the side of the rooftop and launched herself up. Diana crashed into the side of the roof but was able to climb up and go over to look down at where she had seen the causeway branch.

Diana's eyed looked down and saw that the causeway did not go into the same parkade, but instead went underground as it ramped down. A sign above stated, 'Hotel Parking Lot.' There were no guards immediately station at this tunnel, although the ones at the door in the alleyway had a line of sight towards it even though it was about fifty feet from them. Before Diana went down though, she began to explore the rooftop she had access to. She walked over the gravel on the roof and climbed up onto a catwalk that led to some air-conditioning machines at the sides. In the middle of the space there was a white glasshouse with patios at either side. It appeared to be some sort of restaurant. Behind this restaurant there was a large open space of gravel in six large rectangular trays. Hotel windows could be seen looking towards this space. The only doors into the hotel from this area was via the restaurant, but Diana could see people inside, so she backed off and returned to space that looked down to the alleyway. Diana's eyes looked over to the ERT members and then immediately down to a ledge below.

Diana moved her legs over and brought herself down onto the ledge. She then jumped down a one-story jump and then came onto a ledge below as the ERT members were distracted. She finally, quietly lowered herself onto the pavement and then looked across as a taxicab drove by and blocked the view of the ERT by the rear doors so that she could hurry down the ramp of the parkade and disappear into the underground parking lot under the hotel. The ramp curved around and then went down so that she was positively underneath the hotel. Diana walked with caution as she came into the parking lot. She proceeded down and reached the other side where there was a metal gate that blocked access into another tunnel that went further down.

Nearby, Diana saw a concrete half-wall that looked down to where the tunnel went to. She went over and looked down to see more parked cars throughout, but at a risk of a two-story drop. She looked around below and saw a red pick-up truck parked in a stall nearby. Diana went down the half-wall until she was within jumping distance of the truck. She then hopped up and jumped down, landing on the roof of the pick-up truck, and then jumped down so that she was on the concrete floor of the second sublevel of the parkade. Ahead, underneath the initial sublevel were a set of elevator doors with a sign above that read, 'Main Lobby.'

The elevator door dinged, causing Diana to take the grapple gun and quickly shoot herself up and out of visible sight. She brought herself down onto some steady pipes and then looked over as she saw three Syndicate mercenaries with assault rifles, and two agents in black suits. She looked at the group with a suspicious and confused eye. The five of them walked away from the elevator and stood in the middle of the causeway. They began to smoke.

"I'm telling you," one of the mercs expressed. "It's back to the glory days from here on out. I'm glad the doctor could finally see some sense. I might finally be able to book my vacations for the summer."

"Don't be so happy just yet," another replied. "I mean, nothing is set and done. They're just having a meeting upstairs and we still don't know how much heat will be on Paladin when it's set and done."

"If Captain Stirling becomes the new police commissioner, it'll be set and done," an agent remarked. "He's been with the Syndicate since the beginning and is less of an uncertain bastard than Game was."

Diana sighed and began to make her way silently over the group. She then took the grapple gun and shot at the pipe below, holding on and swinging down to introduce herself. Diana swung into a merc, pushing him onto the floor with a sharp blow. Diana pulled down the pipe and caused some steam to shoot out and hit another. She then let go and quickly put the grapple gun back to her belt before raising her hands up to engage the other three. She moved in and kicked another onto the ground as they composed themselves from the fright they had attained. Diana then turned to another merc who dropped his cigar and raised his fists up.

"How did he get in here?" an agent questioned.

"Shut up and take 'im down!" a merc replied.

Diana looked at the three remaining grunts and charged at the nearest one, roundhouse kicking him down and then jumping on top of him to drop her knee onto his neck in a brutal manner. She then turned around to the others. She quickly deflected a punch from the side and fell over. Diana recovered by kicking her legs up and pushing the agent back. Diana then moved to the other, rife with determination and focus. She raised her gauntlets to cover her face as the agent swiped a knife at her. She then lowered her gauntlets as she got a fair amount of space between her and him, continuing to jump back as she dodged the swipes before going in to grab the agent's hand and headbutt him. Diana then looked to the other grunt that stood up from the ground. She raised her fists up to him and he gave a tired punch towards her. Diana caught the punch and took him down onto the ground, dislocating his arm from his shoulder and causing him an immense amount of pain.

Once the grunts were taken care of, Diana walked over to the elevator and called for one to come down to take her up. Diana changed channels on her radio and then brought her hand to her earpiece as she waited.

"Delta-Two-Forty-three, this is Alpha Eight," Diana remarked. "Do you copy?"

No immediate response came.

"Go ahead, Alpha Eight," Macdonald finally replied.

"ERT are at the doors, and I've run into armed private security in the sublevel. Rumor has it that both of our targets are in the building, and maybe more. I need you to call the cavalry to secure the base of the hotel while I go up to the top."

"Negative," Macdonald responded. "Too high-profile at the moment. You'll need to make some noise to give the cavalry a reason to show."

Diana paused for a moment as the elevator door opened.

"Copy that," Diana replied with slight distaste. "I'll give them a reason to show."

Diana hit the 'M' button on the panel in the elevator. The doors then closed, and Diana began to rise up to the surface. She looked up to the ceiling as the elevator went up. Once the elevator arrived at the main floor, the doors opened, and some guests began to enter the empty elevator. Diana looked down from the roof, through the narrow hatch that she had jumped through, and held a smoke grenade in her hand. Diana pulled the pin, and a small cloud of smoke began to pour into the elevator. A woman shrieked while a man gave a worried grunt.

"Fire!" another man shouted. "Fire!"

Diana heard a fire alarm activated by the loud ringing that consumed the main foyer. She hopped down into the smoky elevator and then threw the grenade into the foyer.

"Grenade!" a different man yelled. "Secure the building – we're on lockdown!"

"Hm? Lockdown?" Diana whispered, taking out a pistol.

Diana looked through the smoke and into the hotel lobby. She could see some men in suits produce pistols from their jackets as they looked over to the elevator where the smoke came from. She then immediately turned to some next to her, an agent, who had his pistol trained on her. Diana reacted and pulled the gun down. The agent fired a shot into the floor. Civilians panicked and yelled as the gun was fired. Diana hit the man in the side of the head with her pistol and saw him fall to the floor.

"Get these civilians out of here! Everybody out!" another man yelled.

Diana grappled up and onto a beam within the realm of the ceiling and got a better look of the foyer around. She saw two agents near the elevator with their guns trained on the door. There were nine more in total, all looking towards the elevator door as it closed, but smoke continued to emit from the grenade that had been thrown. Hotel staff evacuated the room, ushering guests and other civilians out. Diana changed her radio channel until she came across a transmission.

"I want that room cleared," a man spoke through her earpiece. "Nobody in or out until the good doctor and Mrs. Dulles have finished their meeting. Am I understood?"

"Roger."

"ERT have secured the exit points. Smoke whoever has infiltrated the hotel out."

"Copy that."

Diana scanned the room and looked to the nine agents that remained. Her eyes shot from one to another, calculating her next move. The hotel lobby consisted of two levels, the main level contained a Christmas tree in the center that reached up and almost touched the ceiling realm where Diana was. From here, there were various sofas and services desks within enclaves in the wall, including the check-in desk behind and a concierge next to it. On the second level, which was shaped in a U with the elevators on the open face, there were tall arched windows that looked out on the lateral faces and two double doors at each of the other sides near the lateral corners of the room. Underneath the second level and protruding through the railings were columns that extended up to connect with the beams in the ceiling where Diana was. At either side, towards the corners, were stairs with red carpet that went up the second level. Behind the second level at the front and rear sides there were gaps with railings that looked down to the entrances. The main doors on the main level consisted of two spinning doors like those at Cabernet Tower, and two regular doors at the side on the face that looked to Campbell Street, and simple sliding doors on the side that looked to the causeway at the rear. The windows of these doors were tinted dark so that it was difficult to see to the other side where ERT was. The agents secured the sliding door and locked it down. The room was decorated in tinsel and garland, leftover from the holiday season. The agents began to spread out and cover all of the ground. Diana began to move along the beam, balancing as though it were a tightrope and going around to position herself over an agent on the second level towards the rear of the hotel.

Diana dropped down with the grapple gun, lowering herself and then scooping her arm around the neck of the agent and proceeding to choke him out as he raised herself slightly to receive the help of gravity. The agent squirmed, kicking his legs mid-air until he was finally out for the count and Diana released him. Diana grappled back up and began to move around to the next beam and then the next beam until she was near the Christmas tree. She looked to two agents at the check-in desk and another two moving up the stairs at the front of the hotel. Another two agents took position at the elevators where the smoke began to dissipate.

"We have the room in lockdown," an agent reported.

"Good. Flush the vigilante out of there," the supervisor ordered.

"Roger."

Diana looked around for her next target, eyeing two agents at the top of the stairwell where they split up. She then changed her glance below to two at the main entrance of the hotel, looking out with their guns drawn. Diana made her way over to them, taking out a smoke grenade and then hooking it onto the belt as smoke began to pour out. She then lowered herself down with the grapple gun and dropped the grenade gently before going over with her own gun drawn and grabbing hold of the agent by the neck, hitting him in the head with her pistol and then shooting the other in the side of the leg. The smoke enshrouded all three of them. Diana finished choking out the agent she had hold of and then dropped him. She then moved to the other and dropped her knee down on his neck before shooting up, climbing up and looking over the railing on the second level.

"Target is moving!" an agent reported.

"We have a man down over here!"

Diana watched as the two agents above began to move back down. She then climbed over as one of them stopped to take point at the other side of the platform. Diana moved in with a knife and took hold of the agent's neck, stabbing him in the thigh and then hitting him in the head. The agent yelled out. Diana put the knife away and then shot up into the ceiling. Three agents could be seen on the ground below, two of which were at the elevator doors. The other two were on the other side of the second level. Diana went around to them and dropped down to perform the same attack as at the other side of the room, but without the smoke. She shot at the thigh of one of the agents and then took hold of then neck of the other, hitting him in the head with her pistol and then hitting him again as he fell to the ground. Diana quickly jumped and landed onto the other with the shot leg and brought her neck down in a quick motion to knock out the other with a headbutt. She then kept low and went to the corner of the railing where she took a flash grenade leftover from New Year's Eve and threw it over. Diana then ran around and jumped down as they were blinded, landing atop of one of the agents and taking the grapple gun and shooting it towards another nearby to pull him over. Diana then shot her pistol and hit the third in the thigh, bringing him onto the ground. She shifted her attention back to the agent on the floor that she had landed atop of. She moved in and brought her thigh down onto his neck, hitting him in the head and then to the other before he could stand. Diana then quickly went to the third as he was the last, putting her pistol away and grabbing him by the jacket, pulling him away from his gun on the floor and towards the elevator door. Diana kicked him in the chest where he had a ballistic vest underneath his suit.

"Where are they?!" Diana shouted. "Where's Dulles and Bishop?!"

"U-up..." the man simply said with fright.

"How specific..." Diana muttered.

Diana took her pistol and hit him in the head, but the trauma of the whip caused the grunt to pass out.

"Woops," Diana remarked, looking at him.

Diana pulled him away from the elevator door and left him on his side. She then called for an elevator, waiting and then entering to go for the top-most floor.

. . . .

Half an hour earlier, Tristan entered through the main doors of the Windsor Hotel and went towards the elevator. He called for an elevator and waited with a small crowd of people before entering in as the elevator arrived. He looked at his phone and read the text message sent by Helene, which said that she was at the penthouse, in the Empress Suite. Her follow-up message said that that she was in distress and needed him to hurry. Tristan made his way up the elevator and to the penthouse suite on the top-most floor. The elevator soon arrived, and Tristan stepped out the emptied elevator and came into a small corridor with light beige carpet floor and gold-framed white walls. In the middle of the room was a table with a lone glass vase with a single black dahlia flower inside. Tristan went around the table and towards the set of double doors at the end where there were two large men in suits at either side of the door.

Upon seeing Tristan, the men opened the door and motioned him to enter. Tristan walked forward with cautioned steps and entered into the main foyer of the penthouse suite, which was a large open space with a chandelier in the center. The curtains in the room were drawn and darkness from outside poured in. Tristan stepped through and looked behind as the guards closed the door behind him. Tristan then looked around to see two sets of double doors at either side. The room had a cold atmosphere to it and the space was quiet.

"Helene?" Tristan questioned, voice echoing in the emptiness of the room.

The doors on the left opened and Helene pushed through and made her way over towards Tristan. Tristan's eyes gave a saddened look as he saw Helene again for the first time since the car crash and noticed that her beautiful face had become disfigured with scars and lesions over her cheeks and forehead. The area around her mouth where the nanomachines had bit through her inner cheeks were the worst. However, her hair appeared much the same if not appearing to be more light brown than dark blonde. She wore a white dress and open-toe shoes. Tristan looked at her as she faced him, and she saw that her green eyes were now a pinkish-red. The white of her eyes were bloodshot.

"Helene…" Tristan said in a quiet voice.

"I know…" Helene replied in her same voice and accent, although it was a little raspy. "I'm a mess."

"You look fine," Tristan insisted.

"No, I don't," Helene remarked. "I'm more of a monster than I was when we last saw each other…"

Helene extended a hand towards Tristan's cheek. Tristan simply looked at her as she caressed his face.

"I almost killed you, didn't I?" Helene said. "I'm sorry for that… I hope that you can forgive me."

"Kill me? No! You tried to save me… you did save me. What you did bought me time to heal and call for help. If you hadn't done what you did, we would have both died…"

Helene didn't respond. Tristan took her hand and held it gently.

"You told me you were in distress," Tristan remarked. "What's wrong?"

"I missed you, that's what's wrong," Helene replied, withdrawing her hand. "I haven't been able to stop thinking about you. I'm sorry I've had to hide away for such a long time, but look at me... I can't even look at myself in the mirror."

"You came back for me?"

"Yes," Helene replied, "especially after I saw you on TV."

"TV?" Tristan questioned.

"Yes, silly," Helene remarked, moving aside and going towards a window to look out. "Do you think I'm stupid? I know that was you on New Year's Eve, in the suit and having the police chase after you. You've decided to take on the Syndicate, haven't you?"

"No..." Tristan denied, looking to her.

"And that other one, that was your sweetheart, Ms. Cambridge, wasn't it?" Helene said.

"Yeah, but..."

Tristan looked at Helene from the rear and saw that a streak of her hair was a light grey.

"Quite the duo, wouldn't you say?" Helene asked.

"It's not like that," Tristan remarked. "We're not together, I mean..."

"What do you mean?"

"I mean..."

"Are you not alone now? She left you, didn't she? After you slept with me?" Helene asked, turning around and walking towards Tristan.

"We didn't *sleep* with each other. I mean, we didn't have sex, remember?" Tristan reminded her. "We only *slept* together..."

"I know," Helene replied.

"And it was a mistake," Tristan remarked. "Just like you said..."

"What if it wasn't?" Helene asked, putting her hands behind her back and looking coy.

"What do you mean?"

"I mean, what if it was fate that we came together? You and me?" Helene replied. "I mean, look at you... and me, as I was. I'm not the same as I once was... I've lost my strength and abilities and have become in some way seemingly mortal. Tell me, does she love you?"

"I... I don't know," Tristan confessed. "I mean, I do know, but I don't think she wants anything to do with me. It's more or less over between us."

"So, why can't it begin with us then?"

"I..."

"You believe that she still loves you?" Helene asked, walking towards him. "Are you infatuated with her now that she isn't yours? So much so that you'd place your life in jeopardy to be with her? Do you truly desire what you cannot have...? If so, then we are the same."

Helene put her hands on Tristan's shoulder and looked at him flirtatiously and lustfully.

"Don't you understand me? I want you, Tristan," Helene remarked. "If she loved you enough to want to be with you, she would be with you, wouldn't you say? I want to be with you though. I want you..." she said. "If my appearance troubles you, do not worry... I have enlisted the best doctor in Harlech to transform this disfigurement and restore me to my former beauty."

"I..." Tristan hesitated to speak. "I love her," he admitted to her. "I'm not infatuated with her. She's special to me and I owe it to her to protect her in these times. Even if I have to put my life down... that's what love is about, isn't it? It's a selfless sacrifice. I was taught that, and I've seen it in practice... it's the noblest of sacrifices, and until I can offer that to her, she won't believe me when I say that I love her."

Helene looked at Tristan with slight envy in her eyes. A knock at the door forced their attention away from each other and to the bodyguard with his hand at the doorknob, looking in.

"The hotel has been placed under lockdown," the bodyguard said. "Should I call for your helicopter?"

"Does it appear that the threat is towards me?" Helene asked, moving her hands away from Tristan and looking to the guard.

"No, but…"

"Then I'll stay."

"Of course."

"What's the threat?" Helene asked before the guard left.

"We have reports of the vigilante in the building."

"Really?" Helene questioned, looking to Tristan with a smile.

"Yes," the guard replied. "All guests have been advised to stay in their rooms, while I suggest that we evacuate immediately."

"No," Helene denied. "Let her come if she's coming for me, but I doubt it."

"Of course," the guard remarked.

"I need to go," Tristan said, moving to leave.

Helene took Tristan by the wrist.

"No, you don't," Helene replied. "Where would you go? The hotel is in lockdown. There's no way in or out."

Tristan frowned at her. The door closed and the two were left alone.

"If Diana is down there, it's because there's something going on. I saw police at the front doors when I got here. I need to leave before she gets herself killed."

"Let her be," Helene insisted. "If she wants to get herself killed, then who are you to stop her?"

Tristan looked back at her with a frown. Helene took Tristan's hand.

"You can leave when the lockdown is over," Helene said. "Until then, it looks like you're stuck here with me."

Helene moved in closer to Tristan. She placed her other hand on Tristan's chest and then raised it up to his cheek. She moved in her lips to his.

"Helene…" Tristan scolded in a light voice. "Stop."

"What is it?" Helene questioned.

"Nothing is going to happen between us," Tristan replied, stepping back and rejecting her attempt to seduce him. "My mind is set on her. I'm sorry."

• • • •

The elevator door opened at the top-most floor. Diana immediately shot out her grapple gun forward towards one of the guards in front of the penthouse suite. She then pulled him over and threw a knife at the other, hitting him in the arm. Diana went over and jumped atop of the one on the floor. She then grappled onto the other and pulled him over. She dropped her knee onto the one of the ground, and then grabbed the other.

"Where is she?!" Diana questioned. "Where's Dulles?"

"She's not here!" the bodyguard remarked. "This is the Empress Suite! The meeting is taking place on the floor below, I swear!"

Diana took her pistol and hit him in the head. She then looked around and over to a vent cover. She shot her grapple gun at the cover and pulled it out from the wall. Diana then went over and entered through, coming down into the interstitial space between the two floors. She moved around and went towards a vent grate that looked down onto the fifty-ninth floor as she heard some voices.

"… still grieving over the loss of Zimmerman? He's yet to be found, but…"

Dr. Bishop could be heard ahead. Diana moved in closer so she hear the rest of the conversation.

"… I was surprised to his return, even in the state that he is…" Dr. Bishop finished.

"I do not believe this man to be who he is," Mrs. Dulles replied. "Not my beloved in the least, nor this other person that you have told me of, but if it is the will of Zimmerman… I will comply."

"It *is* the will of both Zimmerman and the Children."

"Children?" Mrs. Dulles questioned.

Diana looked down and towards the dining table in the room below where Mrs. Dulles was dressed in a royal blue dress and Dr. Bishop in a grey suit. Each of them were at either side of the table in the presence of mercenaries that Diana did not recognize to be part of Paladin Groups' mercenary division. They wore black uniforms and each of them appeared to be like variants of the mysterious stranger by their gas masks, vests, and trousers. Diana eyed a larger figure amongst the crowd with his arms crossed. She looked at this man with intent.

"Alas, I miss him greatly," Mrs. Dulles reminisced, continuing on, "but the emotions of our new Leader are compromised and there is a conflict of interest that I cannot agree with."

"Our Leader knows best," Dr. Bishop replied. "You will see… the union between the Syndicate and Zimmerman Corporation will spell a new beginning… one where you can take your rightful place at the head of Paladin Group once the smoke clears and fulfill the completion of your part of Zimmerman's Legacy. I have done mine."

"What about the Wells Project?" Mrs. Dulles questioned.

"Our Leader will see to the rest of that," Dr. Bishop replied. "You only need to play your part that has been entrusted to you. My people have provided you with the means to which you will be able to act. As we speak, the masses have been mobilized to extort tension in the city through riots as the leadership of Captain Stirling as the Commissioner of the Harlech Police Department is about to be announced. The moment is ripe with what is going on in the United States and the rest of the world… tonight will not present a better moment."

"I will do my part," Mrs. Dulles remarked, raising her wine glass. "I will avenge the death of my beloved Zimmerman and see to it that this ends tonight. After tonight, I will have fulfilled what my own father failed to complete in forty years of his work – total control of Harlech, and then more."

"Let us toast then," Dr. Bishop replied, raising his own glass. "To a New World Order."

Diana took both of her pistols and punched down through the grate, hopping down and landing in the middle of the table with both guns trained over at Dr. Bishop and Mrs. Dulles. She quickly shot at one of the mercenaries in the leg and then another at the arm. Diana then turned around to face the larger mercenary with her gun, but she was instantly grabbed by him and forced to drop her guns. The man picked her up and threw her out of a window on the other side. Diana fell through and landed on a patio below, hitting the balustrade on the other side with a hefty force.

Dr. Bishop and Mrs. Dulles looked down from the window over to Diana where she was. She laid on the ground and struggled to pick herself up, trembling.

"So, it's you again," Mrs. Dulles remarked, looking down.

"A female?" Dr. Bishop questioned, noticing that Diana's hood had been pulled back, exposing her long hair and feminine eyes. "How extraordinary… beat her to a pulp…"

Dr. Bishop and Mrs. Dulles moved aside for the large mercenary to hop down and land on the ground below.

Diana looked over and saw that the man had removed his jacket, exposing his arms as he simply wore a reinforced vest over his torso. There was a glare in the eyeholes of his gas mask that gave him almost dark white eyes from the snow. She picked herself up and confronted him. The man was considerably taller than Diana as he shadowed over her.

"Hello there, Damian," Diana muttered, cracking her fists as she raised them up and squeezed them, "or should I say, Mysterious Stranger."

Tristan's ears poked up as he heard the shatter of glass. He quickly went over and behind the curtains of a large window that looked down to the patio below where Diana was.

"Diana!" Tristan shouted, opening the balcony door so that he could step out.

Helene joined him.

"I need to go down there," Tristan muttered.

"And do what?" Helene questioned, grabbing him by the arm. "You don't have your suit. You're going to compromise your identity and get yourselves both killed. Stay here and watch the show."

Tristan looked at her and then back down to where Diana was about to confront the mysterious stranger below. She approached the man with a confident smirk. The man attempted to punch her, but Diana dodged out of the way and went under him, hitting him before she escaped under his arm. The man span around to face her again. He lifted his arm and swatted her back.

Diana rolled onto the ground. She steadied herself at the end and took out some knives.

The large man began to charge towards Diana. Diana jumped hopped over him and came to the other side of the patio as she was boosted in her jump by his momentum. The man almost crashed into the other side but stopped. Diana held the two knives and looked back over to him.

"Come at me, you ugly bastard!" Diana taunted, legs trembling.

The large man turned around and charged towards her. Diana threw the knives at him, scarring him in the face. Diana moved out of the way as he crashed towards her. She then went over as he was on his knees and kicked him in the side of the head. She then grabbed him around the neck as he stood up. Diana hung behind him like a cape. He grabbed at her arm while she took a knife out with the other and stabbed him in the shoulder. The man shouted out and flung Diana at the side, causing her to crash into the floor. The large man then faced her

Diana struggled to stand on her feet. Her trembling became worse. She held the knife in her hand and looked over to him. She moved to the side so that she was at the center-rear of the patio. The man moved over to her, and she threw the knife at him. He deflected it and caused it to fall over the patio. He then went over and grabbed hold of Diana, picking her up then throwing her over the right balustrade onto a patio further below. Diana hit the side of the patio with a brutal impact. She struggled to stand, her body trembled, and she fell over. Diana then looked up as the man jumped down to finish her off.

Suddenly, a gunshot was heard. Diana lowered her head, but then looked up to see that the mask of the man had been shot off. She looked at the man and saw that he had a generic face with no hair. His eyes were not green as Diana thought, but instead brown. His face was bloodied from the shot that tore off his ear. She looked at him with doubt and then turned around to the helicopter that hovered beside her. It was a police helicopter with ERT at the side.

"Freeze!" a voice projected from a microphone.

Diana looked around for a possible escape, but there was none. ERT jumped down and landed with weapons trained on Diana.

"Hands up!" one of them shouted to her.

Diana raised her hands. They swarmed her and brought her down to the ground, removing her veil and bringing her hands behind her back.

"We have the vigilante," one of them said.

Diana grunted as the ERT kept her pinned to the floor. Another team went over to secure the man they had shot, who was apparently not the Mysterious Stranger. Diana was brought onto her feet. She looked over to the side of the balcony above where Tristan had appeared, looking down with concern. Helene appeared next to him. Diana looked confused as she saw Tristan with Helene.

"What...?" Diana questioned.

Diana began to squirm as she resisted the force of the ERT as they attempted to bring her over to the helicopter. They brought her down to the ground. Diana squirmed and squirmed. She felt something fall from her pockets and come onto the snow. The police finally picked her up and brought her into the helicopter. Diana was then made to sit down as the helicopter flew off.

Tristan watched in horror as Diana was taken away. He then let out a sigh of relief. He turned around and saw some ERT arrive behind them. Among them was a man with fair skin and a baseball cap over his head. He was dressed in an ERT uniform but was unlike the rest. He walked over to them. Tristan looked at him and read his name on the front of his uniform, 'Cpt. D. Stirling.'

"Are you kids alright? Quite a show, huh?" Stirling questioned in a firm voice.

"We're alright," Helene replied.

Tristan frowned at him.

"Aren't we, Tristan?" Helene questioned.

"Well, sit tight for another moment. My team are doing a sweep of the hotel, and once it's clear, the lockdown will be rescinded. Have a safe night, Ms. Köhlen."

"Thank you, captain," Helene replied with a smile.

Tristan continued to frown at him as he walked off. He then looked back down to where Diana had been. The ERT brought the large man up a set of stairs in shackles and then through a door where Tristan and Helene had come out of on the fifty-eighth floor, barging through a suite. Once the police had cleared, Tristan turned around and looked back over to where Diana had been taken. He brought a fist down on the top of the balustrade and growled. He then left as soon as he could to return to Cabernet Tower.

Act 7, Scene 1

Tristan sat at the main computer in the sublevel of Cabernet Tower, two hours after the incident at the Windsor Hotel, musing as he looked down at his mug and the bit of coffee that was leftover. He downed the last bit and then put the mug aside, standing up and going over to Barry's workstation where the TV was turned on above. Tristan was half-dressed in his suit with the rest of the top-piece missing as he only wore the long-sleeve dark grey thermal undershirt that pressed against his body. His helmet sat on his desk and the rest of the suit was in the cabinet. Tristan watched a live feed of the chaos in Harlech upon what happened at the hotel, the arrest of the vigilante, and the announcement of Captain Stirling with the Emergency Response Team as the new police commissioner.

Across all three islands in Harlech, riots had spread out in the major urban centers. On King Island, the riots were concentrated in front of the museum at Dominion Square and throughout that immediate area, including Cabernet Tower. The tower was incidentally on lockdown with bulletproof shutters before the sides of the building and the Protection Squad on alert status with Lukas and Lacplesis in the penthouse providing extra protection for Charlemagne and Allodia. On Jarsdel Island, the riots were concentrated in front of City Hall to the south of the Lincoln and in Cliffe Island the riots were at Thames and Queen Boulevard. The mainland was the only area in which there were no riots, but police had erected a checkpoint at Penultimate Bridge to control traffic fleeing to this area. Less than half an hour ago, the mayor's office released a statement saying that Mayor Simpson would speak in response to the riots close to midnight. The weather was perfect for a riot as it began to snow again with a thunderstorm warning in place.

Tristan waited patiently as it was only nine o'clock and the night was only beginning for him. He walked back over to his desk and sat down, sighing. He then received an alert at the corner of the screen that a GPS tracker was online. Tristan raised an eyebrow at this alert and clicked on it. The computer screen displayed a map of Harlech with a textbox over a location to the southeast of Jarsdel Island where Diana's cellphone was present. Tristan looked at the details, such as the moment the tracker went online, but there was no more information to provide.

"What the hell..." Tristan muttered, looking to his left as he saw Diana's cellphone sitting there from when he collected it on New Year's Eve. "Did she get a new phone...? but even then..."

Tristan picked up the phone and turned it on. The phone had been turned off to conserve battery. He waited for the phone to load and then looked at the corner of the screen where it read, 'No Service.' Tristan picked up his own phone and saw that he had one bar of cellphone service with 3G. He sat his phone and Diana's phone down at separate sides of the desk. He then looked at the history of Diana's tracker to see that she had been active moments before up to Wednesday when the phone was seen around the Cascadia Mall, and then for the most part stayed around Diana's apartment. Tristan went back to where the phone currently was. He then opened an Internet browser and began to check what was around this area. Tristan looked at satellite images of this area in Northton and saw that it was mostly enclosed properties with various warehouses of a sort around. These were studios for various film studios, video game studios, and other sorts of production companies. The location that Diana's signal came from was Hartman-Walker Studios. Tristan looked at the signal suspiciously. He shook his head and instantly stood up, going over to the cabinet where his chest piece, arm pieces, and gauntlets were. He put them on and then attached his belt together around his hips. Tristan put his equipment one-by-one onto his belt, including a grapple gun, albeit an older prototype variant given that Diana stole the other.

Once Tristan was ready, he walked over to the motorcycle, which he recovered from the parkade behind the hotel via its in-built tracking device. Tristan got atop of the bike, inserted the keys and turned on the engine. He then pressed the button that opened the hatch into the parkade, and then shot out in the Cabernet Tower parking lot, going through the nearly empty area and then up the tunnel that went out onto Earle Street. Tristan then sped his way towards the highway so that he could reach the movie studios in Northton.

Tristan got off the highway just before Durham Bridge and went down Riverside Drive to turn on the only road that could be turned right on in the immediate area. He passed over a railway crossing and then came onto Parrington Drive, which looped around this enclosed section of the island. The streets were quiet. Tristan drove right and then stopped towards the furthest reach to the west of the neighborhood where he could see through the gates and detect thermal movement. He quietly drove past and went along to park the bike in an offshoot lane besides one of the lots. Tristan turned off the bike and looked ahead of him.

Durham Bridge and its lights could be seen to the side. Tristan looked around and saw a sniper in a black tactical uniform up ahead from a watchtower within the movie studios. He hopped off the motorbike and moved his way to the left to kneel down and peak over behind the gates of the property further left. Four more men could be seen in the space just behind the gates, moving around in a calm manner with arms positioned as though they were armed with assault rifles. They were mostly concentrated around a large building at the side of a road past the gate.

Tristan changed his vision back to standard and then began to sneak his way towards the outer fence of the movie studios, which was a tall iron fence with hedges at the other side. He snuck down and made his way before the gate where he quickly rushed to the other side and then continued down so that he could reach the closest angle to the sniper tower. Tristan then took his plastic explosives launcher and aimed towards one of the legs of the sniper tower. He then shot a small ball of plastic explosives and watched as it quietly attached itself to the leg. Tristan then put the weapon back on his belt and hit the detonator at the side. The tower leg detonated in a small burst of an explosion, ripping through the metal and causing the tower to come down.

Tristan could hear the panic in the voice of the sniper as the tower began to slowly fall over and then crashed down onto the lot. He took advantage of the noise to climb up the fence and then hope down behind the concrete platform where the tower was constructed. The lot was bright so there were the minimal areas to hide in the darkness. Tristan laid low and looked over as some of the mercenaries went over to assist their comrade.

"What the hell was that?" a merc questioned.

"I don't know," the sniper replied. "It was weird..."

"We'll have to report that to command," another merc said, "even if it was nothing. Are you okay?"

"Yeah, my foot hurts though... I can walk it off."

Tristan snuck down the other side of the concrete platform and then shot his grapple gun up onto the roof of the main movie studio hangar. He flew up and landed on the roof. He then looked down from where he was over to the four mercenaries. The fifth was at the other side of the road, keeping vigilant. Tristan went down the roof and looked down the lane towards the rest of the studios where he could see that it was clear. He then dropped down and began to cross the road, coming around the back and rushing forward before stopping around the corner. He then looked over to where the lone mercenary was while the others took their friend to help him sit down. Tristan closed in on the lone merc and then wrapped his arm around him to take him out.

Once the merc was down, Tristan fled back and went the way he came to come back onto the roof. The four mercenaries had taken position at the side of the main movie studio hangar. Tristan came up over them and took a smoke pellet. He then dropped it down and watched as they found themselves covered in smoke. Tristan hooked his grapple gun into the side of the roof and then dropped down, landing atop of one of the mercenaries. He then took his arms and wrapped them around the thigh of one of the other mercenaries, picking him up and dropping him onto the floor before taking his arm and twisting it out of its socket. Tristan then turned around to the third to grab him and pick him up by the waist and thigh. He rolled him onto his back and launched a brutal punch across the face that knocked him out. Finally, Tristan turned to the sniper who attempted to flee but fell over. Tristan deflected a shot at him with his gauntlet and then took his grapple gun out to disarm him, pulling his pistol away from him. He then quickly went over and grabbed him by the collar, punching him back and then letting go as he fell back unconscious.

Once the fight had finished, the smoke had more or less cleared. Tristan stood up with a straight back and took a deep breath. He then knelt over and scavenged a radio from the mercenaries, taking it into his hand and using his other to remove the back and extract a chip. Tristan took the chip and inserted it into his gauntlet. He then began to walk over to a door that went into the hangar.

"No response from Team Two," a voice broadcasted through Tristan's ears. "Team Three, respond."

"Copy that."

Tristan entered into the hangar and came into an empty garage where there were shutter doors that went deeper into the building on the other side of shutters that went outdoors. Tristan walked over to these shutters and looked through with his thermal vision to see two more mercenaries on the other side, simply standing guard at the doors. Tristan looked at the side and saw a door that went to the other side as well on one side of the wall and a panel at the other. He went to the panel and set the doors to open. Tristan then raised them open and threw a smoke pellet to produce a cloud of smoke that enshrouded them all.

The mercenaries began to cough as they became surrounded in smoke. Tristan rushed over and approached one, knocking the butt of the assault rifle into the torso of the mercenary, and then pulling it off. He then wrapped his leg around the thigh of the man, up the buttocks at one hand, and lifted the man up and crashed him onto the floor with a grip around his arm. He twisted the arm and then looked to the other as he attempted to punch at Tristan. Tristan grabbed the arm and hit the man in the eyes with his other hand before flipping the merc onto his back as he grabbed him by the neck. The mercenaries were knocked out with ease.

Suddenly, Tristan looked up and over as he heard a honking sound and the rev of an engine. He looked ahead and saw two headlights aimed straight for him. Before Tristan could recover from the fight he just finished, he quickly grabbed his grapple gun and shot towards a platform at the side, evading being run over by a forklift that drove past him and crashed into the shutter in the other room. Tristan hopped down and went over to the driver who had his torso outstretched over the steering wheel.

Tristan pulled the man out and then grabbed him by his vest. He pulled him away from the smoking wreckage of the forklift and threw him into some wooden crates. Tristan picked him up by the collar and then pressed him against the wall by the shutter panel, pressing his forearm into his neck to slightly choke him.

"What's going on here?!" Tristan shouted. "Who are you people?!"

"F-figure that out on your own…" the grunt replied, attempting to raise a fist at Tristan.

Tristan caught the fist and began to twist the mercenary's hand as he fell down to sit on the floor. He began to breathe rapidly as Tristan held his wrist.

"Are you trying to piss me off?!" Tristan questioned. "Who are you people?!"

"We're Paladin, man," the merc replied. "We're only here to secure the cargo – that's it! There's a whole warehouse full of them out back – they've got the drones. Please… don't hurt me."

Tristan frowned at him and broke his wrist anyways. He then punched him in the side of the head and knocked him out.

"As if I give a damn about you…" Tristan muttered, running ahead and stopping in the middle of the aisle again.

Tristan was in an empty corridor with emptied shelves throughout. There were various cabins throughout the room, including a large one ahead that took the whole width of the hangar. The cabin was only one-story tall and included a platform above with a door that went out to a room on the other side where the corridor ended. Tristan tapped at his gauntlet and then looked at his HUD as a map of Jarsdel Island showed with Diana's tracker nearby. He then closed it and continued forward. A mild wind of snow began to pickup from outside alongside a flash of lightning. Tristan hurried and opened the door, entering into a small empty room. He went to the other side and entered through to a larger space than the corridor as it was a large warehouse with various shipment containers throughout, similar to the ones at Dock F in Port Burnes with the stamp of Zimmerman Corporation. Tristan walked over to one of the containers and broke the chain around the handles with his gauntlet. He then used both hands to open the door and look inside. A sharp wind could be heard drifting into the warehouse from outside.

A large tank sat inside the container with two large cannons at the front and a main turret in the middle. The vehicle was painted in urban camouflage and looked advanced. At the side was a radar sensor. The machine was off, of course, and still. Tristan opened the container doors wider to allow more light in as the warehouse was dim. He climbed atop of the machine and got a better look at it. The beast was taller than he was at about two meters in height, three meters in width, and seven meters in length. Once Tristan had a proper examination of the vehicle, he returned outside the container and began to look at the dozen other containers stretched out and around. None of them were stacked on top of each other, instead, all of them were firmly on the ground.

Tristan tapped at his gauntlet and looked back on his HUD to see if Diana had moved, but she hadn't. Her cellphone at the least was where it was. Tristan looked back at the containers and then began to rush over to the exit where he stopped just before. He raised his forearm before him and tapped a button. Tristan's helmet began to ring.

"Hello?" Charlemagne answered. "Tristan? Where are you? Your roommate Louis has told me that you haven't returned, and you've turned off your phone."

"I'm... busy," Tristan replied. "I'm on the job. They've arrested Diana."

"I know," Charlemagne responded. "I've phoned my lawyer to meet with her tomorrow so that we can get her out. Unfortunately, the cost may be great, but what about you? Are you safe?"

"Yes," Tristan replied. "I'm alright. What about you?"

"I'm at the penthouse. Lukas and Maris are still out there, and it appears that the police have began to attempt to disperse the crowds. The tower is in lockdown though, so don't worry about me."

"Okay," Tristan responded. "Can you do me a favor?"

"What sort of favor?" Charlemagne asked with suspicion.

"It's serious. I'm following up on a lead and I'm now at Hartman-Walker Studios in Northton. I've found a bunch of illegal weaponry owned by Zimmerman Corporation, but it's weird... Paladin Group are here, and I'm not sure if Hartman-Walker is owned by Zimmerman Corps., or what, but something needs to be done about this tech, Charles. It's heavy-duty stuff, I'm talking about tanks and stuff. Can you call the police and give them an anonymous tip, or something about this?"

"And why should I do that?"

"Because I'm following up on a mysterious broadcast of Diana's cellphone signal, which for some reason is being emitted from this place. I think it's possible that somebody has her new cellphone, so I'm going to try and get it back. I'm also curious about all this weaponry..."

"I thought you were out there to protect Diana before she could kill herself out there," Charlemagne remarked, "and now you're out there fighting the Syndicate?"

"I was only curious about the cellphone signal," Tristan argued. "Everything else is coincidental. I don't like incriminating stuff like this... I'm going to see what else I can find before I report back to you. I'm then going to return to the penthouse for the night. If F- If my roommate calls back, please tell him to shut up and stop worrying."

"Hmph," Charlemagne grunted. "I'll phone HPD about the weapons, but that is it. You can sort your friend out on your own. I'm tired and want to go to bed. Goodnight."

Charlemagne went silent. Tristan turned off his radio and then continued through the door, exiting outside and then following the signal from Diana's cellphone over to another large warehouse further head.

Act 7, Scene 2

Diana stood idle in her cell, sat in the middle with her eyes closed and torso straight as she sat cross legged and her hands on her knees. Diana wore her tunic, trousers, and boots and nothing more as everything else had been taken off her. To the police, she was now known as Jane Doe, and she was the least of their worries with the riots on the streets. The cellblock at the Harlech Police Department HQ in Bromley was far from quiet as many rioters had been moved into the detention center with police officers passing by almost every ten or twenty minutes. Diana took deep breaths and cleared her mind, meditating peacefully while the detention center guards, who were coincidentally Stewards with Paladin Group, passed by every five minutes or so to check the inmates.

"Whoa!" a voice exclaimed from somewhere.

Diana opened her eyes and was met with darkness as the lights outside of her cell and down the corridor of the detention center turned off. Next, the ground began to rumble, and the walls shook. A sudden burst of energy hit the side of the precinct, shattering windows and the lightbulbs above them. Diana stood up and approached the bars of her cell.

"Holy crap," a guard remarked. "What was that?"

"Hold on, let me go and take a look."

Another quiet rumble shook the building. Diana began to look around her cell for a possible escape route. She stood idle in the darkness and could not see much of use. Minutes passed by until the door into the detention center opened. Diana looked over and attempted to see what was going on. Instead, she heard a quiet voice speak to the Steward. A dark figure then suddenly appeared before Diana's cell.

Diana jumped back and squinted to see who it was.

"Hello?" Diana questioned.

"It's me," Sergeant Macdonald replied, unlocking the gate. "Come on, we're going to need you out there."

"What's going on?" Diana asked as the door slid open.

"There's been a massive blackout throughout King Island, possibly even the rest of Harlech," Macdonald explained, ushering Diana out. "There was also an explosion nearby, but not sure where."

"Holy crap," Diana replied, hesitating to exit her cell as he looked out of focus. "It's true then. It's happening… they're going through with it."

Diana explained to Macdonald what she had overheard in the meeting between Mrs. Dulles and Dr. Bishop about taking advantage of tonight to strike against the town.

"Where's my stuff?" Diana asked. "I need to get out there right away."

"Not right away," Macdonald corrected as he walked with Diana down the platform to the exit. "First you need to help me re-establish order out here."

"And get my equipment," Diana reminded him, raising the hood from her tunic up and covering her mouth. "Do you have it?"

"Of course not," Macdonald replied as they came to the exit of the detention center and stopped. "I came to rescue you as soon as I could. I didn't stop to pickup your things. They'll be in the evidence lockup most likely."

"All officers to Charlie Bravo," dispatch projected over Macdonald's radio at his belt. "All available officers to Charlie Bravo. We have a Ten-Thirty-four in progress."

"And that," Macdonald said.

"There's only so much I can do without my stuff," Diana remarked. "We'll need to get it before I help with your Ten-Thirty-four, whatever that is."

"It's a riot," Macdonald replied.

"Great, so how do we get to the evidence locker?" Diana asked.

"Through the central office," Macdonald replied, walking forward to set of double doors and into a corridor on the other side.

Diana and Macdonald went forward, going left and down to another set of double doors where voice shrieked from the other side.

"Let him go!" a voice shouted.

Macdonald looked to Diana as he was about to open the door. She looked at him and he nodded to her. She nodded back. Macdonald pushed through the set of doors and looked forward to an inmate in an orange jumpsuit, standing over a police officer by a vending machine. There was another police officer backed into a corner as two other inmates surrounded him.

"Look at this," the crazed inmate remarked at Macdonald and Diana. "We've got a detective and his ninja friend."

Macdonald raised his fists while Diana assumed a defensive stance. The inmate attempted to take a jab at Diana. She took his wrist and pivoted her body to knee him I the head, taking the knife and hitting him with the handle before kneeing him in the face. Diana then looked over to the other two inmates who backed off from the police officer in the corner and came over to them. Diana approached one of them and ducked back as he attempted to stab her. She then intercepted the second jab and knocked the knife out. She then brought the inmate down to the ground and brought her knee down over his face. Macdonald subdued his target and strapped a pair of handcuffs onto him.

Diana stood up and looked over to the police officer in the corner as she stood up. Macdonald helped the one on the ground back onto his feet.

"How did they get through?" Macdonald questioned the sergeant.

"Charlie Bravo is on lockdown, but some of them got through…" the sergeant answered. "They've taken the central block for themselves, and we can't get through into the next hallway."

"What's she doing out of her cell?" the female police officer asked.

"She just saved your ass, and you're questioning why she of all people is out?" Macdonald replied. "She's going to help us get everything back under control."

"It'll be pointless," the officer replied. "They've blocked the doors, so unless she has a bulldozer, we're out of luck."

"There has to be a way through," Macdonald encouraged, walking past the double doors to the other side with Diana.

The other two police officers subdued the other inmates while they went ahead. Macdonald walked to the end and attempted to get through the door, but it was blocked from the other side. Diana looked around and saw a vent above.

"Help me pry this open," Diana said, pointing to the vent.

"I'll give you a boost," Macdonald replied.

Macdonald stood before the vent and brought his hands together. Diana climbed onto them with her boots and then grabbed hold of the bars. She tugged at the vent cover and managed to rip it off. She then threw it over and climbed into the duct.

"Wait here," Diana said, crawling through. "I'm going to see what I can do."

"Sure thing."

Diana crawled forward and then came to a corner. She went around the other side and began to hear voices from the other end.

"How do we get out of here?" an inmate questioned.

"We just got to hold out with these hostages until they'll listen to us. Would you rather go out into the cold?"

Diana continued to the end of the vent duct and began to turn her body She reached a grate that looked out to the room on the other side and saw that it was dark on the other side. She continued around another corner and then turned to another grate, where this one landed out onto a platform. Diana shifted her body and began to press her boots into the bars to pop the screws out. She then shifted her body again and brought her hands to the grate, moving it over gently, and then exiting. Diana looked left and right and saw through the darkness to see that it was clear and safe for her to be here.

The room that Diana had come to was lit by a flash of lightning. She saw a brief glimpse of the room before the darkness settled in again. Light poured in through overtop windows from outside, but other than that, the room was completely dark. At the sides of the room were platform walkways with wooden railings that connected to wooden pillars every so often. There were approximately six inmates, each with assault rifles patrolling around the room. Two inmates could be seen in the middle cubicle where there were three disarmed police officers who were being held hostage. Diana noticed that a massacre had played out in the room as there were some corpses spread around of fallen officers. Another inmate could be seen on the platform at the other side from where she was, while another two could be seen below spread around the ground floor. The last and nearest inmate was down the platform Diana was on but looking down.

Diana made her approach to this inmate and quietly snuck up behind him. She then kicked him in the shin and brought an arm around his neck and a hand to his mouth to muffle him into silence. She then dropped him over and continued around to reach the other at the other side. Diana stopped around the corner and looked down.

The inmate made his approach towards Diana. She stood up and remained in cover behind a pillar and then began to climb up so that she could take position over a beam that stretched over the ceiling like at the hotel lobby. She then began to go down towards the inmate until she was behind him. She climbed down and then snuck behind the inmate, bringing her arm around him and taking him down to the ground. She then went down a set of stairs at the side and came to the ground floor. Diana picked up a fire extinguisher and held it like a weapon. She eyed the hostages in the cubicle and saw an inmate approaching her.

Diana snuck behind a cubicle wall and looked around the corner to see the direction the inmate was coming in. She readied herself until the man was around the corner and then stood up to hit him in the head with the fire extinguisher, knocking him onto the ground. Diana then went over to him and knocked him back with a headbutt before she continued off.

"Did you hear that?" an inmate questioned as Diana snuck off.

"Hear what?" another replied.

"Is anybody there?"

"I'm still here," a third inmate reported in.

"What about the others?" the first inmate worried as Diana made her way back upstairs and down the platform.

Diana snuck ahead and climbed atop of the railing near the vent access she came out of where an inmate was positioned directly below her. The man began to move again and started to come around the stairs to where Diana was. Diana retreated back and passed the center of the room before she hopped over.

"Hm?" the inmate questioned.

Diana crouched and looked ahead to where she could see the inmate. He continued down. Diana stood up and climbed up onto the edge of the railing, bringing herself up as the man passed by. Diana grabbed the inmate and butt her head into his head before bringing her arm around his neck and dropping down, using the force of gravity as she held on to a rail leg with one hand and choked out the inmate with the other.

Once the inmate ceased to squirm, Diana let go and dropped down again. She then began to a make her way towards the center of the room where the hostages were. She immediately noticed that one of the inmates had left.

"Oh God!" an inmate yelled. "We have a guy down over here! Near the exit!"

"What?!" the other replied. "How?!"

Diana rushed to the inmate near the hostages now that she was alone and went towards her just as she turned around. Diana grabbed hold of the inmate by her jumpsuit and smashed her head into hers before turning her around and wrapping an arm around her neck. Diana then smashed her head into a pillar nearby, causing a minor amount of noise.

"Hello?" the last inmate questioned.

Diana ran over to him and roundhouse kicked him onto the ground. She then hopped on top of him and kicked into his face to knock him out. Diana then stood up straight and turned around.

"Forget about me?" an inmate questioned. "Come any closer, and this little piggy will die! Understood?!"

Diana looked over to the center of the room where an inmate took a police officer and held him at gunpoint. She quickly ran up the stairs and snuck down the walkway, hiding behind the railing and looking through to see the hostage and inmate. She continued forward and dropped down, walking over to hide behind a cubicle. She got to the back of the cubicle that the inmate was behind, which had a glass pane that saw through the other side. Diana looked up and tracked the motion of the inmate.

Once the inmate turned to the side, Diana stood up and reached her hand through the glass to grab the barrel of the rifle with both hands. The rifle fired briefly. She jabbed the rifle back into the torso of the inmate before taking it off him and hitting him again with brute force. Diana then hopped over onto the other side as the hostage scrambled away and hit him a third time to make sure he was out for sure this time. Diana held the assault rifle and watched as the hostages moved out of the way in a minor panic at the sight of her.

"Whoa, whoa, whoa," Diana remarked. "I'm not your enemy. I'm a friend, not a foe…" Diana took the assault rifle and handed it towards the nearest officer. "I've been sent by Sergeant Macdonald to save your asses…"

Diana left the officers and went to the door that was blocked off previously. She began to move the furniture and then opened the doors so that Macdonald could get through.

"Good job," Macdonald said, entering and going over to the center.

Diana joined him. The other officers began to arm themselves again. One of them looked over to Diana.

"You're working with the vigilante?" the officer questioned.

"She just saved you, didn't she?"

"I suppose she did," the officer quietly admitted.

"Let's get these criminals back in shackles before they wake up," Macdonald ordered. "Stay here until backup arrives. I'm going to Charlie Bravo."

Macdonald then looked to Diana.

"Come on, let's go and get your stuff," Macdonald said to her.

Diana nodded. The two then left, crossing the room and going to the opposite-side from where they came through and continuing onwards into the precinct.

Act 7, Scene 3

Diana and Macdonald entered the evidence locker of the Harlech PD precinct. The room was a large storage space with countertops that contained boxes and a series of shelves that stretched back a couple meters. Each box, container, or bag was labeled with the file number the evidence was related to. Diana found her stuff in a box in one of the few boxes that started with the number twenty-one because of the year. She took out her grapple gun to attach to her belt and picked up her knives. She also took the EMP grenades, which were the only grenades she had left. Finally, Diana put on her ballistic armor, her holster vest and then her leather jacket before looking into the box where something was missing.

"My guns aren't in here," Diana reported to Macdonald.

"If they didn't pick something up, then it's not going to be there," Macdonald replied.

"Do you guys have an armory nearby? I need to restock on some goods then."

"Why do you need weapons?"

Diana looked at him and frowned.

"Fine, kid," Macdonald sighed, leaving the room so that they could go to the armory nearby.

Diana and Macdonald walked inside and looked at the rack of weapons and various crates around the room.

"Help yourself to whatever you need," Macdonald said, moving over to equip himself with a proper vest, shotgun and some tear gas grenades.

Diana took some breaching explosives, smoke grenades, and two SIG Sauer pistols along with some magazines.

"Come on," Macdonald encouraged. "We need to help out at Charlie Bravo. We've been putting it off for too long."

The pair left the basement of the precinct and came back upstairs to return to the central block where the officers were patrolling around. They went to a set of doors to the left and continued through, down the corridor, stopping as they saw two officers run around the corner with one clenching the bloodied wound of his right arm.

"We have some felons outside of Charlie Bravo," the female officer explained.

"You're not going to take us alive!" a voice yelled from around the corner.

Diana took initiative and ran down, taking cover at the corner and peaking around to see two armed inmates with a hostage between them. Diana's eyes glanced over to a vent grate above them. She backed off and retreated towards Macdonald to explain the situation.

"Wait here," Diana said, moving over to another vent grate above.

Diana took the grapple gun and launched it towards the cover. She then pulled it down and shot back up to climb into the vent duct. Diana then proceeded to crawl around until she was directly at the side of the two inmates. She quietly repositioned her body to begin pushing the grate out of the wall, and then allowed it to gently fall over on one hinge so that it hung and didn't crash onto the ground. Diana then pulled herself out and quickly approached the inmate before her with the grapple gun in hand.

Diana grabbed the barrel of the rifle, backed it into the torso of the inmate, and shot the grapple gun towards the other to pull him off balance. The rifle went off briefly. Diana dropped the grapple gun and used both hands to beat the butt of the gun into the inmate again, pulling it off him and then hitting him in the head with the butt of the gun. She then took it and hit the other inmate in the back of the head with it before tossing it over and throwing him over. Diana dropped her knee onto his neck and then stood up to look at the other.

"Clear!" Diana shouted back to Macdonald.

Macdonald came around the corner with his shotgun ready. He then went over and helped the officer onto his feet. Diana grabbed the assault rifle and handed it to him.

"Thanks…" the officer remarked.

The ground below their feet began to rumble.

"All units, we're receiving multiple reports from within the city," dispatch called over Macdonald's radio.

Macdonald picked up his radio from his belt.

"Dispatch, this is Delta-Two-Forty-three, go ahead," Macdonald replied.

"Delta-Two-Forty-three, we have reports coming of further pandemonium on the streets," dispatch explained.

"Has the Ten-Thirty-Four out there gotten worse?" Macdonald asked.

"No, Delta-Two-Forty-three. We're receiving multiple reports from officers on the streets of tanks and… robots…? I've been unable to speak with neither the watch commander nor sergeants on the field, which leaves you in charge."

Macdonald was silent.

"Delta-Two-Forty-three, we've received multiple calls from within the city. Cliffe and Jarsdel Division are spread thin," dispatch said. "We've also received reports of attack helicopters in the skies."

"Understood," Macdonald finally replied. "All units, clear the streets and pullback to your nearest point of safety. Hold your ground until we can restore a proper chain of command and keep civilians off the street. Your priority is to keep civilians safe."

Macdonald's radio buzzed as officers responded. He looked over to Diana with an unsure face.

"If I'm in charge, then that means that nobody can get a hold of anyone else… Where the hell is the new commissioner and watch commander?" Macdonald questioned.

"The commissioner's been unavailable. Lieutenant Fleming is here though. He was last seen at Charlie Bravo," the female officer replied. "He should be there still…"

"Where's ERT?" Macdonald asked.

"They're all out there…" the other police officer replied.

"Great," Macdonald sarcastically responded. "It's a war zone out there. The force could barely fight a war on crime let alone an actual war. We need to organize an EOC ASAP," he said, turning to Diana. "Come on. You two stay here and control this corridor."

"Yes, sergeant."

Diana and Macdonald left and went through the set of doors to reach an elevator. They then stepped onto the elevator and began to go down the slow ride into the sublevel of the precinct. The door opened from the other side, and they came out into a dark corridor. Macdonald took out his flashlight and led the way to the other side. He took a card key and pressed it into a panel, forgetting that the power was out.

"Help me push this door open," Macdonald said.

Diana nodded and the two pushed against the heavy door to open it. They came into a junction corridor with doors at either side. Macdonald raised his shotgun and shot at the inmates that were attempting to get into the door on the other side. He fired at a shot at both of them, subduing them and pulling them out of the way. Diana helped with the other.

Macdonald went to the door and knocked on it. Diana looked at the doors at the side to see that they were reinforced with steel blast shields like those around Cabernet Tower at the moment.

"It's Sergeant Macdonald! Let me in!" Macdonald shouted.

The door opened and a police officer on the other side with a pistol raised looked at the two of them. She pointed her firearm at Diana with suspicion.

"She's here to help… We need to get this block under control."

Macdonald pushed through and went over to the control panel in the control room.

"It's no use… Without the auxiliary power or more manpower, we won't be able to get these guys under control," another officer inside remarked.

Diana walked in and looked at the man in a suit on the floor. He had dark hair and fair skin. He looked to be in his late forties. He clenched his bloodied abdomen. Macdonald turned around and looked at him.

"Is he alright?" Macdonald asked.

"He's severely wounded…" the female officer replied. "Another reason why we need to get things under control, or else he'll bleed to death."

"Where's the generator?" Macdonald questioned.

"Down the corridor you came from and to the right," the female officer replied. "We tried to get over there, but we're kind of out of ammo at this point."

"Here," Macdonald said, taking out some magazines and putting them on the table.

Diana approached the reinforced window before the control panel and looked down to the cell block that was Charlie Bravo. The block was much larger than the one she had been kept in. Charlie Bravo was a rectangular three-story room with cells on both the ground and second floors and an open space in the middle. There was no platform on the third floor and instead the top of the control room and a balcony that looked down. Diana could see various inmates had set fire to the detention center and were destroying whatever they could find. Among them was Diana's large mercenary friend from the Windsor Hotel, dressed in an orange jumpsuit with the sleeves ripped off.

"Alright, I'm going to go and find the generator," Macdonald said.

"What do you want me to do?"

"To fight," Macdonald replied. "You seem to be good that that."

"Okay," Diana simply replied, looking back down to the inmates below.

"Once I get the power back on, we should be able to lockup these guys and restore order to the precinct. We'll also be able to get Lieutenant Fleming some help and be able to establish an Emergency Operation Command."

"Good luck," Macdonald encouraged before we left.

Diana looked to him and nodded. She then approached a door at the side that led to a balcony. She climbed onto the railing and looked down.

"Well, look who it is!" the large thug from the hotel celebrated from below.

Diana glared at him with an uneasy expression. The police officers that remained came out to assist Diana, opening fire on the inmates below, causing them to return fire with projectiles thrown towards them. Diana took the grapple gun into her hand and lowered herself down, letting go once she was a couple feet above and landing below. She then put the grapple gun away and assumed a defensive stance.

Two inmates began to make their way towards Diana, prompting her to shoot both at them in the feet as she produced her two pistols from her jacket. The large grunt began to charge towards her. Diana shot at his feet and then jumped out of the way, landing on the ground nearby as another inmate tried to punch her. Diana kicked back at him and then jumped up as an inmate jumped down from above towards her. Diana swiped his legs with hers, knocking him off-balance and then moved in to dislocate his arm.

The large grunt panted on his knees where he had been gashed by the bullets. Diana ran towards him and hit him in the head with her guns. The grunt recuperated and grabbed Diana by her waist. He then threw her over, forcing her to lose grip on her firearms. She quickly stood up, watching as the man picked up an unconscious inmate, and then throwing him towards her. Diana jumped out of the way by hopping over an inmate nearby, causing him to get hit by the body instead. The large grunt then began to charge towards Diana again.

Diana produced two knives and threw them towards him as she did at the hotel. The grunt grabbed his face and crashed into the metal bars of a cell, running his hand over his bloodied nose as he fell over and sat on the ground like a very large toddler. Three inmates approached Diana as she recovered. She raised her legs to kick one of them onto the ground before kicking herself back up and kicking another onto the ground. An inmate attempted to punch Diana, but she avoided it and evaded another punch before grabbing his arm and knocking him onto the floor to dislocate his shoulder. She then looked at the other and blocked his punch with her gauntlets, closing and head-butting him in the head before looking over to the large grunt. Diana rushed over and grabbed her pistols. She then began to beat at the man before he could recover. Diana jumped backwards and dodged out of the way before he could grab her.

"You're the reason I'm locked up in here, freak!" an inmate taunted.

Diana took out her last knife and threw it towards the large grunt as he attempted to charge at her again. The knife hit his thigh and caused him to come crashing down. She then quickly ran towards him, shooting at his feet before hitting him in the side of the head until he grabbed Diana by the side. Diana retaliated by kicking off him, launching herself off and flipping over to land on her feet.

"Who is this guy?!" an inmate questioned.

Diana looked over as three more inmates approached her. She shot at their feet and quickly turned to the large grunt as he was about to crash into her. Diana jumped out of the way and then refocused on the grunts ahead as the larger man hit the side of a metal column and fell onto his knees to recover for a moment. Diana approached the inmates and waited for them to approach her. She then jumped back and took her gun to hit him in the neck before looking to the other two. One of them charged at Diana. She lowered herself and picked him up as she pushed her body towards him, picking him up with both guns in her hand and then tossing his body over. She brought her knee down onto his neck and knocked him out. Diana then shot at the leg of the other grunt and went in to hit him in the head.

The large grunt then recovered and began to face Diana. She shot at his legs again as he was about to charge at her before jumping out of the way. She then quickly ran towards him with her emptied guns and hit him in the head with them. The grunt fell over and landed on his hands. Diana hit him again once and then jumped up, pushing stepping onto the back of the large grunt before going over to smash his face into the concrete, knocking him out once and for all.

Diana looked around and saw that most of the inmates had been more or less dealt with. She put her pistols away and then shot her grapple gun upwards to rejoin the others.

"Who *are* you?" the female officer questioned.

"The riot has been dealt with," Diana replied instead.

Diana walked back into the command room. The lights flickered and power was restored into the detention center.

"Good riddance…" Lieutenant Fleming remarked as he looked over.

Macdonald quickly returned and joined up with Diana.

"Is it over?" Macdonald questioned.

"Yeah, it's over," Diana remarked.

"Good work," Macdonald replied. "We need get the lieutenant upstairs and set up an infirmary STAT."

Macdonald helped the lieutenant onto his feet.

"Sergeant…" Lieutenant Fleming said. "You have shown remarkable leadership tonight…"

"Don't thank me," Macdonald replied, assisting him out of the cell block. "You can thank the vigilante. She's done most of the leg work…"

Diana followed from behind.

"No," the Lieutenant denied as Macdonald helped him down the corridor. "Not a vigilante… a hero."

Diana expressed a mild smile as he heard the words. Macdonald turned over to her and nodded.

"Thanks for all your help. I won't hold you any longer," Macdonald said. "I'm going to establish an EOC and reorganize the police force once I get the lieutenant upstairs. Where are you going to go?"

"Zimmerman Tower," Diana replied, "except I have no idea how I'm going to get over there when it's a war zone out there."

"Go down this hall then," Macdonald said, looking over to the right. "It'll take you to a garage. You'll find a manhole there, which goes down into the old Harlech Tunnel System. That'll take you to the underground subway line, which goes to Durham Station underneath Zimmerman Tower. Why Zimmerman Tower though?"

"It's most likely the command point for all this," Diana replied. "All of these drones are Zimmerman technology, so if I'm going to find some answers about all this, that'll be the place."

"Right," Macdonald replied. "Okay. Good luck."

"You too," Diana replied before she left.

Act 7, Scene 4

Approximately an hour beforehand, Tristan looked down from atop of a tall green screen wall in the hangar at Hartman-Walker Studios. There was a replica of a large airplane torn apart ahead with various mercenaries around. He eyed one as he set down a circular device onto the ground.

"Why are we setting up mines?" a merc questioned.

"Boss said so, that's all there is to it," another merc nearby replied.

"I thought the vigilante was behind bars. Who else could the boss be anticipating?"

"There's two of them, remember? Boss wants us to slow down the other…"

"Boss, we've secured the room. Nobody is getting through here," a voice projected over the communications that Tristan could eavesdrop on.

"Good," Dr. Bishop replied. "I'm busy at the moment, so contain the situation where you are. Do not interrupt me. The least you dogs can do is buy me more time than put this operation in jeopardy."

"Who is he calling a dog?" a merc remarked.

"Shut up and keep watch," another scolded.

Tristan looked around. He could see approximately eight mercenaries in total throughout the room. A sniper included made nine of them. He could see atop of the scaffold to the side, some spaces of which were covered by square panels. He looked at HUD and saw that Diana's cellphone signal was close. Tristan then looked back down as his eyes went between each mercenary below. Two mercenaries could be seen by a doorway at the westside of the hangar that went towards Diana's cellphone signal. Another four were spread out around the wreckage of the replica plane. Another could be seen making his way behind the green screen, while another was last seen going underneath the scaffold. Tristan turned around and looked down at the merc as he came just about behind the large screen. He went forward onto a beam that connected the wall onto the wall of the hangar and prepped his grapple gun to drop down.

Once the mercenary began to walk down, Tristan kept his grapple gun attached to his belt and used it to lower himself towards the mercenary and grab him from behind. He lifted his arm around his neck and chocked him out. He then dropped him and continued on foot as he detached from the beam and went towards the scaffold ahead. He stopped around the corner and looked ahead as the merc approached him. Tristan shot his grapple gun at him and pulled him towards him, pulling him in so that Tristan could strangle him into unconsciousness. He then began to climb up the scaffolding with his grapple gun, climbing up so that he could sneak behind the mercenary. Tristan brought his arm around him and proceeded to choke him out before hiding him behind a panel. He then looked ahead.

A mercenary could be seen at the front of the airplane. Tristan took his bow and prepared to fire it towards him. He then shot an arrow and threw a smoke pellet over so that he could go in and grab him by the thigh and tackle him onto the ground. Tristan then punched him out and proceeded into the nose of the plane wreck. He took out his bow and pulled an arrow back, firing at a merc ahead.

"Ow!" the merc cried out. "I've been hit with an arrow!"

Tristan tackled the man onto the ground before he could say anything more. He then punched him out, growling as he punched him and then stood up and continued forward.

"What's going on over there?" a merc questioned.

"Where's our sniper?" another merc questioned. "What's going on?"

"No, no, no," a third mercenary remarked. "This can't be happening."

"What the hell is going on?"

Tristan grappled up onto the roof of the airplane. He then went down to the left onto the top of a wing as he made his approach over to the two mercenaries by the door out of the hangar. He threw a smoke pellet at them and enshrouded them in smoke. He then hopped down and moved over to take them down. One of the mercenaries raised his hands towards Tristan. Tristan grabbed them and then pivoted his body so that his back was against his front. He then grabbed him around the thigh while his other arm held onto an arm. He then lifted him up, rolling into him so that he was firm on the ground with Tristan on top. Tristan then elbowed him in the head to knock him out before rolling back onto his feet. The other mercenary tried to punch him through the smoke, but Tristan dodged and then grabbed him by the arms before sweeping his foot at his legs, quickly taking the hostile down and then landing on top of him to knock him out with a punch. Tristan then took his grapple gun as he stood up and shot towards the scaffold to make his escape.

The remaining two mercenaries converged at the left-side of the plane as the smoke cleared and the two mercenaries were left unconscious by the door.

"Where the hell did he go?!" the mercenary questioned.

Tristan shot across back to the green screen wall and then slid down with his gauntlet, shooting his grapple gun towards the mercenary by the nose of the plane to pull him down. He then hopped on top of him, shooting the grapple gun at the other mercenary and pulled his assault rifle off of him. Tristan dropped onto the mercenary he was on, elbowing him in the head before standing up and taking his grapple gun to pull the sidearm off of the merc as he was about to shoot. Tristan caught the pistol into his hand and then threw it back at him, hitting him in the head. He then went forward and picked him up, slamming him onto the ground and then punching him out. Tristan pushed off him to stand up again, panting and looking around. He then brushed his gauntlets with his hands and began to make his way towards the exit.

The room on the other side was a dark corridor that went down the left side. Tristan switched on his night vision and then began to go down, looking at the doors at the side and reading the names on the front with star insignias around them. He read some names that he didn't recognize until he came towards the end and saw one that read, 'Helene Köhlen.' Tristan opened the door and entered through. He entered and came into an empty room.

Helene's dressing room had luxurious furniture positioned around and a large dressing table with a large mirror. There was a lounge sofa and some armchairs in one corner and various racks of clothing on the other side. On the wall behind the lounge set there were movie posters of films that she had starred in. He finished looking around and then turned on his HUD to see where the signal was nearby, but not where he was. Tristan exited the room and continued down the corridor to a door at the end where the signal was behind.

Tristan approached the door and read the title over it that said, 'Film Archives.' He then brought a hand to the doorknob and listened in as he could hear a voice speak on the other side.

"It is done…" Dr. Bishop said.

Tristan opened the door gently and then looked through. The room was dark on the other side. He slipped through and found himself in a small aisle behind a shelf with various film canisters with light seeping through the other side. Tristan walked down the one-way route out of the aisle and came around to another. In the middle of this aisle, more light seeped through from the rest of the room. Tristan walked over and hid at the corner, peaking across the other side and over to a man ahead behind a dressing table atop of a thin platform. The man wore a lab coat and looked at his subject in a salon chair. He had a needle in his hand and set it down on the table. He grinned fiendishly as he looked at his subject before looking over to Tristan.

"He is here," Dr. Bishop said, frowning.

Tristan came out from around the corner and entered into the room.

"I believe you have something of mine," Tristan stated. "A cellphone."

"Tristan," Helene said in a soft voice from the salon chair.

"Helene?" Tristan questioned as the seat turned to face him.

Tristan raised his visor and looked over to Helene. Her face had been reconstructed so that it was it returned to its prime smoothness. Her hair had also been dyed so that it had the color it once had. Her hair had also been straightened. She wore black lace dress with long sleeves that covered her arms. Nonetheless, her legs were as smooth as Tristan knew them and at her feet were black high heels. Tristan looked at her eyes as they were the only part of her that had not changed – they continued to have a reddish glow to them instead of the former green.

"I knew you would come if you thought Diana was here," Helene said, standing up.

"Your face…" Tristan remarked in awe.

"I know," she replied, bringing a hand to her cheeks. "Its former beauty has been restored. Am I beautiful enough for you now?"

Tristan didn't reply.

"There's more," Helene remarked. "I've also regained some of my strength, not all of it, but enough to be myself again."

"What's going on here?" Tristan questioned. "What is he doing here? He's with the Syndicate."

"My love," Helene said with a smile. "Isn't it obvious? He's my personal doctor… a good friend of mine who helped me recover these last few months. Through Hyacinth, another seemingly old friend, I was able to assume leadership of all of this."

"What are you talking about?"

"Isn't it clear?" Helene questioned. "I thought you were supposed to be a smart boy. Nevertheless, I'll explain it to you. I am the Leader of the Syndicate now, relinquished by my dear friend here and Hyacinth who have come together in the spirit of a common cause, uniting the remains of Montgomery's legacy with what remains of Zimmerman Corporation. Thus, the fulfillment of more than just Zimmerman's Legacy – the complete domination and eradication of human life on Earth and the establishment of a new world. Hyacinth knew that her father would betray her and give command of the Syndicate to his adopted son instead of her. She overthrew them both so that she could began to mobilize and initiate Zimmerman's Legacy, using the Syndicate as a front to move around the city. My friend here though fought on my behalf to do so much more. He recovered my corpse from the Mayfair where Hyacinth kept me. He healed me and kept me safe until I was ready to surface again. Through him, I was also able to recover a key instrument of Zimmerman's that was a part of his contingency plan, and what I sought after more than anything. Once I was ready to make an appearance, I brought them together, and now it is all ready. Today, the world ends."

Dr. Bishop presented her with a radio. She took into her hand and spoke into it.

"Hyacinth," Helene spoke into the radio.

"Yes, Helene, darling," Mrs. Dulles replied.

"Initiate the invasion," Helene ordered. "Put an end to all of them and raze the cities of the world to the ground."

"Yes, my dear," Mrs. Dulles affirmed.

"Stop!" Tristan shouted.

Shutters at both the left and right side of the room opened, and mercenaries dressed in black, like the ones that rescued Mrs. Dulles at Durham and Hunter, appeared with assault rifles pointed towards Tristan. Helene raised a hand at them and then looked back over to Tristan. One of the mercenaries approached Helene at her right-side and whispered into her ear.

"So, he's betrayed us," Helene remarked. "No matter."

"Should we evacuate?" Dr. Bishop questioned.

"Not yet," Helene replied, looking to Tristan and approaching him. "This world has grown old. It is time for the two of us to run away together and start our lives together. Join me, please, and we can run to another time and place where it is only you and me, for eternity."

Helene placed her hands on Tristan's chest.

"Isn't that what you want? Certainty?"

"You're insane," Tristan simply remarked. "All of this is insane."

"Don't be silly…" Helene replied, grabbing Tristan by the side and bringing her mouth close to his.

Tristan pushed her back.

"Back off," Tristan said. "You'll kill millions of innocent people. I can't take part in that. Even more, I will never be with you. Even if you were the same person you were two months ago… Diana is my other half, and I can't be tempted to abandon her like I was last time."

Helene frowned at him. She grabbed him by the neck and then threw him to the right, past some mercenaries and out of the storage room where he landed outside in the snow. Tristan hit the snowy concrete hard, causing his HUD to glitch and show some static for a moment.

"Oh my God!" Helene shouted with regret. "Tristan, I'm sorry!"

Tristan slowly recovered as he heard a helicopter fly overhead. He looked over saw it land at the other side of the storage closet. Helene walked over to him as he was still on the ground.

"Please, the world is about to come to an end and your Diana is nowhere to be seen," Helene said to him. "You would really give up the chance of eternal life, with me, the two of us in intertwined passion for eternity?"

Tristan looked back at her in all her beauty. He then looked to the ground.

"No…" Tristan denied.

"Fine," Helene replied. "We'll see each other again before it's over, I'm sure. Maybe then you'll change your mind."

"Ma'am," an elite mercenary spoke from behind.

"What?" Helene questioned, turning to him.

"An armor division has sieged the precinct in Bromley," the merc reported.

"Is that so?" Helene replied with a smile. "Maintain the drones. We must capture the Alpha Target," she said before looking back to Diana. "We'll see each other again, Tristan. Try and stop me, and all of the Syndicate and Zimmerman Corporation combined, or save your dear beloved Diana at the police precinct or save yourself and escape with me to a better world. The choice is yours."

Helene left. Tristan remained where he was as he felt back onto the ground in pain.

"Tristan!" Charlemagne remarked over Tristan's headset. "Your bio-readings are critical. What's going on?"

"I had a… hard fall," Tristan replied, attempting to stand up again.

Tristan watched as Helene's helicopter lifted and flew off.

"Sceafa's informed me that the situation on the streets has intensified with reports of those tanks you told me about," Charlemagne said. "I've taken Allodia down to the basement where we've been told to hide out. The rest of the team have taken defensive positions around the tower. Where are you?"

"I'm at the movie studios still," Tristan replied.

"I have word about Diana," Charlemagne went on and said. "I've been listening to the police dispatch and transmissions, and they're received an order to treat her as a friendly. It appears they've released her to provide assistance…"

"Where is she?" Tristan questioned.

"I'm not sure, but if I knew her, then she'll be going to the center of all this. I've acquired control of a Cabernet satellite to get a visual of the situation below."

Tristan finally stood up and took his grapple gun to shoot up and leave the studios. He began to run down a roof and then shot towards a beam at the Durham Bridge so that he could look down at the city around. Tristan looked around at the chaos where tanks were shooting at random buildings and columns of robots were shooting at cars. The entire city had been set aflame with smoke pouring into the sky above. Tristan could hear the eerie scream of civilians shouting for their lives around as the evil of destruction swept through Jarsdel Island and the other islands around.

"It's a nightmare out here, Charles..." Tristan remarked. "We have to stop this."

"I know," Charlemagne replied. "The entire city is still in a blackout, but I'm seeing a bizarre energy reading from Zimmerman Tower. You should make your way over there at once..."

"Okay," Tristan agreed, watching as helicopters fired missiles at random buildings around. "I'm on my way."

"Please hurry," Charlemagne replied. "I have no way of contacting Diana, and my best guess is that she'll be going there too. You'll need to help her to bring an end to this massacre."

"Dammit, that reminds me," Tristan muttered. "I forgot to retrieve her phone."

"Nevermind that," Charlemagne responded. "Get over to Zimmerman Tower at once before anybody else has to die!"

"Sorry, yes," Tristan agreed. "Stay safe, okay? I'll go as fast as I can so that we can try and bring an end to this."

"Godspeed, my boy," Charlemagne replied. "Godspeed."

Act 8, Scene 1

Diana hurried down the raised concrete ledge of the underground railway track that ran from near the Harlech Police Department HQ. The tunnel had been lit by a dim red light that was difficult to see through. She passed various stations until she finally began to see some white light at the end of the tunnel. She followed along the quiet narrow passageway where no trains had run past, and vaulted over the gate at the end when she entered the large room that was Durham Station beneath Zimmerman Tower.

Durham Station was wide with two trenches where the northbound and southbound trains would pass through. In the middle of these two trenches was a narrow platform with a plastic glass divider. On the lateral sides, there were two raised platforms on each respective side with benches and advertisements behind. At the north and south sides of these platforms were stairs that went up and around to the second level where there were shops above. A bridge connected these two sections at the far-side away from where Diana had come out of. At the lateral north and south faces of these platforms, on both sides, there were stairs that went to the surface of downtown Harlech, but these stairs were blocked off by shutters. At the bridge that connected the two platforms, there was an elevator with a rectangular tube that continued upwards into the ceiling and presumably up into Zimmerman Tower. The shaft of the elevator was transparent, and it could be seen that the elevator was currently resting ahead.

However, Diana could see various elite mercenaries around the station, patrolling the area. There were at least seven mercenaries in total, some of which wore heavy-duty vests on their front that covered their necks. There were two of these, one nearby and the other to the left on the right upper platform. Two more mercenaries could be seen at the base of the northbound stairs on both sides, another in front of the elevator shaft, one on the lower left platform, and a final one directly ahead by the tunnel, looking northbound.

Diana dropped down into the trench and began to make her way over towards the mercenary that looked down the tunnel. She then climbed up and knocked him onto his knees by kicking his calf, and then proceeded to strangle him. Once he was out, Diana pulled his body into the trench and kept him there before going up and looking over to the mercenary with the reinforced armor. She avoided him and instead climbed over the glass barrier between the two trenches, jumping down to the other side. Diana proceeded to make her way around to the mercenary there and then proceeded to strangle him. He fell quietly. Diana moved his body away from the open and against the wall. She then began to climb up and look over at the two mercenaries that were left and right. Diana looked up and saw that there was a plain ceiling overtop with lights beaming down – no possibility of lurking from above.

Diana backed away and took her grapple gun to launch it towards the bridge where the mercenary in front of the elevator was. She attached a smoke grenade at her belt and then launched herself up. She caught the edge of the platform with one hand and began to quickly climb up. She then launched the grapple gun towards the man and dropped down to pull him over with her, launching him off with a frightened yell.

"Contact!" an elite mercenary shouted. "Central platform!"

Once Diana landed below, she quickly went over and knocked out the mercenary as he landed in the trench. She then climbed up and tossed the smoke grenade towards the mercenary with the reinforced armor. Diana took both her pistols and went over to him, shooting him at the feet, and then going in with her gauntlets to slice at his face. She then began to hit him with the grips of her pistols, knocking him over, and finishing him off with the kick. Once he was down, Diana began to move up the stairs, putting her guns away and taking the grapple gun. She shot at the mercenary at the base of the stairs and pulled him over. She then went over and took his rifle, hitting him in the back of the head with it before slamming his head down into the concrete floor.

"I've lost sight of the target!" an elite merc shouted from the other side of the room.

Diana quickly moved into cover at the corner of the platform that extended into an arched bridge over the two trenches. She then kept the grapple gun ready as she waited for the reinforced mercenary to come on over the bridge for her to grab onto him. Soon enough, he came to the apex of the bridge, causing her to grab onto him and pull him over. The man didn't fall over, but he did drop his rifle. Diana threw a smoke grenade and covered them in smoke. She then went forward with both pistols and sliced at his face with her gauntlets, temporarily distracting him before she could beat him down, onto the floor, and then delivering the finishing blow. Diana put her guns away and then went over the bridge.

The elite mercenary raised his rifle towards her as he saw her. Diana shot the grapple gun at him and pulled him over. She then took a knife and threw at him, hitting him in the thigh. Diana quickly went over and kicked him over, taking the knife out and dropping a knee down on his neck to take him out. With all of these elite mercenaries taken care of, Diana scavenged some equipment off the body of the last one she had taken down, taking a key card.

Diana went to the elevator next and pressed the call button to have the doors open. The doors opened and she walked in. The elevator did not go too far and only went up to another sublevel above and then the main floor and second floor. Diana selected the main floor and then watched as the elevator car rose up and go through the earth to come to the main lobby of Zimmerman Tower.

Zimmerman Tower was a near mockery of Cabernet Tower. The main floor consisted of a shopping sector similar with the main floor of Cabernet Tower, but instead of a gold and white color scheme, the lobby had a silver and black color scheme with black marble floors and silver frames atop of the glass railings, sides of the elevator shafts, etcetera. The elevator door opened behind her, and she came out to face some closed shops. At the sides of these shops was a diagonal corridor that connected with stairs at the side, which went to the sublevel below and which connected with a parkade and the subway station based on a sign above pointing towards the stairs. Diana went around where there was an enclosure with some shrubs surrounding the other faces of the elevator shaft that only went up another floor. In the middle of the main lobby was a circular space with some coffee tables and a coffee shop behind the elevator shaft. The rim of the circular floor was silver and had a shine towards it by the bright lights above where a chandelier hung from the ceiling. A second level circled the entire space and was accessible by escalators further ahead or the elevator that also went up to this second level. There were shops around this entire area. Unlike the station below, the room was quiet and nobody could be seen. All of the shops had closed and Diana was alone.

Diana came around and took a closer look at the lobby. Left and right from the circular space in the middle of the foyer were corridors with more shops at the side and doors that exited out onto the streets. Diana could not see outside though because the front of the doors and windows were protected by a blast screen. Directly ahead, to the south of the door at the opposite-face from the elevator was another corridor that went towards the main entrance into the tower and was where the escalators were that went up to the second floor. In the middle of this wide corridor was a replica of a statue at the Zimmerman Tower in New York City and it was a statue of Prometheus. Around the statue was a fountain where water sprouted out and wrinkled around the shallow pool. Water also cascaded down the sides of the base platform of the bronze statue of the titan with a ball of fire surrounded by a ring. Diana began to walk around the central area of the tower lobby and looked up to see some elevators on the second floor just like with Cabernet Tower.

"How original," Diana muttered, going down the main corridor towards the escalators to reach the elevators.

Diana stopped before the elevators and tapped the button to call for a car. A shaft door opened, and Diana stepped in. She then tapped for the top-most floor, which was the observation tower at the very top of the tower, but the button quickly faded out and the door did not close. Diana repeated the action, tapping the card she extracted from the mercenary below into a panel, but the door would still not close.

"Hmph," Diana groaned with a sigh.

Diana kicked off the side of the elevator shaft and punched the hatch above. She then shot the grapple gun and climbed out of the elevator car to enter the wide shaft, looking up to the many floors that were above. A chill fell upon Diana as she looked at the height above. She took a deep breath and then looked over to a ladder for her to climb. Diana hopped atop of all the elevators that were parked and reached the ladder. She then began to climb up to make her way to the observation tower more than a hundred meters above. Diana climbed up and up, looking at the large numbers printed on the side of the shaft that read the floor number she was at.

By the time that Diana was near the sixtieth floor, she began to hear some cries nearby. She slowly continued upwards, climbing until the sound was most concentrated. Diana held on and looked down at the sixty-floor or so drop that followed. She wrapped an arm around the side of the ladder and then hit an emergency release on the elevator shaft door she was at. The door opened and revealed the lobby ahead. Diana took the grapple gun and shot through, using the momentum to zip in and then roll her landing as she arrived onto the sixtieth floor.

Diana looked around and took in the atmosphere. Unlike Cabernet Tower, there was more of a futuristic sense in the floors of Zimmerman Tower. The floors continued the dark, shiny marble from the main floor, but the walls were composed of a thick dark grey metallic panel, although with the red lights that shined down, the walls and floor took on a slightly burgundy color. Diana proceeded to follow the echo of a woman crying. She saw that based on the rooms in the corridor she came down, she was in some sort of research lab component of the tower as each room had windows that looked in to a laboratory. Diana reached the end of the corridor and came to another wide corridor that went left and right.

To the left, Diana saw a group of scientists against a wall while two elite mercenaries held rifles and watched them from the other side. Another mercenary came around the corner at the end of the corridor, holding a scientist by the arm and throwing him to the others.

"That's all I could find," the elite merc reported.

"It'll do," the other replied. "Let's get this over with…"

"Please…!" a scientist cried out. "I have a family!"

"Your family is probably dead, buddy," the merc responded. "Everybody against the wall!"

"Oh God!" another scientist remarked.

"No…" Diana muttered, running towards them.

Diana took a smoke grenade and threw it towards them. She then took the grapple gun and hooked onto the closest merc to pull his rifle off him. Diana then kicked him back with a roundhouse kick, causing him to fall into the other merc behind him. She then took a knife and threw it at the third, moving over to the closest mercenary to take her pistol and hit him at the side of the head with it. Diana looked over to the third merc as he took his sidearm and pointed it towards her. She jumped up, dodging a shot at her, and landed atop of him, kicking the pistol off and then stomping on his face. Diana then brought her leg down onto his neck to knock him out. Lastly, Diana knocked the second merc out before looking over to the scientists as they covered their heads.

"You're safe!" Diana exclaimed to them. "Nobody is going to hurt you."

Diana watched as they slowly stopped to cower and stood up. She approached them and put her guns away.

"You're that vigilante, aren't you?" a scientist pointed out.

"I am," Diana confirmed. "What's going on here? Why were these mercenaries trying to kill you?"

"Because we're not worth anything to the company anymore," the scientist replied.

"Also, because some of us may know too much about what Zimmerman has been up to over the last couple years," another scientist opined.

"Which is?" Diana questioned.

"Too much…"

"Hm…." Diana responded. "I'm here to stop the attack on the city. Do any of you know how it can be stopped, if it can be stopped? I understand that this has all been planned for a long time."

"Almost a decade…" an older scientist remarked. "I'm the chief technician and have been here since Zimmerman was just a wealthy board member."

"What's going on then?" Diana asked. "How do I put an end to all this?"

"It's an ambitious mission, but the only way you'll stop the drones is if you take out the command relay on the roof of the tower, but that's a protected area few have access to. The observation tower was converted into a command center, and it's powered by a source of permanent, renewable energy – our fusion reactor."

"Fusion reactor?"

"It was a secret project Zimmerman put us up to and it was only recently completed. Ever since Mr. Zimmerman went missing, Mrs. Dulles has taken over everything and continued his work. She had us continue production of the drone army, the fusion reactor, and something else codenamed the Wells Project."

"The Wells Project?" Diana questioned.

"Mr. Zimmerman was deeply invested in all these projects, and we never questioned his motives and only followed his orders. We were paid handsomely…" the scientist admitted, slightly ashamed. "If only we knew that something like this was in mind…"

"Zimmerman's Legacy…" Diana murmured.

"I'm afraid so," the chief tech agreed. "Here," he said, giving Diana a key card. "I don't if this'll be of any use, but it's my access card. You should be able to access most, if not all of the doors in this building with it."

"I picked a card like this off of one of the mercs, but it wouldn't work on the elevator."

"You have to tap on the panel once and then select the floor you want," the scientist explained. "It should work... You can try mine to see if it's just the card you picked up that was at fault or not."

"Okay," Diana replied, putting the card into her jacket. "How do you suggest that I shut down the command relay?"

"The access control panel would give you direct access. There's a supercomputer with an advanced AI that controls all of the drones simultaneously with option to receive orders from the field commanders... People like this guy over here."

"Who are these people? I don't recognize them as Paladin mercenaries."

"They're members of Zimmerman's private army – Shadow Company, an American private military company. Zimmerman Corporation owns them and they're responsible for security on all of Zimmerman properties, while also doing his dirty work, I suppose."

"I thought Zimmerman contracted his dirty work to a Russian-based company known as Huntsman Legionnaires."

"Well, yes, but also no," the chief technician replied. "Shadow Company is a small company and while he did used to contract Huntsman, he only did so in public. Shadow Company, as their name implies, do work that he did not want anybody to know of, or so I've heard. When it came to public affairs, Huntsman has always been there, but it's never been perfect. Often times, the two mercenary groups would come head-to-head, which was always a point of tension between Zimmerman and the commander of the Huntsman. Shadow Company was more of an amphibious team too, specializing in that sort of thing. Also, Huntsman was always larger than Shadow Company... a lot larger in terms of members and equipment. Zimmerman did not want to rely on manpower too much, which was also why he had us develop this drone program. From what I understood, at least at the time, these drones were meant to compose the core of Zimmerman's private army, but it seems like there's so much more to it... All of these drones fall under the direction of Shadow Company, and the de facto head of that would be Mrs. Dulles now."

"Dulles... where is she?"

"I'm not sure, but if I had to guess, in the command center under the watchful eye of these men," the chief technician replied.

"Okay," Diana replied. "I'm going to go and stop her and put an end to the massacre. If you can, find a place to barricade yourselves in until this is over. Hell, arm yourselves with their guns if you have to, but be aware that they will wake up within five minutes."

"Okay," the chief technician replied. "Thank you for saving our lives. Please, put an end to this..."

Diana nodded and stepped to the side to leave.

"And wait!" a female scientist remarked. "There are more of us out here, trying to hide from these mercenaries as they try to put us down. Please, stop them before they kill our colleagues. There should be at least four more of us out there."

"And be careful," the chief technician remarked. "There's more than just these Shadow Company men lurking around. There are some drones in these halls..."

"Got it," Diana replied, nodding. "Thanks."

Diana left the scientists and proceeded to run down and around the entire floor until she reached a fire escape that allowed her to go up to the next floor. She made her way down another corridor and then found herself at a four-way junction. She looked around and chose to go down the left corridor where she heard some voices nearby. Diana moved forward and stopped as she heard some heavy and robotic footsteps followed by the smashing of glass. She found herself at the end of a corridor and looked into the room to her right where there were scientists setting some documents aflame. They pulled each folder out from a filing cabinet and lit them in a pile in the middle of the room. Diana also looked at a robot on the ground, sparks flying out of it with its limbs pulled off.

"Ah!" a scientist shouted as he saw Diana.

"Easy there," Diana responded. "I'm friend."

"You're... you're the vigilante!"

"Yeah, yeah," Diana replied in a dull tone, rolling her eyes, "I know. What are you doing? What is that?"

"One of those vile droids," the other scientist answered.

Diana looked at the robot and saw that it was significantly different from the robot seen in the Arctic, which Charlemagne kept one of in his office, but closer in appearance to the robots she saw in Russia years ago. The robot had a cubic form to it now though, with dark grey armor and a lack of a head. Instead, its eyes pierced out from its torso.

"How did you manage to deactivate it?" Diana questioned.

"It wasn't hard," the scientist replied. "Just a lot of patience and knowledge..."

"Cease and desist!" a robotic voice projected from the other side of the room.

"Oh God, there's more of them!" the other scientist remarked, hiding behind the counter.

Diana took her pistols and opened fire at the robot at the other side of the room, breaking the glass. The bullets impacted the torso, causing it to flinch backwards. Diana spent her entire two magazines and released them. The robot looked at her and then began to point its arm towards her. The forearm then span up. Diana quickly ducked down to join the scientists as it began to shoot a hail of bullets towards her, hitting the top of the countertop instead and the glass tubes and flasks above. The robot stopped firing as soon as Diana was out of its sight. Diana reloaded her guns and then went to the corner as the robot stepped through the doorway. She shot at its legs, but it was severely ineffective.

"Hit it at the core!" a scientist whispered. "The core!"

Diana looked to him and then nodded. She stood up and began to shoot the robot in the center of the torso, near the eyes. The bullets ripped through and sparks began to fly. The robot fell over backwards. Another robot pushed its wounded comrade out of the way and began to fire towards Diana. She ducked down again, stayed crouched, and began to move up. She heard the fallen robot detonate, while the other ceased to fire. Diana then stood up and shot at the robot with the rest of her magazines, tearing through the core.

The robot began to glitch and fry. Diana kicked it back out of the doorway and then saw it detonate, giving off a minor shock of an explosion. Diana covered her face with her gauntlets and then looked over to the scientists.

"You can come out now," Diana said to them.

The scientists stood up.

"What are you doing here? Shadow Company mercenaries are looking for you and were just about to execute a bunch of your colleagues."

"Sorry," the scientist apologized. "We had to destroy some files about our work here."

"Fine, but you've been warned, "Diana replied. "I'm going to the command center above and putting a stop to the drone attack."

Diana moved to leave.

"Wait!" the other scientist remarked. "There should be two more of us somewhere on the next floor," she said. "They went to destroy some of their own files but haven't returned. Please rescue them... they could be in danger!"

Diana sighed and then nodded.

"If they're alive, I'll see what I can do."

Diana left and continued down the corridor, stopping to hide around a corner as she saw a group of three robots approach from ahead. She quickly reloaded her guns before reaching down to an EMP grenade on her belt.

"Hm..." Diana remarked.

Diana took the EMP grenade and tossed it around the corner. The grenade detonated and gave off a flash. Diana looked around the corner and saw the robots begin to malfunction and then shut off. They all fell down without a fight. They also didn't detonate. The flash from the grenade left behind some sparks in the air that began to produce static with Diana's radio. She turned it off and then continued through to reach a fire escape to continue up to the sixty-second floor. Diana raced up the stairs and then came out to continue down another corridor as she searched for these last two civilians.

Act 8, Scene 2

"Stay back!" a scientist shouted, moving against a wall in the middle of the sixty-second floor as Diana approached.

"Easy there!" Diana warned, raising her hands. "I'm a friend!"

Diana looked over to the other scientist who was on the floor.

"Crap!" the other scientist cursed as blast doors fell down at either side, entrapping them in a segment of the wide corridor. "Not good!"

"What the hell?!" Diana questioned, looking around the dark red enclosure they were in.

"Stop right there," Mrs. Dulles' voice echoed through a PA. "You're not going a step further."

"Look!" a scientist pointed out.

Diana looked over to a monitor at the center of the wall behind her. Mrs. Dulles looked towards them through the television screen. She was dressed in a lab coat and wore a teal sweater with a brownish silk scarf. Her dark hair was tied in a bun. She had a strict look on her face and crossed her arms.

"I should have known that it was you all this time, Diana," Mrs. Dulles noted. "The lone survivor – the ghost of the nuclear power plant incident. I'm afraid that you may have escaped death once, but you will soon come to join my father, brother, and even my late husband soon."

One of the blast doors to the left opened, but before they could escape, they were met with a line of droids that walked forward with their arms pointed towards them. Diana flinched as she was met with them, but they didn't fire at them yet. They entered into the enclosure and then the blast doors closed again. Diana counted six of them. The scientists crawled away from them before the other side opened and another six walked in, cornering them in the center of the room. Diana looked both ways with uncertainty.

"How about a dozen of our finest drones ever created, eyeing you – targeting you. If you try anything, then they'll open fire, and send you and those two doctors into a bloody gore on the floor. Your trek ends here, hero. The cities of the world are under my control, and you cannot stop us this time."

Diana felt uneasy, holding her guns steady as she looked around, feeling outnumbered and entrapped.

"Should you survive, the room will be filled with a powerful neurotoxin. The gas is quick and painless, but the choice is yours. Either way, you'll be finished once and for all. Say 'Hello' to Damian when you meet him in hell."

The monitor shut off and displayed a counter starting at two minutes. The time quickly began to tick away.

"What are you going to do?" a doctor questioned.

"Uh…" Diana replied as the drones began to spin up their guns.

Tristan quickly shot down from a vent in the ceiling, tossing some EMP chips onto some robots nearby, causing the robots to instantly malfunction. He turned around to Diana and looked to her.

"Don't just stand there, toss those grenades you stole off me!" Tristan remarked, prepping his bow.

Diana quickly took an EMP grenade and threw it over. She then hid her head as it set off, terminating almost all of the robots instantly. Tristan shot an arrow over to one in the corner that didn't set off, hitting it in the very center of its torso to cause it to malfunction.

"Tristan…" Diana said with a bit of relief.

"We need to get out of here," Tristan stated, looking to the clock as they had a minute left. "We'll each take one and go into the vent. You first."

Diana nodded and waved over for one of the scientists to come over to her. She then took her grapple gun and shot up into the vent that Tristan came out of, going up and through. Tristan helped the other onto his feet and then took him over to the vent where he followed behind. Diana began to crawl ahead.

"If you follow up, we'll come to the floor above," Tristan said.

"How did you find me?"

"Charlemagne told me to come to Zimmerman Tower because it was the one place in Harlech with power and a major energy reading, and I found you where you were because of CCTV."

Diana didn't respond. She came to the end of the tunnel and looked up the vent that Tristan had come down. She climbed out and then helped the scientist out. Diana saw some robots on the floor with arrows through their armor. Tristan came out of the vent and helped the scientist behind him out. Diana looked to him as the two stared at each other.

"So, are you going to arrest me? Take me back to Cabernet Tower, or whatever your plan was with me?" Diana questioned. "To stop me from achieving my goals?"

"No," Tristan denied. "You were already arrested once, and the police went ahead and released you. Besides, we've got bigger things to worry about with what's going on the streets. I'm here to help you."

Diana looked at him and nodded. She then turned to the scientists as they recovered.

"Find someplace to hide," Diana told them. "Your other colleagues are safe."

"Thank you," one of the scientists expressed.

"Are you okay?" Tristan asked Diana.

"I'm fine," Diana replied. "I'm just starting to get a little tired… it's been a long day."

"Understandable," Tristan responded. "Lead the way."

Diana nodded. She began to jog forward. Tristan followed. They came to the center of the sixty-third floor where there were some elevators.

"The command center is on the observation deck at the top of the tower," Diana explained to Tristan. "If we want to shut down all of these drones, then we need to shut down the supercomputer up there that's controlling all of them."

"How do we do that?" Tristan questioned.

"The chief technician told me that we might be able to access the control panel, but do you have anymore of those EMP chips?"

"Yeah," Tristan responded."

"Then that should do it too," Diana remarked.

The elevator door opened, and the former couple stepped in. Diana tapped the key card she got from the scientist and then hit the button for the top-most floor marked by an 'O.' Tristan watched. The doors closed and the elevator then began to move up.

"Diana…" Tristan said, looking to Diana and raising his visor. "I just want to let you know before we head on out that I'm truly, deeply sorry about what I've done to you."

"Please don't start," Diana interjected.

"The pain that I caused you is irredeemable. I don't expect you to forgive me… but I don't want to live in a state where we hate each other…. I'm just sorry for what I did, and even though I said it was irredeemable, I'm going to try and make it up to you and prove myself to you."

Diana sighed and then replied, "If that's the case, then I forgive you."

"What?" Tristan questioned. "Just like that?"

"I don't want to live in a state of frustration against you either, nor do I want you straining yourself thinking that we can be together again if you try hard enough. So how about I simply tell you that you're forgiven, because it's my Christian duty to forgive people that trespass against us as Christ does the same for all of us when we approach him with a sullen heart."

Tristan looked forward and didn't reply. He clenched a fist and lowered his visor. He cleared his throat and began to change the subject, explaining to her what he found at the movie studios, to which Diana replied that she saw these items at Dock F. Tristan then explained his encounter with Helene and Dr. Bishop. Diana was silent about Helene, but nervous. Tristan finished off by explaining the goal of the invasion – the complete eradication of humanity to lay the foundation for a new world.

Before Diana could respond, they were met with a screech from the PA.

"What do you think you're doing?" Mrs. Dulles questioned. "You cannot stop what has been set in motion. The world is about to enter into a new, permanent age. This is the end for you. This is Zimmerman's Legacy – a world without humanity to corrupt what Mother Nature has given us. A world in which a new humanity will be able to grow and develop, and I'm afraid neither of you are invited."

Tristan frowned at that word. He cleared this throat. The elevator came to a sudden stop.

"Should we get out?" Tristan questioned.

"Obviously," Diana replied, eyeing the open ceiling panel as this was the same elevator she had come through earlier. "Give me a boost."

Diana was boosted through. Tristan began to hear the run-up of the machine gun arms that the robots had from the other side of the door. He quickly took his grapple gun, shot himself up and then climbed up to join Diana as the doors opened. Diana looked below as bullets riddled the inside of the elevator before stopping.

"Targets out of sight," a robot remarked.

Diana and Tristan looked at each other from the top of the car. Diana looked upwards, seeing that a blast door had extended ahead, blocking off their access to the observation deck via the elevator shaft.

"Hm..." Diana pondered. "We'll have to travel the rest up by foot. Come on, let's deal with these bots..."

"I've wanted to have a go at these bastards ever since we came up against them in Russia."

"Yeah, well, don't think about trying to kiss me when it's all set and done."

"Me?" Tristan questioned. "You were the one that leaned towards me!"

Diana looked back at him with a strict face.

"Are they dead?" Mrs. Dulles questioned over the PA. "I can't see..."

"Zero hostiles located," a robot reported back.

Diana took her second-last EMP grenade and readied it. She then dropped it down and watched as it set off on impact. They then heard the robots at the other side malfunction and fall over. Diana took her pistol and readied them.

"Ladies first," Diana said to Tristan.

Tristan frowned at her and hopped down on his own. He looked forward and saw that some of the robots were not terminated. Tristan quickly grabbed his bow and shot at the closest robot. Diana hopped down to join him, opening fire ahead. They both looked forward and saw there to be four drones left. One of the drones had a riot shield integrated into its arm, while another two had stun batons. The last had a cannon and began to spin it up. The environment around them was cold as they had been taken to a rooftop just before the observation tower that looked out to the city.

"Cease and desist," one of the robots said.

Diana lowered her pistols as her bullets failed to penetrate through the riot shield. Tristan put his bow away as he raised his fists instead. Each of them stepped out onto the rooftop as they confronted the four robots. Diana fired at the robot with the cannon as it was about to shoot them and caused it fall over.

A robot with a stun baton lunged towards Diana and jabbed her in the leg. Diana shouted out in pain as it electrified her.

"Diana!" Tristan yelled.

Another robot bashed Tristan in the side with the riot shield. He bashed back at it, but the robot held its ground. Diana took her pistols and opened fire at the robot with the riot shield, tricking it to lower its guard before she shot at him through the core and causing it to fall over. Meanwhile, Tristan jumped over and grabbed the robot, picking it up in all its weight and then tossing over onto the side of the half-wall at the edge of the roof. The pair then faced the final robot from each side. The robot attempted to jab Tristan in the leg. He grabbed the stun baton and lowered it down. Diana quickly moved over and hit it in the side with the butt of her gun, shooting it through the back with the other. Tristan then kicked the robot back. The robot began to malfunction and then self-destruct.

Tristan patted his hands and then looked around. Diana walked over to the edge of the roof and looked below to the rest of the city. Helicopters patrolled the skies, firing missiles into skyscrapers while tanks rolled across the emptied streets. The entire city had been lit aflame. The sky above them was a dark grey from the clouds that covered them. At the height they were at, it was extremely cold. The snow stopped though and there hadn't been anymore thunder or lightning.

"We need to move," Diana encouraged, turning around.

Diana looked over and saw an iron fence that blocked off a platform, which gave access to the rest of the roof. The fence had a sign that read, 'Maintenance Only.' The rooftop deck where they were only composed a single side of the whole roof. Tristan followed Diana as she went to this gate, which she opened by shooting the lock.

The belly of the observation deck loomed over them. They were only a short distance away. From the exterior, Zimmerman Tower (formerly Durham Tower) was an eighty-story concrete tower with a lookout at the top, which was disk-shaped and composed three additional stories. Atop of the lookout tower was a large radio antenna. The lookout sat on top of a three-story concrete stand on the rooftop they were on. The floor they were on consisted of the open rooftop, and a maintenance room with sharp hooks protruding from the corners of the edge to stop birds from nesting nearby.

Tristan followed Diana onto the maintenance platform. They then reached a steel door that went into this maintenance room on the eightieth floor, but ignored it in favor of climbing up onto a platform two meters above that continued along the side of the maintenance box. They then climbed over and came onto the rooftop of the top-most floor so that they were right underneath the observation tower and its three-story pedestal. Tristan stopped in the gravel they were on and knelt down.

"I see something over there," Diana reported, turning around to look at Tristan. "Are you okay?

"Yeah, just a second," Tristan replied. "My HUD began to act a little screwy. It's okay. I turned it off so it shouldn't be a problem anymore. Let's go."

Diana pointed over to a steel platform at the side of the concrete pedestal beneath the command center. A helicopter with a spotlight passed them as she did, causing them to lower down. The platform that Diana pointed at was a sort of balcony with a steel door that went inside. At one end of the platform, there was a ladder that could extend down, but was raised up. Diana took her grapple gun and shot towards it. Tristan followed.

Once they were atop, the pair approached the panel that went inside. Diana scanned one of the cards that she had and then the other. None of them worked. The helicopter made another pass as it obviously looked for them.

"Can you hack into this?" Diana questioned.

"Sure," Tristan replied, taking a chip from his belt and placing onto the panel.

The panel began to fry. Tristan tried to open the door, but it wouldn't open.

"Nice job…" Diana muttered, taking some explosives from her own pouch. "Step back."

Diana placed the explosives she retrieved from the precinct and then set the timer. The pair of them walked away to the other side of the platform and then watched as the door was blown off. They then continued through into the small maintenance room.

"Up there!" Tristan said, pointing over to a grate above them.

Tristan took his grapple gun, aimed it at the vent and fired it before locking his control so that he could pull the grate off its hinges. He then grappled back over and climbed through. Diana followed from behind.

The pair moved through the duct system until they could see some grates above them as they came to the bottom floor of the lookout tower. Diana looked above and saw that there were metal beams stretched across the ceiling of the observation deck. She opened the floor grate and stepped out. Tristan followed. The pair then shot up and came to the ceiling and looked below.

The lookout tower was large. Around the ground floor was an open space around the perimeter of the tower where there were various crates of equipment, some machines, mostly servers and three mercenaries patrolling about. The middle layer, or second floor, contained the fusion reactor in the center alongside all the support equipment, wiring, and turbines, which created a mess of machinery. The core of the fusion reactor was hidden to their sight. The third floor, which was a simple, small platform at the very back, cutting through the first floor, contained a small room accessible via a ladder from the second floor. The second floor was accessible both by ladders and stairs around. In total, there were six mercenaries with another two on the second floor. On the third floor, Hyacinth Dulles could be seen on the other side of the control room. All around the lookout there were windows that looked out to the city.

"Six mercs," Diana whispered to Tristan. "Three for each of us. Let's take them out."

"Keep quiet and communicate with me via signals," Tristan whispered back. "We'll guide each other through this, being our eyes in the sky for each of us."

Diana nodded. Tristan launched his grapple gun to a beam further ahead. He positioned himself overtop of a mercenary below. Diana made an okay sign to him. Tristan lowered himself and came behind a mercenary on the second floor, looking over the side of the railing. He then choked him out.

"They've breached the command center!" Dulles shouted from her control room over a PA. "Kill them, you fools! They'll ruin everything – they'll put it all in jeopardy!"

Tristan rushed his takedown and smashed the head of the mercenary onto the railing before shooting back up. He repositioned and then looked over to Diana who took point over another merc. Tristan moved to be near the merc directly ahead of that mercenary. They looked at each other and then nodded. The pair then dropped down and each quickly took them out. Tristan grabbed his merc by the thigh and gave him a Sambo takedown as he smashed him into the floor before dislocating his arm, while Diana knocked her merc over and then dropped her knee on his neck.

The former couple then disappeared upwards and repositioned as Dulles shouted over the PA, "Fools! They're on the second floor!"

Tristan balanced himself over the beam and then made his way over to look to where Diana was going. She positioned herself over a merc. Tristan looked around the immediate area and then over to Diana who was looking to him for confirmation. Tristan gave a simple nod to her, and she dropped down, lowering herself with the grapple gun and choking the mercenary out. She then shot up and looked to Tristan who was eyeing the second-last mercenary. She examined the nearby area and then gave Tristan an okay sign. Tristan lowered himself down behind another mercenary and quickly strangled him with his bicep before lowering him to the floor.

"By the railing!" Dulles shouted. "Hurry!"

Tristan dropped a pellet of smoke as gun shots passed him. He then shot up to the ceiling and repositioned himself. Diana took a knife and threw it at the last mercenary. She then dropped down and ran over to him, kicking him down and then quickly dropping the knee on his neck while Tristan lowered himself outright to join her.

"You imbeciles," Dulles remarked. "You absolute imbeciles. What kind of men are you, anyway? You call yourselves the best... You've ruined it all!"

A light from outside shined into the lookout. Diana and Tristan quickly grappled up as the helicopter began to open fire into the tower.

"Let's take her out once and for all," Diana said to Tristan.

"After you," Tristan replied.

The pair went over to the platform outside of the control panel and lowered themselves down. Diana approached the door and kicked it down.

"You haven't won," Hyacinth remarked to her.

Diana grabbed hold of her and slammed her head into the desk.

"Shut up," Diana replied. "I'm sick of hearing you talk."

"How do we shut this off?!" Tristan questioned her.

Diana moved towards the front of the keyboard.

"Maybe if we find something that says, 'Off?'" Diana suggested, looking around the unfamiliar desktop.

"You... you can't," Mrs. Dulles murmured from the ground. "Please don't... It's all I have left of him... My dearest Audric... I've failed him."

"Hm..." Tristan groaned. "Plan B. I'm going to go and plant some chips onto each of the servers and hopefully bring this thing offline without causing another Cabernet Tech incident with the fusion reactor."

"The girl..." Mrs. Dulles muttered. "Helene... she's all I have left... Goodbye, dearest Helene..."

"Whoa!" Diana reacted as the monitor shut off. "What did I do?!"

The monitor displayed a ten second count. Diana looked down to Mrs. Dulles who had a bracelet around her arm with a counter that matched the counter on the screen. She quickly stood up and ran out of the control room. Tristan looked towards her as Diana ran after her.

"Get out of here!" Diana said. "It's going to blow!"

Tristan looked to the counter as it said five seconds left. He followed after Diana onto the second floor. Mrs. Dulles threw a chair through the window, shattering it, and then running through. The control room detonated, which caused a chain reaction of other explosions.

"Oh no she doesn't," Tristan remarked as he saw Dulles jump out.

Diana went out after her. Tristan jumped out after both of them.

The rest of the lookout blew up in a fiery blitz that caused even the radio antenna to collapse into the roof. There was then a larger explosion that rose up in a mushroom cloud fireball, decimating the higher levels of the roof. Diana looked up to the blast before looking below to the streets she was about to impact into. Tristan on the other hand dived forward, grabbing hold of Dulles, and then shooting his grapple gun towards the tower, which caused him to swing towards the side and crash through a window. He crashed into a floor below and landed into an office cubicle, Mrs. Dulles in his arms, knocking himself out by the intense impact he had.

Act 8, Scene 3

Tristan woke up with a grunt. A strong wind blew past him with a gentle breeze of snow that fell through the broken window he had crashed through. Hyacinth Dulles laid atop of him, still unconscious. He pushed her off and then stood up, looking around and tearing off his visor as he couldn't see anything through it as it had cracked again. Tristan also raised the rest of the helmet, exposing his hair and dropping it to the ground.

"Tristan?" Charlemagne questioned through his headset. "Are you awake?"

"Charles..." Tristan grunted, coughing. "Yeah, I'm here."

"Good," Charlemagne replied. "Your suits readings went low for a moment, so I thought something had happened. Where's Diana? Is she alright?"

Tristan walked forward and looked down below the twenty or so stories towards the streets. It was still early in the morning before the sun could rise. Tristan could see some tanks frozen on the street, while some of the robots were fallen over. The missile fire and gunshots had come to an end in the least as had the screaming.

"I- I don't know where she is," Tristan admitted, looking around in confusion. "We jumped off the tower and got separated. I have Mrs. Dulles though. You can tell the police they can find her in Zimmerman Tower, tied up."

Tristan took some ties from his belt and went over to secure her against a column.

"Will do," Charlemagne replied. "Oh..."

"What is it?" Tristan asked.

"You have a... phone call. From Helene Köhlen?" Charlemagne questioned. "Should I... patch you though?"

"Yes," Tristan replied. "Helene?"

"Did you see the picture I sent you?" Helene asked, hiding the amusement in her voice.

"What picture?" Tristan questioned. "I've been kind of busy…"

"I hope you didn't forget about me, Tristan," Helene said. "I can understand why you would be so obsessed with her. She is quite beautiful…"

Tristan gave a deep frown.

"Your dilemma between us will soon come to an end," Helene remarked.

"Where are you? Where's my Diana?!" Tristan barked.

Helene laughed and replied, "This is very cute. Your little Diana… Don't you worry. She's alive and asleep. She's had a long day after all and could use some rest after stopping the drone invasion that threatened this God-forsaken world."

"Where are you…?"

"You will know soon enough," Helene replied. "We're not ready for you yet."

Helene hung up. Charlemagne cleared his throat.

"The photo she sent to your phone is of Diana, asleep and on the ground of an unknown location," Charlemagne said. "I'm unable to trace the signal of the call and there is no metadata to the photo."

"You don't have to," Tristan replied. "Where's Diana's cellphone signal? Helene still has her phone."

"One moment…" Charlemagne replied. "Ah, she's at Pentateuch Cathedral nearby."

"Okay, I'm going to go and rescue Diana. Tell the cops about Hyacinth at Zimmerman Tower."

"Understood."

Tristan went to the window he broke through and then jumped down, using the grapple gun to break his fall before he came onto the streets. He then made his way towards the alleyway where he hid his bike, coming onto it and then racing off to make his way towards Bromley. Tristan got off his bike in another alleyway and then shot up to climb onto a roof.

Despite the fact that it was early morning, the city was still dark, especially due to the buildup of smoke as most buildings continued to burn. Tristan looked across the street towards Pentateuch Cathedral, but could see some snipers around, all pointing towards the entrance of the cathedral. There were approximately four of them in total.

Tristan made his way towards the first of them and snuck behind him as their eyes were focused down the scope of their rifle. With a look of fright and aggression, he strangled him unconscious and then made his way over to the next one down the west-side of Bailey Drive. He made his approach behind the second and gave him the same fate. Tristan then looked across the street to a building on the east side.

Tristan made his way over and climbed over the edge of the roof. He then went behind the mercenary and knocked him onto his knees, bringing his arm around his neck and choking him out cold. He then shot himself across the street and made his way around to the other building on the east side, towards the north. Tristan climbed up the side of the building and approached the merc from behind, strangling him and then pulling him onto his side before he dropped down and went down the sidewalk to reach the steps that went up to Pentateuch Cathedral.

As Tristan made his approach to the front doors, he stopped before the entrance and looked up to the rose window. He took a deep breath and shuttered for a moment. He closed his eyes for a moment and then continued onwards only to notice a red dot at his hand as he placed it on the door handle. Tristan turned around and froze as Shadow Company closed in on him from nowhere and then knocked him out.

Diana watched from the floor as two elite mercenaries pulled Tristan's unconscious body down the aisle of the cathedral and dropped him near her. Helene stood ahead, before a large monstrous machine that took up the entire chancel and transept before the altar. The device consisted of a platform shaped in a hexagon and six arms stretched out and bent with the claws of the arm facing down to the center of the platform. At the rear of one of the claws was a panel. Helene was not near this panel, but instead by a table where she plucked pedals off a flower. She hummed the classic wedding tune to herself while Tristan woke up.

"Leave us," Helene commanded the mercenaries.

The mercenaries left. Tristan was stripped of all his weaponry like Diana. Diana's face had even been exposed as her hood was pulled back and veil removed. Tristan's hands were tied behind his back as were Diana's.

Helene finished deflowering the flower and then placed it in the vase. She then turned around and looked at the pair.

"Isn't this nice?" Helene smiled. "Together again. My boys found this one falling of the side of the tower. She had a rough landing, but put up quite the fight before she was hauled over here."

"We... we destroyed the drones..." Tristan said in a weak voice.

"I don't give a damn about the drones!" Helene yelled back in a sharp voice.

Helene then took a deep breath to calm down.

"That is not why I have brought us together on this glorious day," Helene said, returning her smile.

"Glorious?" Tristan questioned. "Innocent people have died because of you…"

"Ah…" Helene replied. "Are they innocent? What is innocence? You assume the best of people, but you do not know that all of us are sinners. All of us have sinned at least once in our life. Your human judgement leads you to believe that we are all good, which is surprising given what you've been through."

"What are you talking about?" Tristan asked.

"Zimmerman and I never saw eye to eye," Helene expressed. "From the beginning, I understood that his intentions were never with us. His 'legacy' as it seems, represents his attempt to rebel even against us and assert his own vision – flawed as it obviously was. Good riddance he has left us. Such a simple objective and yet such a complicated manifest when the same could be achieved with this…"

Helene pointed towards the monstrosity before them. She turned around and approached Tristan with seductive eyes.

"You're such a handsome boy, Tristan," Helene remarked in a lustful voice. "Could you imagine the love that we could make, you and me? The hours we would have, especially as I give you the gift of eternity that has restored my strength. We could look like this, youthful for the rest of our eternal lives. Do you not want that?"

"N-no…" Tristan denied, "no future without Diana is worth living…" he grunted.

Helene frowned.

"What do you see in her that you cannot see in me? Look at me! I am gorgeous and look at her! Her mannish face! Her ugly, dark hair! I am the very essence of beauty, and you deny me?!"

Tristan looked to Helene as he remained on his side.

"She may not be perfect," Tristan admitted, "but she's my other half. We're both imperfect."

Helene flinched at Tristan's words and held a deep frown. She looked over to Diana, picking up a handgun on the table and going over to her.

"Let's see how much you value you her when she's dead!" Helene shouted, pointing the gun over to Diana.

Diana looked over in horror. Her body froze and she ducked her head in. Tristan's eyes widened. He instantly pushed himself up to stand and jumped as the gun shot twice towards her. The bullets hit into Tristan's torso, causing him to crash into the floor before Diana.

"No!" Helene shouted. "No! No! No!"

Helene lowered the gun. Diana looked over to Tristan who was immobile where he landed. Helene looked at him and his closed eyes.

"T-Tristan?" Diana questioned, looking over to him as he didn't move. "Tristan!" she cried out, eyeing watering.

"No!" Helene shouted again towards Diana. "You're supposed to be dead! Why?! Why can't you not stop taking things from me?! First my body, and now him! I'll kill you!"

Helene raised the gun again and pointed it towards Diana. A wind then flew into the cathedral, shattering the rose window and all windows looking in from the narthex. The wind flew over Diana.

"You will not harm her," the voice in the wind whispered.

Diana ears twitched as she heard the feminine voice.

"N-no…!" Helene remarked, bringing her hands to her head as the wind span around her.

"Leave my body, you terrible demon!" the voice then said.

"No, it cannot be!" the evil spirit within Helene's body remarked.

Diana watched in horror.

"Leave," the voice called out, "and let the parents of this holy one be!"

Helene's body began to twitch. Her arm stretched out and as if by possession, it began to bring the barrel of the pistol to Helene's head. A gunshot then fired, and Helene fell over dead.

Diana panted as she looked around her; Helene dead ahead and Tristan next to her. She began to crawl towards him and brushed her head into his back as she continued to cry.

"Tristan…" Diana muttered. "Please don't die… Don't die, Tristan. Please…"

Diana slowly opened her eyes as she heard Tristan cough.

"Tristan!" Diana chanted, raising herself up and burying herself into his side with tears falling down her cheeks. "Oh my God, Tristan. I thought you were dead – God, the amount of times I've had to be scared by your death!"

"To think, Barry gave me the option of a lighter armor…" Tristan remarked.

Diana gave a light laugh. She continued to lean over Tristan until he began to squirm. She pulled herself off and knelt over him. Tristan tensed his wrists and flexed his arms, breaking out of his ties and then standing up. He used his gauntlets to break Diana out of her own ties and then looked at her. Diana instantly brought her hands to his cheeks to feel them and then brought her arms around to hug him. She continued to cry.

"Please… please… for the love of God," Diana remarked. "Never scare me like that ever again, Tristan. My heart cannot take anymore of it…"

"Deal," Tristan replied, "but only if you do the same."

"Yes, of course," Diana remarked.

The couple looked over to the front doors of the cathedral as they heard gunshots. Tristan held Diana in his arms as they waited in anticipation. He stood up and fetched the gun that

Helene had shot herself with and then looked over to the door to defend them both. The door flew open, but not with Shadow Company on the other side, but the Protection Squad. Tristan lowered the gun and embraced Diana at the side, kissing her on the cheek.

"Sorry to keep you waiting," Lukas remarked, waving over to them, "but we've got orders from Charlemagne to get you to safety at once."

Tristan nodded and replied, "Thanks, Lukas. Tell Charles, 'Thank you,' because we really needed it."

Tristan stood up and helped Diana onto her feet. The pair walked with Lukas and Lacplesis out of the church and joined up with the rest of Charlemagne's private security detail as they took them towards the armored cars outside, where they were then promptly taken to hospital to check in for their wounds. Tristan held Diana in his arms as they rode to the hospital, kissing her on the head as the couple reunited once more.

Epilogue

Diana sat in a stretcher in the Emergency Department of St. Luke Hospital in downtown Harlech. The curtains at the side gave her some privacy and she looked healthier than she appeared days earlier. She was alone in her stall of the busy hospital where hundreds checked in after the attack that killed many worldwide. Diana read her latest read, 'Demons' by Fyodor Dostoevsky, and then looked out towards the corridor before her stall as a white light flashed.

"Code White," an announcer over a PA announced. "Code White."

Diana stood up and grabbed her IV pole. She then began to exit to look out as hospital security stormed down the corridor and tackled an aggressive man on a stretcher. The three of the Stewards body-piled atop of the man while the nurse in blue scrubs held a needle and quickly approached him, while another joined security in holding the man down. The rest of the patients in the room looked, especially as the nurses struggled with the man. He soon settled. Diana moved back into her stall and sat back down in her bed.

Diana's nurse, one of the ladies in the altercation, came by with a computer on wheels.

"Ms. Cambridge," the woman said. "Sorry about the wait... We just had a bit of a non-compliant patient."

"Interesting job you have..." Diana remarked. "I'm intrigued."

"It's just another day here at St. Luke's, I'm afraid," the nurse remarked. "Nothing's different..."

The nurse looked at her computer screen and typed something out. She then went over to Diana to take some readings of her blood pressure and heart rate.

"Good…" the nurse remarked. "The doctor's going to come and see you so that you can be discharged. There's just one thing he has to talk to you about…"

"Oh God…" Diana replied. "What? Does it have anything to do with my blood?"

"No," the nurse answered. "It's actually about your urine. You're pregnant."

Diana dropped her expression and took in one of stun.

"What…?" Diana questioned.

Diana's heart-race rose to a steady hundred beats per minute. Her blood pressure lowered.

"I'm what?" Diana questioned again.

"You're pregnant," the nurse repeated. "From the looks of it, you're somewhere just over four months in. The doctor will come to speak to you about that, book you in for an ultrasound, but otherwise, you're good to go… Congratulations."

The nurse left Diana on her own.

"Oh my God…" Diana muttered, wiping the tears from her eyes. "How…? Oh my God, I completely forgot I haven't had my period in months! But four months…! That's… Oh my God, of course! The island!" she whispered.

Diana raised a smile. She brought a hand to her previously thought to be subcutaneous belly fat and took in deep breath.

"Praise be to God in the highest," Diana remarked. "He has blessed me with a child."

• • • •

Moments later, Charlemagne arrived at the hospital to pick-up Diana. He smiled and hugged her as she was discharged. She was provided with a change of her own clothes, and the Protection Squad took all of her equipment and vigilante dress with them when she was admitted and changed into a hospital gown.

"I'm glad you're all better," Charlemagne remarked. "You sustained quite the injuries…"

"Yeah," Diana replied. "Let's go and see Tristan. I have to talk to him."

"Certainly," Charlemagne said.

The pair took the elevator and went upstairs to the second floor and then down towards the Intensive Care Unit. Charlemagne buzzed in and said that two visitors were here to see Tristan Merrick. The doors then opened, and they were guided in and taken to a private room where Tristan was inside, awake and watching TV. Tristan smiled as he saw Charlemagne and Diana arrive.

"I'll be a moment and then you can have some personal time with him," Charlemagne quietly said to Diana.

"Okay," she replied.

The pair walked through and met with Tristan.

"How are you doing?" Charlemagne remarked with hands in his blazer pocket.

"I'm doing a little better," Tristan replied. "I'm worried about school though. I'm glad you've been discharged."

Diana smiled.

"Any news on your condition?"

"Apparently my spleen's been ruptured," Tristan said, "so they've booked me in for surgery to remove it… Not that I really needed a spleen to begin with given the way I am. They're going to move me to the surgical ward soon."

"Ah, good," Charlemagne replied, feeling his phone vibrate.

Charlemagne took it out and looked at it. He had a text message from an unknown foreign number that said, "Meet me outside the hospital at Venus Street. We need to talk."

"Hm…" Charlemagne muttered. "Excuse me, I have to take a phone call."

Charlemagne left Diana and Tristan alone. Diana smiled and walked over to sit on his bed. She brought a hand down onto his.

"Diana," Tristan said, "I'm sorry about what happened between us on Halloween."

"Hm?" Diana questioned, looking confused.

"You know, the Halloween Incident?"

"Oh," Diana replied. "Do you have amnesia or something? You already apologized for that like fifty times, and I forgave you, at least twice now if not more."

"I know, but this is another apology, because I was weak, and miserable… Not that I blame my actions on that alone, because they were my actions to do what I did. Nonetheless, it was a stupid thing, and…"

Diana closed her eyes and smiled.

"Tristan, we're both at fault," Diana confessed. "What kind of woman would I be to you if I didn't take part blame in what happened? I ignored you as much as you ignored me."

"The onus is on the man to take initiative, but if you feel any fault, I suppose I can forgive you too."

Diana gave a smile of disbelief at him.

"Actually, now that we have the chance, there's some things I need to talk to you about regarding Helene and what happened that night after you fell unconscious."

Diana explained her perspective of the incident, from Charlemagne calling her, her ignoring him, her talking to Iustina (who she had to explain to Tristan from when she first met her), and then her talking to a man named Cardinal Calavera to her lust for revenge against Iustina and Helene after being manipulated by the cardinal, to her transactions with people she had no idea to be the Children of Moloch, and then the assault on the castle, fight with Iustina, fight with the Shapeshifter, and then Helene's sacrifice that left her thought-to-be-dead.

"When I left Helene at the castle, I was more than positive that she was dead," Diana remarked. "I have no idea how she presented herself to us until we were in the cathedral and she shot you. Something… supernatural happened, and it was like the ghost of Helene had drifted into the room. She began to tell this imposter to get out of her body, and referred to the spirit as an evil, terrible demon. After a while of thinking about this, I think this Helene we met over the last week wasn't Helene as you knew her. When Helene charged at the shapeshifter, I think something happened with their bodies in the Fountain of Youth that caused Helene to die, but the demonic spirit of the shapeshifter, or cardinal, to merge into her body and awaken after I left."

"Gross…" Tristan remarked. "You mean, that woman who placed her hands on me… and who tried to lure me into that sick fantasy world, or whatever, was some old dude?"

Diana shrugged.

"What the hell…" Tristan replied. "No more adventures for us. I think this last one is it… I'm done."

Tristan laid his head back into his pillow. Diana smiled at him. She took his hand. Tristan looked back at her with a smile, noticing that she looked anxious.

"What's wrong?" Tristan questioned. "Everything was okay with the doctor, right? You're all medically good?"

"Yes, I'm as healthy as… a horse," Diana replied.

"Your hands are sweaty."

"Oh," Diana responded, looking down, "well, on the subject of catching up, there appears to be something else I have to tell you. Something that I've only found out about recently, but is about the both of us."

Diana stood up to close the shutter door behind them. She then sat down again and looked to bed before looking over to Tristan who smiled at her.

"What is it?" Tristan questioned.

• • • •

Charlemagne stepped out onto Venus Street in front of the hospital and looked around. He then turned around as he noticed someone approach him from behind. Director Eleanor Black looked at him with a frown. She wore her traditional black blazer and skirt with dark leggings and black high heels.

"You have got a lot of explaining to do this time," Eleanor said. "I'm still upset over what happened in China and Zimmerman's mysterious 'disappearance.'"

"Eleanor," Charlemagne greeted, "it's been a while. Still working for a den of pedophiles?"

Eleanor ignored his remark.

"For once, I can speak to you in a congratulatory manner. Diana and Tristan have us in a large debt for their services, which keep up with the mandate of the Global Defense Project. They've managed to avoid a total destruction of Western Civilization and also brought the wife of Franklin Dulles to justice, although the whereabouts of Dr. Cohen are unknown."

"Dr. Cohen?"

"You may know him as Dr. Nash Bishop. He is an Israeli citizen formerly with Mossad and his whereabouts are unknown to us. His real name is Dr. Naser Cohen."

"Cohen – Bishop, clever," Charlemagne remarked. "Well, I'll keep an eye out for him," he sarcastically replied.

"Because of what Diana and Tristan have done for the world, we have decided to pull some strings and see to it that neither of them are charged. Apparently, the Harlech Police Department would not arrest them anyways, so… consider this a gift."

"I'm sure they'd be very relieved to know that heroic actions are rewarded for once," Charlemagne replied. "Anything else?"

"No," Eleanor responded. "Stay out of trouble for now and be sure those two lay low. Goodbye, Charles."

Charlemagne watched as she left down the road and disappeared around the corner. He then turned around and came across Tristan's roommate who was nearby. The two of them looked at each other with plain faces. Charlemagne approached him.

"You're Tristan's roommate, aren't you," Charlemagne said. "Louis, right? The one that phoned me when he didn't return, and the one who was with Diana that day that Tristan was unfaithful."

"Yes," Finn replied.

"I've heard from Tristan that you're with the Faculty of Applied Science, attempting to gain a degree in mechanical engineering. Is this true?"

"Yes," Finn answered.

"I've also heard from him that you'd like to intern with Cabernet Industries."

"You have?"

"Yes," Charlemagne replied. "He said it was the least I could do for the help you've given him."

"My help wasn't a service…" Finn remarked. "It was friendship."

"Do you accept the offer?" Charlemagne questioned.

Finn's face dropped.

"Mr. Cabernet… there's something I have to admit to you," Finn remarked, looking aside with a difficult face.

Charlemagne looked back at him with surprise. Finn looked back at him, taking a deep breath for confidence.

"What is it, my dear boy?" Charlemagne questioned.

"My name is Finn, sir, not Louis – Finn Louis Cunningham to be exact," Finn clarified. "I'm your son."

Charlemagne's expression dropped and took in one of stun. The pair simply looked back at each other.

"There is, despite all corruption, enough eternal youth left in the world to fight to the last against the doctrine of despair."

– William Joyce

www.ingramcontent.com/pod-product-compliance
Lightning Source LLC
Chambersburg PA
CBHW051939220626
47052CB00004B/715